CW00409610

*Books by Nancy Cato available
from New English Library:*

ALL THE RIVERS RUN
NORTH-WEST BY SOUTH
BROWN SUGAR

BROWN SUGAR

Nancy Cato

NEW ENGLISH LIBRARY

First published in Great Britain in 1974 by William Heinemann Ltd

Copyright © Nancy Cato 1974

All rights reserved. No part of this publication
may be reproduced or transmitted, in any form
or by any means, without permission
of the publishers.

First NEL Paperback Edition February 1982

Conditions of sale: This book is sold
subject to the condition that it shall not,
by way of trade or otherwise, be lent,
re-sold, hired out, or otherwise circulated
without the publisher's prior consent in
any form of binding or cover other than
that in which it is published and without a
similar condition including this condition
being imposed on the subsequent
purchaser.

NEL Books are published by
New English Library,
Barnard's Inn, Holborn,
London EC1N 2JR, a division of Hodder and Stoughton Ltd.

Printed and bound in Great Britain by
Cox & Wyman Ltd, Reading

0 450 05362 8

For Kath Walker

Contents

Book One: The Dark Brown and the First White

1   The Pacific

    1   The ship   14
    2   The Islanders   19
    3   The missionaries   30
    4   The blackbirders   38

2   Queensland

    1   The homestead   44
    2   The establishment   54
    3   Maryborough   63
    4   The Kanaka village   69
    5   The hunt   76

3   Reaping the whirlwind

    1   Revenge   83
    2   Sugar town   90
    3   The ball   95
    4   Zachariah   104

4   The loves of the parallels

    1   Helga   110
    2   Dougal   114
    3   Emily and Joseph   117
    4   James   129
    5   Amelia and Andrew   135

5   Developments
    1 Rose   141
    2 Joseph   146
    3 The Black Police   152
    4 Burnt sugar   158
    5 Marriage at Mackay   161
    6 Andrew Duguid   168
    7 Return to Chindera   174

Book Two: The Second White and the First Yellow

1   Aftermaths
    1 At Chindera   180
    2 White and brown   187
    3 The Efate family   194
    4 Graham   198

2   The second generation
    1 David   206
    2 Pamela   214
    3 Tula   221
    4 Kanaka go home   227
    5 Angus Johnstone   230

3   A tale that is told
    1 May   237
    2 Fiona   241
    3 Joseph   246
    4 Helga   249
    5 Tula again   253

The Duguid and Johnstone Families

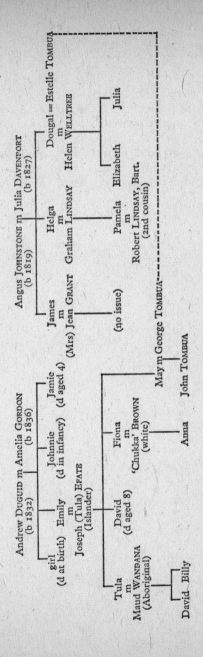

Acknowledgements

In collecting material for this book, I wish to acknowledge the assistance of the Freyer Memorial Library, University of Queensland, and the Oxley Library, Brisbane, for making available manuscripts and early books; the Maryborough and Wide Bay Historical Society, the Bundaberg Library and the many individuals, descendants of both Islander and plantation owner, with whom I have talked from Murwillumba in the south to Mackay in the north.

Nancy Cato

The *First White* is a clear, dry, beautifully grained sugar

The *Second White*, though not so clear, is quite dry and would rate in the highest class

The *First Yellow* is dry, well-granulated and apparently as perfect as such sugar can be made

The *Second Yellow* is a very excellent sugar for domestic purposes, far removed from

The *Dark Brown* or 'Ration' sugar (suitable for Kanakas).

Report on the quality of the 1890 sugar yield
at Bundaberg, Queensland.

Book One

The Dark Brown and the First White

1 The Pacific

1 The ship

At seven o'clock on a clear blue morning the schooner *Jason* sailed through an opening in the sheltering reef round the island of Lifu, lying between the New Hebrides and New Caledonia. The temperature on deck was about 85 degrees, the water temperature not much less. A long, lazy swell came rolling in from the north-west across a thousand miles of the Pacific, to break in gouts of foam upon the outer walls of coral. At the base of each curling wave showed a momentary flash of translucent green, to be lost at once in a smother of white.

Like curving jaws the opening in the coral swept past on either side of the schooner. She had beaten on and off all night, waiting for daylight to negotiate the reef. It would be easy to come to grief on one or other of the white fangs grinning and gleaming on each side.

Now the ship sailed through a flat calm, the blue surface broken by a few streaks of white where some larger wave had flung spray across the barrier. Her mainsail came tumbling down opposite a shallow beach of dazzling sand. The anchor was dropped into water as clear and green as emeralds; the crew waited on deck for the native canoes to come out to greet them.

Always in the Islands you kept your rifles loaded and at the ready, but no trouble was expected here. The village had been a Christian one for many years; a Presbyterian mission based in Australia had now taken over from the London Missionary Society.

On land, nothing moved but for a faint breeze stirring the feathery fronds of palm-trees to a wave of welcome, gentle, beckoning. Captain John Coath, not an unduly sensitive man, watched the empty beach impatiently. He would have to think of something to attract the attention of the natives. Yet some obscure feeling held him transfixed on the rather cramped deck of his command.

There was a sense of waiting, of arrested time. The green water, gold-white sand, blue sky and the lazy movement of palm fronds seemed to be speaking, silently, insistently, of something which had been for always and would go on for ever, if men were there to see it or not.

He turned abruptly, shaking off the mesmerism of that beckoning shore. 'Irving!' he called roughly. The mate, a red-faced, blue-eyed, dark-bearded Englishman, put his head above the hatchway. The Kanaka crew leaned indolently on the rail. 'Irving, we'll have to try the "missionary trick". Get your black hat and some books for Bibles, and I'll put on my white mackintosh, and we'll walk round the deck singin' hymns. That should fetch 'em.'

Sandalwood traders had been visiting the Loyalty Islands for years past, feuding with the resident missionary who tried to prevent the men working for them, the village women from becoming their willing partners. These newcomers were seeking not sandalwood but men, strong young men to work in the sugar-cane in the new plantations of the Queensland coast.

Captain Coath and the mate began striding solemnly round the deck, each with a book open in front of him, chanting aloud, and frequently raising their eyes to heaven. The crew giggled at this charade.

'Oh, look will ye look?' chanted Irving, with his eyes apparently on the hymn-book, 'I think – they are com-ing!'

The crew began to murmur excitedly, and Captain Coath swivelled his eyes to the side. He saw the first Islanders splashing and swimming out from the beach – for they were like fish in the water – pushing gifts of floating coconuts and yams threaded on sticks ahead of them. Then the canoes followed, full of cheerful, muscular young men with flowers in their black, woolly hair, strings of shells round their necks, and little else in the way of clothing but a sulu round their loins, no doubt a concession to the sensibilities of the missionary's wife.

They paddled strongly. Irving noted with approval their sleek skins and rippling muscles, which would bring good money – at least £6 a head – on the Queensland labour market.

The men came nearer, laughing and waving.

The missionaries had told them to beware of white men in ships. This was why they had hidden when the schooner was sighted. Mr Duguid, the missionary in charge, was away visiting another island, and they were afraid. But since this seemed to be a 'ship bilong mit-on-a-ree', with someone who looked like a bishop on board, all must be well.

They were welcomed aboard and swarmed all over the ship, handling or picking up everything movable, talking in deep, rapid voices and laughing in a high falsetto. Some were busy prising copper nails out of the woodwork. The tobacco they had received for the yams and coconuts was stuffed into the tops of their sulus, or stuck in their hair. Those who spoke English conversed in pidgin:

'You like more yam? You buy yam? You got plenty knife, plenty nail?'

While the captain stood on a vantage point with a loaded pistol loose in his belt, the mate indicated that down in the hold were all sorts of good things: bright calico and beads, mirrors, nails and iron tomahawks. Eagerly the Islanders climbed down the rough wooden ladder without a thought of danger. They grabbed handfuls of trade goods, chattering like children.

The ladder was quietly drawn up again. A sudden darkening of the light, a crash overhead, and they looked up to find themselves trapped. The hatches were rapidly being secured. Now to their terror they heard the vessel being made ready for sea, the anchor being winched in, the sails run up and the sound of waves slapping against a moving hull. A howl of rage and fear went up from the men, trapped like so many wild possums in the hold.

The *Jason* spread her mainsail to the breeze and turned for the opening in the reef. On shore, the village women saw the canoes drifting away empty, the stranger-ship sailing off. Those who had come out to the ship began swimming despairingly after her (for women were not allowed in canoes), calling to their men to come back. Some followed for two miles, and then, caught in the tidal rip running out through the reef, were too tired to return. They were never seen again.

*

Only one man, Tanua, was left on deck when the hatches were closed. He was trying to prise a copper nail from a piece of planking. When he saw the ship begin to make way, he ran to the side and flung himself overboard, diving deep and coming up on the port side well away from the ship. But the white men were waiting for him to come up. With a long boathook of wood, cruelly barbed with the metal which so fascinated the Islanders, he was hooked through the cheek by the mate, gaffed like a great fish, and hauled struggling and bleeding on deck. The pain in his face was excruciating, especially when the barb was pulled out. Now they were at sea the hatches were opened, and he was flung down in the hold with the others.

One of the men was Wamu, a son of the chief, the head-man of their village. He had been baptized by the missionary and given the new name of Taniela, or Daniel.

Wamu was angry and humiliated at having fallen into the white man's trap. It was he who had said, 'See, they are good men, mit-on-a-rees, they read from the Good Book and sing hymns. Let us go out with yams and fruit to greet them.'

Fortunately the men whose wives were swimming and calling and drowning behind the ship could not see out. At first they had sat cowed and silent, too stunned to protest. Then as the ship made out into open sea and began lifting to the big, slow rollers, a babble of angry talk arose. Where were they going, and why?

They knew of bad men in ships who sometimes stole women from the villages. But it was unbelievable that they would kidnap all the strong young men, and take them away over the sea, perhaps never to return to their beautiful island.

They lost count of time in the dark hold. The air began to stink with their own excrement. Their only food was boiled rice and a few vegetables. Then the ship ran into a storm, and besides their other miseries they became seasick. Water began to leak through her ancient hull; they were terrified.

Seven of them were almost unable to eat, and what they ate passed straight through without nourishing them. Their dysentery made them weaker. Tanua, the man with the hole in his cheek, became feverish as the wound turned septic. He was the first to die.

The howl which went up from the hold when he died brought the white men running. The ladder was put down, and two men were allowed up into the fresh air to carry the body of their companion from the hold, while the rest were covered by rifles. Then, to their horror, they saw him thrown overboard without ceremony to the sharks. One man at his head, one at his feet; one, two, heave, splash!

All around, the blue Pacific lay calm and deeply blue, almost purple, without a streak of white. The bad weather had gone, leaving only the great slow swell humping the sea into glassy hills and hollows which slid beneath the keel diagonally to their course. No land, not even a land-cloud indicating an island, was to be seen anywhere.

The two Islanders, used to seeing always some faint peaks upon the horizon or some nearer landfall, felt lost and 'properly fright'.

'You all come big-feller island along white man,' said the big boss. He had a black beard and an ugly red face in which the eyes were as blue as the ocean, but harder, like chips of blue glass beads.

'What-name?' they asked, stupefied.

'Big island, him called Queensland, very good place, plenty kai-kai, plenty calico, shirt, trouser, tomahawk. Sposem you work three year, we bring you back long your home island. You bring gun, knife, shirt, all-a-same white boss.'

'T'ree moon?' they asked, brightening. 'You bring us back our own islan' after t'ree moon? You no gammon?'

'Three *year*. Twelve moon,' said Irving mendaciously. He decided it wasn't worth while trying to explain time to niggers.

Captain Coath thought it would be best to 'let all the poor bastards up on deck to get some fresh air' now they were out of sight of land; but Irving was cautious. They seemed quiet enough; only the moans of the sick came up from below, together with the stench of their humanity. He had seen too much of their 'treachery', sudden murders of whole crews by Island men. He suggested they be let up in twos and threes for exercise, since every one that died meant £6 less in Maryborough.

Three more had died and had to be thrown overboard, and then they lost another man, perfectly healthy. He had been allowed up on deck, when with a sudden despairing yell he ran to the side and dived over the rail.

'Back the mains'l! Bring her round! Get that lunatic back on board, Irving,' shouted the captain, seeing some of his profit disappearing.

By the time they had lowered a boat the man's head was just a black dot, like a distant floating coconut. Suddenly it disappeared altogether. Had he simply given up and let himself sink? Or had a school of sharks attracted by the dead bodies thrown overboard, been following the ship?

They rowed about aimlessly for a while, but there was no sign of the escapee. It wasn't worth wasting time over one man. The sooner they got the rest of their human cargo to port, the more would be left alive. Captain Coath ordered the boat back again, and sailed on.

2 The Islanders

Joseph Efate, who used to be called Tula, sat numbly in a corner of the hold, on top of a heap of hard iron ballast. He tried not to breathe too deeply of the stench, telling himself that this was all a dream and he would wake up in his own village, in the men's house smelling sweetly of woven palm fronds, with warm, fresh air blowing through the chinks of the walls and clean, springy sleeping mats of pandanus fronds beneath him.

Joseph and his friends had heard of the 'snatch-snatches', though they had not been to their village before. They were less to be feared than the 'kill-kills', who were after human heads to trade with the headhunters who lived to the north and east. These bad men would fire terrible weapons and destroy whole villages. They would drop heavy rocks on friendly canoes which had come out to trade, and then kill the men as they were pulled from the water.

Though he was only fifteen Joseph was big and strong for his age, and regarded himself as a man. He had been wary, hiding in the shelter of pandanus and breadfruit trees, until the others said that there was no sign of the frightening 'bang-bangs' which could blow a hole in the side of a hut; while the white men seemed to be reading from the Good Book and singing hymns . . . So they had put out trustingly in the canoes.

Now, to while away the dreadful tedium of the voyage, to forget his thirst for pure stream-water and a swim to wash the sweat and stink from his body, Joseph let his mind go back to the time when the missionaries first came.

Of course they were not the first white men the villagers had seen. Before there had been the sandalwooders, who had given Chief Louela a top-hat to wear with his porpoise-tooth necklace and his coconut-shell codpiece. Then had come the Samoan missionaries and the London Missionary Society. Most of them had sailed away again, disheartened, to leave the Islanders to return to cannibalism and war; while the sandalwood vessels left nothing but some bright beads and mirrors that soon got broken, and had taken away some of the prettiest girls.

So that when Mitter the Reverend Duguid, as he said his name was, arrived one day to teach them more about that great God of the white men and Jesu his son, they were at first suspicious. When the ship's boat deposited him on the beach they let him walk up the coral path unharmed, but in the bushes a dozen arrows were aimed at his heart.

Then someone noticed that the other figure, which remained sitting in the boat with the native crew, was that of a white Mary. This was something they had heard of but never seen, so that it was said the intruders came from a big, rich island to the westward where there were many men, but no women.

The man walked very firm and upright and he carried the black book which they recognized from earlier times as the Bible, the Good Book. Mitter Duguid wore a white pith helmet, and his long beard was like gold in the sun.

They rushed out to greet him.

At first they had been very curious, lifting the white Mary's long skirts to look underneath for her legs, but she screamed and Mitter Duguid looked angry so they did not do this again.

Joseph began to dream. He forgot the crowded hold, and the

moans of the sick. He became Tula again, swimming in the small lagoon in water as clear as air, enclosed on three sides with a wall of coral so that it was safe from sharks and sea-snakes.

Eyes open under the water, Tula glided along. He watched the gold-netted sunbeams dance on the sandy bottom. That solid black patch was a shoal of small herrings, yards across. He feinted towards them, and they moved as one in a swift flowing movement. He tossed a small piece of coral rock among them and the mass divided, to close up again instantly, like healing flesh over a white wound. Tiny turquoise fish flashed jewel-like away from his floating shadow; an octopus slid into a crevice of coral rock. It was too small to harm anyone, too big and tough for eating. He surfaced and looked quickly towards the shore twenty yards away, shaking the water from his short curls.

His two charges were playing in the bright, coarse sand, one letting it run through her spread fingers, laughing, the other digging and heaping it up with a concentration and purposefulness that Tula would never have shown at that age.

For they were only babies: white babies, smooth and chubby, with a delightful pale golden tint from the tropic sun. Their hair was like finest coconut fibre, so fair as to be almost white, and quite straight. Tula never ceased to marvel at their hair. Every child he had ever known had been born with tight, black, frizzy curls in a cap about his head.

The bigger child, the girl, deliberately tipped sand on the head of her smaller brother, who was constructing something so busily. The boy hit her; she yelled, and slapped him back. Tula quickly swam and waded towards them.

'Em'ly!' he said sternly. 'You no-more fight-fight longa Jamus. You be good girl now, or I tell you Mumma.'

She screwed up her blue eyes at him, her tears turning to a bewitching smile. She slowly dusted sand from her fingers. She knew he wouldn't tell, of course; he was her slave, divinely appointed to guard and care for her, to carry her when she was tired or when she had to cross sharp coral rock or mud.

Her mother, busily binding hymn-books or helping her husband write out prayers in the Island vernacular, always knew that the children were safe with him, Tula. Her husband made many trips in the missionary vessel to other islands in the Loyalty Group or to the New Hebrides, and Tula, even at twelve, had made himself responsible for the safety of the little family. He slept on the floor of their house when Mr Duguid was away.

Now, in Tula's dream of remembrance, Emily was exploring a ghost-crab's hole. Her arm and pink, dimpled fist reached as far as they would go into the sandy tunnel. Then she gave a scream. The tenant of the hole, always alert for something to eat, had nipped one of her soft fingers.

Tula had held and comforted her while he sucked the blood from the tiny cut. He did not spit it out. He drank the spot of red blood — surprisingly it was not white, nor blue, as he had half expected from the colour of the veins under her transparent skin. He felt he was drinking the whiteman magic, his strength and *mana*.

'Ah, *mana*!' the men cried in unison when the kava-drinking ceremony began. Tula could remember the men decked in green leaves and hibiscus flowers, the long ritual of question and answer, the soft clapping of hands. He had been too young to attend, but had watched from the darkness outside.

The missionaries did not approve of kava-drinking, and they made the men wear a sulu and the girls long dresses to cover their figures, where they had only a few strings of beads made from shells before, and a bark waist-belt. (It had taken a long time to make tapa-cloth by the old method of beating bark, and it was used only for chiefs' robes or for decorating houses.)

In those times there would be great feast-days for the birthday of the chief's eldest son; formerly, before the white men came, it was said that the boy was allowed to choose the plumpest of the latest batch of war-prisoners for his meal. More lately it was a whole roasted pig, with baked yams and bananas. After the feast came the sing-sing, with dancing and beating of drums to an insistent rhythm which warmed the blood, so that many a young girl found her lover on those nights 'under the palm-trees' as the saying was.

That was where Tula had first proved his manhood. Before,

22

he had preferred fishing on the reef to playing around with girls. They were always giggling and putting their arms round you and making mysterious remarks which sent them into shrill peals of laughter. That was why he preferred the missionary's house, where the girls never dared to make jokes like that – though Susanna, who worked there, would sometimes flash him a look of invitation, though usually she was scornful.

'Have a banana, O Tula,' they would call mockingly, and one would add, 'Oh, he don't want a banana, he got big banana already. Is it big enough yet, young Tula?', and they would fall into each other's arms with laughing, while he hung his head and walked away.

His mother had died in the great measles epidemic, the first one, when he was only a baby. The second epidemic had been even worse, wiping out many of the people on Tanna in the New Hebrides, the next neighbouring group. The minister there had threatened them with a pestilence from Heaven if they did not mend their ways. On Eromanga the people rose up and murdered the white missionaries whose God had brought the disease.

On Lifu, the Duguids had watched their house burned down. The Reverend Andrew had punished the men severely with thirty lashes, then calmly set them to building him a new and better home, of coral blocks cemented with white burned lime. The best plaiters of palm fronds in the village had settled to weaving a new roof.

He and Mrs Duguid had gone about their tasks so unperturbed and unafraid that the people had to admire them. Joseph Tula had always been fascinated with the white people, and especially with the first little boy who died.

There had been a little girl as well who did not live more than a few hours. But Johnnie, that boy-baby, was fat and strong, and would kick vigorously in his cot when it was set in a beam of morning sunlight on the verandah.

He had hung about watching the child playing with his dimpled fists until Mrs Duguid hunted him away. But after the baby's death she had noticed him one day looking in at the empty cot with two big tears in his brown eyes. A bond of sympathy grew up between them. From that time on she seemed to accept him almost as one of the family.

Oh! Would he ever see Mrs Duguid and little Emily and Jamus again? thought Joseph, sitting in the stinking hold of the blackbirding ship.

Little Johnnie, that boy-baby, he could never see because he was buried under a palm-tree on the highest part of the island.

'Dysentery', Tula had heard Mrs Duguid say, and 'it's the constant heat – he is getting dried out.' Mr Duguid had told her to give him coconut milk, anything, but to keep giving him fluids. Little Johnnie, flushed and pale by turns, had become too weak even to drink. From a plump, healthy child he had wasted away to a tiny living skeleton with a big head in which his sunken eyes looked enormous. He suddenly looked old and wise and solemn, as if he knew his fate.

Tula had watched the procession that carried the small home-made coffin to the peak. Mrs Duguid did not go. She lay in her darkened bedroom with her face to the wall.

She did not even seem to care about Emily any more, and Tula had to look after her a lot of the time. Mr Duguid was busy as usual, going the rounds of his parish, to the other side of the island, across the lagoon, or on long trips in the mission-ary schooner.

His wife would scarcely speak to him because he had wanted to bury the baby at sea, and not 'in this heathen land'. Tula had heard them arguing. She demanded that Johnnie should be buried beside his little sister who had scarcely lived to see the day.

Tula understood Mrs Duguid's feelings. She had told him once that her baby was buried on the highest point of land, 'the nearest to Heaven on this Island'. The Islanders themselves always buried their relatives and friends on land; only enemies were thrown to the sea, or in the old days, eaten at a great feast.

These days they rarely had a feast, and hardly ever danced. Now they had other, Christian ceremonies. The younger men had been baptized with new Christian names: Taniela, Tavita (or David) and his own name, Joseph.

They liked to sing hymns and to say the 'Our Father', their

voices blending in the half-understood words. But 'The power and the glory', he understood that. It was what he felt when he leaned far out from the top of a coconut palm, letting the wind rock him like a bird. It was when he sang and shouted at the moist blue sky which seemed near enough to touch; or swam against a strong surf, thrusting his muscles against the muscular hills of water, diving through their green translucence before they could bury him in foam.

And it was the feeling he had when, after long and boring lessons in the mission house with Mrs Duguid, he suddenly understood. The funny little black marks, like men standing on their heads or with their legs crossed, or kneeling with their heads or bent in the 'S's – suddenly instead of pictures they were sounds, and he could read. And now he was learning to write.

He picked up little Jamie and dusted the sand off him, distracting his attention from his 'work' by the sight of a hovering sea-eagle, white-breasted and russet-winged.

Taking Emily by the hand and carrying Jamie, he followed the white coral track winding through the rain-forest, not quite jungle, which led to the house. Mrs Duguid was at the stove in the outside kitchen. The girl Susanna was setting the table, moving on silent bare feet. She wore a loosely gathered Mother Hubbard which reached almost to her ankles and effectively hid her burgeoning figure. (Nakedness was a sin, the missionaries taught.)

Susanna walked out to the kitchen with an exaggerated twitch of the hips which in an earlier day would have set her beaded belt swinging provocatively.

'Joseph, is that you?' called Mrs Duguid. 'Will ye no' give the bairns a wash whiles I finish dishing up the kai?' Her voice was busy and abstracted. Joseph washed the protesting children with a rough, scratchy flannel. Susanna, who was dotty about little James, lifted him into his chair, crooning over him. 'You my Jamus, yes, you plenty good boy.' He grabbed a handful of her black frizz and hung on, laughing, till she disentangled his fingers and straightened up.

'Joseph, you may sit doon wi' us. Ye've no eaten yet?'

'No, Ma'am.'

'Well, sit ye doon then. Susanna, come and fetch the food if ye please.'

Susanna had dumped the plate of baked taro and banana, with green tops boiled in coconut milk, in front of Joseph with a scornful emphasis. She did not approve of coloured boys sitting down to eat with white peoples. And this Joseph was already above himself for a boy of twelve. (Oh yes, Joseph knew what she was thinking.)

Mrs Duguid came in, sat down, and began to say grace:

> 'Some ha'e meat an' canna eat,
> Some wad eat that want it,
> But we ha'e meat an' we can eat,
> And so the Lord be thankit . . .'

Tula was hungry. He waited impatiently to begin his food.

*

'Down you go, you black bastards!'

Joseph Tula Efate was rudely awakened from his daydream of friends and food by the crash of a ladder being put down into the hold. Two dozen men half-fell, half-climbed into the dimness and stench, where the only sleeping accommodation was a rough double row of shelves running round the sides.

Five more men had died of seasickness or homesickness, making it a little less crowded; now here was this great crowd of strangers coming down on top of them! The prisoners felt the irritation of passengers who have settled down on a long voyage, to find a lot of newcomers embarking at a later port. The first-comers felt superior, and made room grumblingly.

Wamu, the chief's son, had been protective towards Tula from the start. (Because he was young, the older men had been inclined to bully him and take the best bits out of the mess-buckets of boiled rice and vegetables lowered to them twice a day.) Wamu and Tula had made a corner of their own, sleeping head to feet where two shelves joined, helping to brace each other when the ship rolled.

Sometimes Wamu sang a mournful song of farewell, while

Tula kept time by clapping or by beating with his cupped hands on the boards. When they were allowed on deck together, they stood holding hands, gazing back over the limitless ocean to where they believed their island lay, far below the horizon.

The newcomers seemed dazed at first. Many of them were bleeding from gashes, or bruised and scratched. They came from a different island group altogether, with a different language. They explained, with the help of those who knew pidgin English, that the 'snatch-snatch' had come into their bay looking innocent and friendly. They had rowed out to meet the ship, carrying garlands of flowers in welcome.

Then, as the canoes clustered round the bows, suddenly heavy pieces of iron and stone fell out of the rigging: old cannon and sharp pieces that crashed through the canoes and sank them, injuring some of the men. All had started to swim for shore, but a ship's boat was put out after them, its crew hitting on the head with their oars any man who would not climb aboard. Some had drowned, a few had got away; the rest were prisoners.

As their numbness wore off, the new Islanders began to argue about sleeping places. They were a warlike, headhunting people and not popular with the Lifuans, whom they despised as 'missionary boy'. One man tried to take Tula's place in the corner of the shelf.

'That this man's sleeping-place,' said Wamu surlily.

The other gazed at him from bloodshot dark eyes. He had a graze above one eyebrow and a swelling under the other eye. He was in no mood to argue. He gave Wamu a push in the chest. Wamu sprang at him. Two of the other newcomers prised lengths of wood from the sleeping-shelves for weapons, and attacked Wamu and Tula, who had gone to his help.

The white men on deck heard the noise. They thought a riot was breaking out and that the prisoners were smashing the ship's hull. Two of them began firing down into the hold.

First Lui of Lifu was shot dead, then a bullet hit Wamu.

He raised himself on one arm, lifted his head, and began to speak in an oracular way, reproving the men with the guns. Another bullet cut him down, and he was heard no more.

'Try not to kill them,' Tula heard a rough voice from above. 'Don't forget every one means about £6 a head to me in Maryborough!'

Tula made his way to Wamu's side, but he was already dead. He sat there with the dead man half across him, stupefied with grief. It was already dark in the hold; night was falling over the sea. Once or twice in the night men came and threw pieces of burning paper down, but all was quiet save for the groans of the wounded.

Somehow the hideous night passed.

Tula dozed off, and woke to find Wamu stiff and cold in his arms. A pink, yellow-whiskered face peered down from the hatch-way: a young man stood there with a steaming cup of coffee in his hand. He seemed to be counting bodies.

'I say,' he called to someone behind him, 'what would people say to my killing twelve niggers before breakfast?' He was a tall young man fresh out from England who had shipped with Captain Coath 'to gain experience'. He was finding the whole voyage most exciting.

During the morning the ladder was put down in the hold and the chastened men were told to come up on deck. Ropes were placed round the badly wounded and the dead so that they could be hauled up. Slipping in the blood of his fellows, Tula helped.

He saw that they were passing close to an island, whether it was the one the new men had come from he did not know; but as they sailed closer the white men began tipping the wounded overboard with the dead.

Some sank at once, others tried feebly to swim. Their blood spread out in the blue-green water, turning it red and cloudy. Some who were not so badly wounded dived overboard themselves and swam for shore. It might be a cannibal island where they would lose their lives, but anything was better than the dreaded kill-kills who had kidnapped them. They firmly believed that they would be eaten anyway when they reached the white man's 'island'.

In this way twenty-five to thirty men were disposed of, and now there was no argument over places in the hold.

Before he was sent below, Tula looked round the horizon, taking in great gulps of fresh air. The white crew had been down in the hold directing the Kanaka crew to clean and whitewash the walls to remove the stains of blood. At least it would not smell when he was returned to his prison. The lime-wash would sweeten the air and lighten the darkness of the hold. But the pictures of horror would never be erased from behind his eyes.

Always he saw his friend Wamu raising himself on one arm, lifting his head to speak in a proud, strong voice: then the bullet smashing into his chest and the blood gushing from his mouth, mixed with pink froth. Then a picture of his sturdy, dark body turning and sinking down in the green translucent depths beneath the boat, where the great fierce fish they used to hunt beyond the reef would be waiting to eat him . . .

It was such a beautiful morning. How could such dreadful things have been done in such lovely surroundings? A gentle wind just ruffled the surface of the sea; the island, dark green and wooded, lay close by; beyond, coral cays and larger islands, floating softly in a blue haze, clustered on every hand. This must be part of the New Hebrides, it was not the Loyalties Group, for he had been all over those islands by canoe and launch. His experience of the large boat belonging to the missionaries, and of white men's ways generally, helped Tula to overcome his terror and homesickness. He was even young enough to feel a sense of adventure at sailing off to the great 'island' of Queensland. He had no mother to weep for him, nor wife nor children; he was only fifteen.

But to have gone without saying goodbye to his father, or to his friends the Duguids, and most of all to little Em'ly! He hoped they would not think he had gone of his own free will. And he hoped the three moons would pass quickly before he would be back.

Chief Louela would certainly avenge the snatching and murder of his son, Wamu. If this ship was going to return them to Lifu it had better be very quick about it and get away as fast as it could. He himself would help to split the skull of that young man with the cup of coffee, if he had a tomahawk in his hand. He had not heard the word 'niggers' before, but the tone of voice told him it was a term of contempt.

Perhaps they could all get guns in Queensland, and take them back to defend their island against white slavers and black headhunters.

3 The missionaries

The Reverend Andrew Duguid lifted his white topee and wiped the sweat from his brow. The missionary schooner *Dayspring* had just dropped him on its way to Uvea, putting him over the side in a light dinghy which he had to row to land.

Usually, two or three canoes would put out to meet the schooner, and he would be rowed ashore in triumph by his 'boys' of the Presbyterian New Hebridean Mission. It was strange, but today there were no canoes. There was not a soul on the beach, and no women or children came swimming out to meet him. Had some sickness struck the village? He had been away only a week.

As he took up the oars again he looked over his shoulder at the thick mantle of jungle sloping up to the low hills in the centre of the island. He longed to see a real mountain again: the bare, misty mountains of Scotland washed with the mauve-red of heather, instead of this endless green. But he had exiled himself here of his own free will, and Amelia had come with him. Without her he could never have kept going. She accepted everything: the heat, the discomforts, the never having a white woman to talk to, the drudgery of teaching the girls to read and sew and to conduct themselves modestly.

They had achieved something, he felt. The women were decently covered, in loose dresses they made themselves, instead of flaunting about in a few strings of beads. The men no longer drank kava until they were stupefied, nor did they collect enemy heads as a proof of virility, nor strangle widows, nor eat human flesh. They had given up their more reprehensible habits and heathen customs. Yet he was not at ease about the work.

There were still backslidings, illegitimate births, bloody fights between rival villages, and worst of all, a deep indifference to religion. His own boys, like Joseph Efate or Tula as his uncles called him, were docile, cheerful fellows who would work hard in the mission taro patch if asked. But he felt the deep, dark, spiritual inertia under all the singing of hymns and prayer meetings.

They loved singing and they sang well, with good harmony. He had taught them hymns translated into their own Melanesian tongue, which he was still learning. Lifu was a small island and had long been subject to missionary influence. Most of the people were nominally Christians. In the early days, though, he had become disheartened. When he finished speaking of Jesu's love and suffering for mankind, they would look at him with an indifferent or incredulous expression, or even burst out laughing. It was disconcerting.

And when he invited them to the house, and a great black, nearly naked fellow sat casually with his bottom right on the dining-table, Amelia's face was a study. Basically, he felt, they were a lazy, good-for-nothing people, disappointing in many ways. Yet he knew he should not be always shouting at the men to get up from their long midday siesta, to work harder. The women were more energetic than the men. Yet when the sandalwood vessels called, he had to prevent the men from working for the visiting Europeans, for the sake of their souls.

Now and then he let them have a feast in the old style for someone's birthday: whole roast pig, baked bananas and yams and sweet potato and cassava cooked in the earth. They spent a week preparing the feast, and needed another week to sleep it off. It was a fearful waste of time. Andrew was always conscious of the passage of time. (He took out his large silver watch now, and consulted it.)

He rested on the oars and wiped his upper lip. The beauty of the curving golden shore, the green feathery line of palms against the sky, a few thatched houses showing grey-brown shapes in a clearing; all meant nothing to the man of God.

He was here because he had been called to the task, because he was needed. He took up the oars again. Strange, how quiet it was! Amelia would be waiting to greet him at the house, set high to catch any breeze from the sea. A corner of its white coral-block walls showed above the trees, and its palm-leaf roof.

On the way from Maré they had passed a strange schooner, black-hulled, making towards the New Hebrides. She might have been French, but she carried no flag. More likely a sandalwooder from Australia. Those ships knew they were not welcome, and gave the mission schooner a wide berth.

He grounded the little dinghy with a soft crunch in the coral sand, expertly shipped the oars and jumped out, pulling her well up the beach above the tide. He left most of his things to be carried up later, and feeling rather flat at the lack of welcome – for he had been expected home today – he toiled up the soft, steeply sloping beach to the welcome shade of the jungle.

Just then he heard the wailing of women.

They were gathered outside the village meeting-house, crying and gesticulating. Children howled in sympathy, dogs barked, babies yelled. There seemed to be no young men about. Were they all out fishing?

'Ah, Man-of-God!' cried one of the women, seeing him and running to meet him. 'A great disaster has struck like a tidal wave while you were from home!'

'Not my wife!' His lips were white, almost too stiff to form the words. 'Not Missie Duguid?'

'No, no, it is the young men, all, all are gone. And women also, they swam after the snatch-snatch, calling and crying for their men, and are washed against the reef or sunk beneath the waves.'

'Now what's this ye're telling me?' He lifted the topee from his wet hair in the shade of a breadfruit tree. 'The men are gone, ye say? They did not wish to go? They have been stolen by the sandalwood getters for slaves! I told them to have naething to do wi' those wicked white men.'

'Ah, but these look alla-same mi-ton-a-ree, sing alla-time, readim Bible. Men go out to this God-ship. Then she sail away, quick-time, and our young men all gone, our strongest, our best. Ai-eee-ai!' and they went off into another long wail of despair.

'Aye, we saw her sailing past the island. No wonder she kept well away!' He was talking to himself, hurrying up the slope. 'I must write at once to the Moderator.' He had forgotten that he was hot and tired.

He flung his hat on the table in the outer room. 'Amelia!'

'Och, is it you, Andrew. I didna hear ye.' She spoke as she came through the bamboo curtain from the bedroom, smoothing her brown hair back into its knot with her thin, fine-boned hand. He kissed her, but distractedly, then flung himself into a chair and demanded pen and paper.

'I must write to the Moderator, and to the Reverend Robert Steele,' he said.

'Yes Andrew; but first let me mak' ye a nice cup of tay. You must be clemmed.'

'I dinna want tay, woman! Those dastardly black-bir-rders; I've been hearin' what they've been up to on Malekula. And now they've struck here, and I from hame.'

Amelia went on quietly stoking up the stove and bringing the big black kettle to the boil. The stove was outside, under a palm-leaf shelter, to keep its heat from the house. She called to him through the open door:

'I kenned naething aboot it, till I heard the women screaming and carrying on. By then the schooner was sailing awa', and some of the puir things swimming after her.'

'You're sure she was schooner-rigged? Not a brigantine – the *Syren,* for instance, with that villain Ross Lewin in command?'

'No, she was a schooner, dark-painted.'

'They can't be allowed to get away with this!' cried Andrew, slapping the table. 'It's straight-oot kidnapping, it's slavery!'

'You know what these wretches call it? "Blackbirding" – like trapping animals or birds for the market. They're supposed to bring them back to their own islands after three years on the sugar plantations. And what will happen to our Christian young men like Joseph—'

'Joseph! They haven't taken Joseph!' cried Amelia.

'Ay; he's gone with the ither young men.'

'How will I manage without Joseph? He was so devóted to Emily. Forbye, he is only a bairn.'

'But well-built and muscular. He will need to be strong for the canefields, which is where he will be set to work. All so that the grrand families o' Maryborough can hold their balls an' drive oot in their carriages, never mind that their plantations are built upon ruined homes and martyred black men.'

'Andrew dear, here's a sup of tay now. Sit ye doon and drink it while it's hot ... I'll fetch the pen and paper. And here's an oatcake. Ye're too thin,' she said, looking with anxious affection at his bony face, the fanatical eyes sunk deep in their sockets. Oh, it was good to have him back. He might look frail, but he was a man, masterful and fearless, and she loved him dearly.

While he was away she did not sleep well. And during the last week some premonition had been weighing on her, like a physical pressure on her chest. She was Scottish, and her mother before her had this same uncomfortable gift of precognition.

It was like the time before Johnnie died. One night, in a waking flash – she was sure she had not been asleep – she had seen him lying pale and still in his cot. A great flying cockroach, a disgusting black shiny creature, had landed on his arm, and he did not flinch nor move.

It was only a flash on her inward eye, yet so vivid that she had got up, quietly without disturbing Andrew, and hurried to look at the child. The hot grease from the candle fell on her wrist. Johnnie was asleep, of course, breathing gently, faintly flushed, his fair floss of hair damp with sweat against his forehead. There was no cockroach. She raised the damp hair with one finger, and unable to resist the need to feel his living warmth, lifted and turned him on his other side. His eyelids fluttered, his lips made unconscious sucking movements as he settled back into sleep. She tucked the mosquito net firmly round his cot and went back to bed. Three weeks later he had died of dysentery.

She often dreamed of him, always that he was alive, and then would wake to the realization of her loss. He had been so small, he held on to her long skirts as he made his first staggering steps in the world. And now he was gone, to join the baby sister already buried beneath the alien palms of Lifu. When they sang, in church service, the hymn 'Around the throne of God in Heaven, Thousands of children stand', she began to weep. She did not care about those thousands of angel children, she wanted her child, flesh of her flesh and bone of her bone.

'We will have another,' Andrew had tried to comfort her. She felt alienated from him in her grief, which she knew he did not share. Then little James had been given to them. For a while she had wondered if the Lord did not mean her to have any more children, if perhaps He was punishing her for her dependence on the physical side of love. Even Johnnie she had loved with a sensuous delight in his silken floss of hair, his clear skin, his tiny lips playing with her nipple when he was full of milk and content. For Amelia Duguid was a warm and womanly person, with a passionate nature overlaid by generations of stern Presbyterian ancestors and their dour prohibitions.

In truth she did not want any more children, now she had Emily and James to bring up in this heat and isolation. Perhaps she should no longer sleep with Andrew? Yet he had little enough of comfort in the hard vocation he had chosen. And she loved the way he mastered her in bed.

Now, while he sat composing a fiery letter to Dr Steele in Sydney, having eaten his oatcake and gulped his tea without tasting it, Amelia looked round the spacious room. As she was given to do, she began counting her blessings.

The house was clean, cool, and airy. The large open windows with louvres of woven palm frond let in the sea-breezes while keeping out the heavy, vertical rain of the tropics. The walls were lined with calico, and the windows with neat muslin curtains that she kept laundered and fresh, and looped back with her one frivolity, lilac-coloured ribbons. A set of rough shelves lined one wall to hold her sewing things and their collection of Divine books and sermons (they did not read novels).

The comfortable cane furniture they had brought from home had all been lost in the fire; but they had saved the solid dining-table and chairs, and for the rest she had covered packing cases with bright cretonne and chintz.

Beyond the door lay the Pacific Ocean, beautifully blue; and resting on it like a faint cloud a distant island which Amelia thought of as 'her' island, though she had never been there.

She had written to her mother when they first arrived, trying to describe the beauty of the view:

'A deep blue sea interrupting the breakers on either side shows the passage through the reef. And as I look up, every now and then a line of dazzling white catches my eye. It is like a slow, even smile spreading outwards into a wide grin, like the smile of one of the native boys, who have the most perfect white teeth I have ever seen, no doubt due to their diet of fruit and vegetables with a little pork and fish.

'The early mornings are most beautiful . . . The area between us and the beach is filled with coconut palms and other bright green things. The nearest coco palm raises above the level of the horizon its feathery crest in front of the pale blue sky; while its lower leaves have the deep blue sea for background. A breeze keeps all in graceful motion . . .'

She had attempted a water-colour, but felt she could not do justice to the brilliance of the scene. Indeed, she never seemed to have time for painting. Though various girls helped in the house, and did the washing in one of the nearby streams, they were indolent and needed much supervision. But Andrew insisted that she must have help. She had found the heat exhausting when Jamie was on the way, and had never recovered her strength.

There came a whimper from the inner room where little James and Emily were asleep. Emily was getting too big for an afternoon sleep, but she too became tired and pale with the heat. Amelia went through and lifted her from the cot. One of her cheeks was flushed a bright pink where she had been lying on it. She smelt hot and acrid with sweat; her blond hair, lighter than Andrew's sandy thatch, clung to her wet neck.

Emily grizzled all the time her dress was being pulled on and her hair brushed. 'I want Jo-seph,' she whined. Amelia had dreaded this demand. How to explain that her devoted slave and guardian was gone?

Joseph Tula: broad-shouldered Tula, with his shining deep bronze skin, his chest hairless as a child's; Joseph with his close-curled cap of black hair clinging so neatly to his head; Joseph of the smoky dark eyes and charming smile. Amelia had always liked him, and trusted him with her children. He had been baptized into the Church, and was almost a member of their family, like another son to her.

'Daddy's home!' she whispered now, to distract Emily.

'Daddee!' Emily struggled from her mother's arms and ran to the other room to fling herself on her father's knee. To her a week was an eternity in which she had not seen her father. She jolted his arm and a blot fell from the nib upon the letter to Dr Steele.

Andrew Duguid frowned. He took one of the small soft arms in a steel grip and held her away from him while he admonished her. 'Little gels must not act like tomboys. Now go out of the room and come in again, quietly, and give me a kiss.'

Emily's flush of joy was gone. Pale and silent, she crept out the door and came in again. She stood several inches away and leaned forward to touch her father's sallow cheek, above the sandy-coloured beard, with her lips. He patted her kindly, but two big tears stood in her blue eyes.

Amelia, who often thought Andrew was too strict with the children, said nothing. He bent to his writing again, his fierce, fanatical gaze under his overhanging brows bent sternly upon the paper as if on those thieving blackbirders themselves. His pen flew along the lines, making a dry, vehement scratching, as he underlined words for emphasis:

'. . . these depraved and soulless villains have taken away almost *all* of my Christian converts among the young and able men of the village; and have indirectly *murdered* some of the women, who were lost when swimming after their husbands.

'Such actions cannot and *must not* go unpunished. From the description she will have been a labour vessel from Queensland – indeed, I think I caught a glimpse of her myself while still at sea.

'By tracing some of my men, such as the chief's son, Wamu, it should be possible to discover the name of the ship, and of her captain and first mate, and to bring them to justice . . .'

He signed the letter with a flourish, blotted it carefully, folded it and sealed it down. There would be a mail ship calling, though not perhaps for weeks. Meanwhile it was written, and the writing had helped to relieve his feelings.

The schooners which visited the Islands with 'trade' goods, he realized, were there only to make money and had no regard for the spiritual or temporal welfare of the native people; but at least they had not until recently begun abducting the young men. Some had gone willingly before as crew members, for short voyages, but this was different. They would be sold at so much a head in Maryborough, like merchandise.

Sandalwood had brought the traders here first. They found they could purchase labour, and load the ship's commissariat with fresh fruit and vegetables, in return for a few worthless glass beads which could be bought in England for 2/6d for ten thousand, and some cheap calico. The sandalwood could be sold at a good profit on the China coast to wealthy merchants who would turn it into joss sticks and sell them for burning before the shrines of ancestors.

As Andrew Duguid put away the writing things, young Jamie began to whimper in the next room. Amelia went to him. He was dry and burning hot to the touch. Fever! Her heart gave a lurch and then seemed to settle, low in her chest, heavy as a stone.

4 The blackbirders

Captain John Coath of the *Jason* felt at peace with the world. Down below he already had a dozen new recruits, some of whom had been snatched by his men when they came too close in their canoe. As they reached up their hands for tobacco in exchange for the bananas and yams they had brought to trade, they were grabbed and hauled aboard by the arms.

In the store-room he still had a good quantity of trade goods for enticing more Kanakas or paying their relatives. The trade box held clay pipes as well as tobacco, and knives, tomahawks, mirrors, nails, knobs of Reckitt's blue, and thousands of coloured beads. There were also some old muskets (in great demand and also illegal, since the Queensland Government had brought in a law prohibiting their export to the islands), and rolls of colour-printed calico.

Much of it could be used again on another trip; they only had to get the men on board, and then sail off with them. But it was more politic to buy them with goods, so that he could return peaceably next time to the same islands. He was running out of islands where his black-painted schooner was welcome. But he had found that to come from the port of Maryborough helped. Many of the Islanders now knew about Maryborough by word of mouth. 'What name cappen?' they would ask first, then 'where you from?' When he replied 'Maryborough' they said, 'Mallybulla velly good place. You buy boy? How long he work?'

To this crucial question the answer had always been 'three moons', but since he had to carry a Government Agent these days to see that the 'boys' understood their contract, he had to say 'three years'. But Captain Coath did not let the presence of the GA worry him unduly. He showed the man from the beginning, by veiled threats and bullying, that he had no authority on this ship. When one of them had proved too interfering he'd had him clapped in irons and put below with the recruits, claiming that the GA was violent and unbalanced and had to be confined for his own good.

He knew that the recruits would very likely settle down to enjoying the life at Maryborough with its gambling and women at the week-ends, and would likely sign up for a new term. They would be given an English name, like Albert or Jim or Tommy ('Tommy Tanna' was a nick-name for a Kanaka, just like 'John Chinaman' or 'Jacky' for an Abo). And after five years or so they would not even want to go back. So he was really doing them a favour by picking them up, even if sometimes they did not seem to appreciate it.

39

They had been standing off and on all night waiting for daylight before making an entrance through the reef. As the sun rose clear and golden out of the Pacific a soft breeze, warm as new milk, began to stir the air. Before, the faintly heaving sea had not a ripple on its polished surface. The reflection of the land with its feathery palms was unbroken. Even the wake formed a row of glassy curves without a break of foam.

All night the spicy, scented land breeze had come sifted through leaves and flowers. Now it came gently from the sea, smelling of salt and ocean. They slipped easily through the reef and dropped anchor in glass-clear depths to a sandy bottom.

A crowd of natives appeared on the beach and signalled for a boat to be sent ashore. This was unusual; he had expected the usual canoes to put out, filled with fruit and vegetables to trade. But he felt no suspicion. This was a missionary island with its own native teachers.

The ship's boat soon came rowing back with Irving, the mate, and the GA and several new recruits. Each of the new men had a long-handled tomahawk because they were frightened, they said, of the recruits already on board, who might be their enemies from a rival island. The men were jaunty, voluble, laughing in high falsetto giggles. Their tomahawks swung carelessly from their belts.

Coath ordered them up for'ard where he could watch them. He did not want a fight breaking out below between these and the earlier recruits. The new men were in such high spirits, anything was likely to happen.

John Coath felt a twinge of uneasiness. He told Irving to stay aboard while the GA went back for another boatload. He and Irving were both armed, and he had no fear of a handful of niggers. He left Irving on deck and went down to his cabin to clean his spare pistol just in case.

Just as he went below and the boat reached the shore, it was raked by musket fire from natives hidden in the jungle greenery. The GA fell dead, the native crew dived overboard, but were shot as they surfaced or cut down as they came ashore.

Irving was sitting on deck, his feet on the rails, surveying the beach when the first shots were fired. Instantly, as at a signal, one of the new recruits who had crept up behind his deck-chair (a mistake to have turned his back on them!) with one stroke of a tomahawk split his face from the chin upward.

The captain, rushing on deck at the mate's terrible cry, met him stumbling blindly down the companionway, his hands pressed to his face. Blood streamed between his fingers.

Captain Coath dragged him down to the cabin and laid him on the floor, locking the door behind him. Judging from the yells and cries the first recruits were being despatched in the hold. He was stupefied at what had happened, at the clever planning of the attack while the ship's crew was separated. But he should have been more cautious. He listened intently.

Now they were gathered round the cabin scuttle, chattering excitedly, waiting for the two white men to come out. They had cut the schooner's cable and she was fast drifting ashore.

The captain was still hoping for help from land. Surely the boat must come back soon? The mate had not been able to tell him what had happened while he was below.

He looked out of the porthole and saw they were adrift. Next moment the *Jason* grounded on the shallow fringing reef with a sickening crunch, and heeled over. He heard bare feet pounding overhead, and loud cries, then a series of splashes, and silence. The natives had dived overboard to swim ashore.

They kept up a harrying fire from the beach, while the captain fired back through the cabin skylight, now pointing towards shore as the deck slanted more and more. The wounded mate, too weak to hold a gun steady, crawled around keeping him supplied with ammunition.

All the next day they lay quiet and unmolested, and at low tide that night they crept out and down the side without being seen, and waded ashore. The mate was by now weak and wandering in the head from loss of blood. He could neither eat nor drink without help through his split jaw.

For five days they managed to hide in the jungle, living on bananas and green coconuts and drinking their milk, while the Niuta hill men who had attacked them prowled about looking for them.

'It's no good, Skipper,' said Irving at last. 'I'm buggered. For

Gawd's sake put a bullet through me and finish me off.'

'Nonsense, man. Pull yourself together. We'll be all right if we stay put. They'll leave eventually and then we'll get away.'

'These murderin' bastards will get us first.'

'Not before I've accounted for a good many,' said Coath grimly.

'I tell yer I'm finished! I can't stand it.'

Coath was tempted to take him at his word. The poor devil looked terrible, greenish-white, with clotted blood and pus in his black beard from the suppurating wound, his eyes red from lack of sleep. It would be a kindness to put him out of his misery. But a shot would draw the natives.

'Don't make such a row!' he snarled. 'They'll hear you, and murder us both.'

'I don't care! I don't care!' Irving began to scream as he rushed towards the beach, perhaps with some idea of bathing his poor mutilated face in the cool sea. Instead he wandered about raving, calling on his old mother at home.

It was not long before the Niuta came running on swift bare feet, with exultant cries. They dragged him from the paths to a clearing in the jungle. Two men fired at him from point-blank range, while a third hacked off his head. It was not much use as a trophy in its damaged state. They left it there and went looking for the other white man.

Less than twenty-four hours later, a schooner from Fiji arrived, also looking for recruits, and saw the *Jason* on the reef. The Niuta, in fear of punishment, fled back to the hills. The Fiji trader rescued John Coath and helped him salvage what he could from the schooner.

Coath vowed that he would get his revenge for the loss of his ship and his whole crew. He was given command of another schooner, but from that time on he never bothered to trade. He took recruits at the point of a gun. He helped to spread the legend of the cruelty and treachery of South Sea Islanders, not stopping to reflect that it was he and his kind who first supplied them with iron tomahawks and guns, who abducted their women and kidnapped their young men, and taught them to regard the white man as an enemy.

If any of Coath's 'recruits' took sick on the long voyage back to Australia, and it seemed they would not survive the journey, he did not waste time or money on treatment. He tipped them overboard, whether near an island or not. Because he would not trust the 'treacherous black bastards' he kept them always in the hold, often for long hours without food or water. If they clamoured for a drink he would go to the hatchway and urinate on them, shouting 'Right, here's some water for you.'

Coath and his new vessel, aptly named the *Cerberus*, became notorious all over the South Pacific. He never went ashore again without a bodyguard of armed men, rifles at the ready. But sooner or later one of the men he had mistreated would get him, as they got Ross Lewin and 'Bully' Hayes and others of the same brutal kind. He knew he was hated. But his black schooner still ventured to head-hunting islands where no-one else would trade.

'I'd sail her to Hell and back, if there was profit in it,' he boasted, and most people believed him.

2 Queensland

1 The homestead

Breakfast at Chindera was a leisurely affair, especially when the weather was fine and warm enough for the meal to be taken on the verandah. The family would straggle out of doors one by one, 'like Brown's cows' as Mrs Johnstone described it. They would begin the meal with good Scots porridge because Angus Johnstone liked it winter and summer, eaten with butter and salt and fresh milk delivered by Annie Fallon the milkwoman.

She came round at dawn, pedalling a delivery-cart attached to a bicycle which she rode with a fine disregard for the proprieties, riding astride and letting her underwear show. 'There goes Annie Red-pants,' the Maryborough children called after her, for in winter she wore red flannel drawers under her skirt.

Dougal was first on the verandah this morning, a big, full-bearded man in the vigour of his youth and masculinity of whose effect on the opposite sex he was fully aware. Many young women found him irresistible, while an almost equal number could not abide him. His eyes were of a hard, bright sea-blue and his mouth had a sensuous redness and fullness which went oddly with his gingery whiskers.

As a child he had been most beautiful, with sturdy build and milk-white skin contrasting with his red-gold curls. Now his pomaded hair, the curls carefully smoothed down, was more orange than gold, more pink than orange. At nineteen the skin of his face was already taking on the ruddy, choleric hue of his McEachern grandfather.

Dougal had inherited also the formidable McEachern nose, hooked like an eagle's beak; and his teeth were remarkably white and sharp.

'Dougal came in, grinning like a fox', was his brother James's rather uncharitable description. And indeed there was something predatory about Dougal, though it was more aquiline than vulpine.

He ladled himself a bowl of porridge from the iron pot keeping warm over a small spirit stove. He splashed milk and sugar over it and began eating in swift gulps as if he had a train to catch.

Helga, one year older, came out to the terrace trailing a pink morning-gown with wide sleeves like butterfly-wings. She wore a wide satin ribbon of an identical pink to hold the wild tumble of dark curls which grew low on her forehead.

Looking at her, Dougal thought with irritation that Helga couldn't even come down to breakfast without making an entrance, as if appearing in her private box at the opera. (He had never seen an opera and didn't want to; but he had seen pictures of them in books and journals, and had read about private boxes and the romantic intrigues which sometimes took place in them.)

Helga glanced with distaste at the back of his head, drawing down the thick dark brows she got from her father. She left him bent above his hasty porridge-slurping and went to the rail of the Italian balustrade.

She leant there, one hand on the sun-warm stone, and framed by a climbing bougainvillaea blazing with improbable papery blooms of bright cerise. The wistaria vine which twined round the balustrade in living ropes as thick as a wrist had finished flowering two months earlier. It was now green with summer leaf.

Honey-eaters called and chattered among the flowering poinciana, and rainbow-parrots flung screeching overhead. At the foot of the lush, semi-tropical garden shone the river, holding all the light of the morning sky.

Helga turned back to the table and selected a slice of pawpaw and another of rock-melon, adding a sparing dash of sugar. Already at twenty she was what her mother called 'well-formed', and though tight-laced stays kept her waist small she was worried about the size of her bust.

She had exchanged not a word with her younger brother. Now she said irritably, '*Must* you eat every meal as though it was to be your last?'

'Better than picking at my food the way you do, like a hen,' he said, but good-humouredly. 'Why be scared of putting on a bit of weight. You're tall enough to carry it.'

'Exactly. I don't want to be known as "a big woman". It's all right to be tall if you're slender with it. "Willowy", they call it in books.'

'Willowy!' Dougal snorted as he went to the chafing-dish for sausages and bacon. 'Who wants a girl to look like a tree?'

Mrs Johnstone sailed majestically on to the terrace, a light wool lace shawl about her shoulders in spite of the early heat, a small white lace cap on her greying hair. Dougal stood up dutifully and his mother kissed his cheek in passing. She sat down at the wrought-iron table before noticing her daughter with a cool 'Good-morning, dear. Your father is just coming. Better put out his porridge, and don't forget to warm the plate from the kettle.'

This was one meal where they liked to do without servants as much as possible, an informal gathering compared to luncheon in the family dining-room, or dinner in the great formal room with its solid carved table to seat a dozen guests, and its massive sideboard of gleaming mahogany and mirrors.

Helga composedly finished her paw-paw before getting up to obey her mother. She poured water from the simmering kettle into a bowl, then emptied the water over the balustrade. Next, the porridge was ladled in and left to set in a smooth lake of oatmeal, to which she added two knobs of butter, and which she set in her father's place.

She selected a boiled egg from the silver stand with its set of cups and silver spoons that had to be polished after every meal by Eliza, the kitchen-maid, for the egg turned them black. Helga rarely entered the kitchen.

'Gude-morning, gude-morning, and a braw fine day it is. Ye can almost hear the cane growing.' Grey sideburns, sleek and black eyebrows bristling, Angus Johnstone settled genially in his place, radiating content.

('The Old Man's in a good mood, might be a good idea to ask him for that new hack,' thought Dougal swiftly.)

At fifty-one Angus did not think of himself as 'old', and he certainly didn't feel it. He was a tall, solidly built man who held himself well, with an almost military carriage. He had married late in life for good economic reasons: 'Dinna marry for money, ma son, but love whaur money is,' his old mother used to tell him. He was content with his two sons and one daughter, and Julia was now past producing any more after a series of miscarriages since Dougal was born.

The two boys would carry on the plantation and the mill when he was gone. There was James with his good brain to do the accounting and watch the tallies at the mill; and Dougal for the practical side, hiring and firing managers and foremen, making sure they were not too soft with the Kanakas and that each knew his job.

And then there was Helga. He glanced under his brows at her, sitting nibbling at a piece of dry toast. Helga was a strong-minded, wilful, difficult girl, too much like himself in some ways. Helga declared that she did not intend to marry, but meant to go abroad and study music and acting. A daughter of his wanting to go on the stage! Angus had a strong sense of family dignity, and he regarded play-acting as a most disreputable profession. They must get all that nonsense out of her head. Marriage and a few babies would soon cure her. He stirred the melted butter into his porridge and sprinkled it liberally with salt.

'And whaur's James?' he asked, fixing piercing blue eyes upon his wife. 'Time he was up, this bonnie morn. Gi'e him a call, Mither.'

There was no question of just calling 'James! Come to breakfast.' The great house that spread behind and above them was modelled on an Italian palazzo that Angus had seen on his tour of Europe when he was a young man.

James's room was upstairs among a dozen other bedrooms and guest rooms opening on to the first-floor balcony. The lower rooms, the reception rooms and the dining-rooms, opened through full-length windows, screened with persiennes, on to a long, roofed verandah and the terrace where they now sat.

The great carved front door had come from Florence, as had the fountain in the garden with its bronze putti and dolphin.

The balustrades were of white Italian marble from Carrara. On the highest point in the acres of garden, Angus Johnstone had built a little Roman temple with stone seats and stone pillars, and here he liked to sit and contemplate his estate and the façade of his imposing mansion.

Chindera had been built for show with its arches and balustrades and tower, but it was comfortable too, and cool in summer. Set on the verdant banks of the Mary River, where not long ago a thick vine jungle flourished, its lawns sloped down through clumps of giant bamboo and traveller's-palm, past feathery-leaved jacarandas and shady mango trees where the flying foxes came at night to eat the golden globes of fruit.

Julia Johnstone rang the little handbell on the table. Sun, slanting through leaves, dazzled back from white cloth and silverware, and slanted a golden beam through the honey jar with its swinging lid to keep out bees and wasps.

'Harriet,' she said to the parlour-maid who appeared from the adjoining dining-room, 'you can bring some fresh coffee, and just give Mr James a call, will you? Tell him we are nearly finished.'

'Yes'm.' Harriet gathered up the empty porridge plates before leaving. Helga preferred to drink coffee in the mornings because she felt it was Continental and European, whereas the others usually took tea.

Angus helped himself to more sausages and bacon while his wife busied herself among the teacups with an elegant tinkle of thin china. She poured boiling water into the pot.

'I have asked young Mr Lindsay to dine with us tonight, Helga,' she said.

'Why tell me?'

Julia Johnstone's eyebrows rose right to her hairline, which, combined with her arrogant, bony nose, would have intimidated most people; however Helga was unmoved. She added, 'You will want to look your best, I presume, when we are entertaining a guest. I suggest you get Estelle to iron your pale green gauze, its suits you well.'

'I am not interested in Mr Lindsay, Mamma. He bores me.'

'Nevertheless, he is very obviously interested in *you*. In any case, you as daughter of the house will do your best to make yourself agreeable. At least it will be a chance to exercise your voice.'

Helga's black brows almost met in a scowl as she decapitated her boiled egg with a sharp blow of the spoon. She made no reply.

Harriet came back with the coffee as James appeared, rather tousle-haired, slender and darkly handsome, as unlike his brother Dougal as it was possible to be. His drooping moustache made him seem older than his years, and gave his pale face a look of melancholy. With a muttered 'Good-morning' to the family he bent his tall frame to kiss his mother, then took a piece of fresh pineapple over to the balustrade. He ate the juicy slice in his fingers while staring out as Helga had done at the green and gold of the morning. A flock of rainbow-parrots swooped recklessly overhead, seeming to collide with, rather than perch on, the bare twigs at the top of a bunya pine. They arranged themselves like brilliant glass beads on a string, like the beads the traders used to entice the simple Islanders to Queensland to work in plantations like Chindera.

James looked over the velvet lawns sloping down to the river. All this wealth and comfort, the house with its long cool dining-room behind him, its shuttered windows opening on to wide verandahs, the drive lined with mango trees, the acres of ordered cane-fields beyond: all depended on coloured labour, men working a twelve-hour day for the magnificent return of ten shillings a month and their keep, with a shirt, a hat and a blanket per year.

Four hundred Kanakas were employed at Chindera besides half a dozen Chinese and ninety Europeans. A local paper, the *Tribune*, had announced recently in its columns that 'In employing coloured labour, Queensland has the possibility of becoming rich beyond the dreams of avarice; while without it, the sugar industry could not survive.'

James sometimes wondered if he were the only person in Maryborough who felt a twinge of conscience over the connotations of 'coloured labour'. (He threw the core of the pineapple slice down among the fallen blossoms of frangipani, lying like creamy-yellow stars on the grass, and joined the family at table.)

To read the southern newspapers was to realize that the *Tribune* and the *Chronicle* were slanted to the plantation-owners' point of view; all the same he did not believe all the stories of piratical, blackbirding captains like Bully Hayes and Captain Murray of the schooner *Carl*. Yet he knew that Islanders on arrival were often sick and unhappy, pining for their lost homes; and when they first arrived and understood from their fellow-workers that it would be three long years, not three moons, before they returned, they would gather together to wail harmoniously through the night, and sing strange songs full of sorrow and yearning.

It proved at least that black men were human beings, with hearts and feelings, whereas some people claimed that they had no more souls than animals. They were human beings, yet he had seen them huddled on deck like cattle, as unknowing of their fate or destination as beasts sent to the slaughter.

He had seen them with labels round their necks, being sent north to the Johnston River with other merchandise. There they were, on the ship's manifest: 'From Maryborough, 1 horse, 35 bags sugar, 13 Kanakas, 1600 ft pinewood, 1 bar of iron, freight £27.12s.'

Then there had been the disquieting case of the schooner *Jason*, based at Maryborough, whose skipper John Coath had after a long inquiry been recently jailed for 'offences against natives'. The scandal had embarrassed Maryborough not a little, for it had been supposed that such things as kidnapping and shooting occurred only in the Fiji trade, or among unscrupulous Sydney captains.

The death rate was very high among new recruits at Chindera. They had a lot of sickness on the plantation, considering that almost all were men in the prime of life. And now he was forced to believe that many of them had been intimidated, starved and beaten before being purchased. He had also suggested that their ration was inadequate, but any idea of increasing it was ruled out by Dougal and his father, who said that if they gave Kanakas white men's rations, it would not be economic to employ them at all.

The *Jason* case had served to confirm his uneasiness with the whole operation of importing Islanders to Queensland.

It was William Brookes, writing for the *Courier Mail* in Brisbane, who had brought the case into the open. Brookes referred to recruiting of Kanaka labour as 'the slave trade'. He was well hated by the Maryborough establishment. Mr Johnstone had taken up yesterday's *Courier Mail* as he drank his tea. 'Aye . . . aye,' he muttered. Then he spluttered in his cup and put it down on the saucer with a crash.

'Lies! Dom'd lies!' he cried. A vein stood out on his forehead; he flushed dangerously. There goes his good mood, thought Dougal gloomily.

'Leesen to this, Julia! "This Colony has attempted to introduce slavery to her shores . . . Coloured labour means ruin, social and moral, to Queensland!" It's yon sancteemonious William Preacher Brookes agen. And some eediot ca'd the Reverend Sunderland of Sydney says he "veesited the Kanakas on one Queensland plantation who had all been taken by fraud, were ill-treated, ill-fed and frequently flogged". The mon's haverin'! And where was this plantation, I'd like fine to ken? It's no' in Maryborough I'll be bound.'

He picked up his cup and gulped tea angrily.

'And yet, Father,' said James in a reasonable tone (for though he was of course on the side of the planters he had this uncomfortable faculty for seeing both sides of every question), 'isn't there more than a grain of truth in this man Brookes? I mean—'

'What! Slavery?'

'I mean it *is* true that you can do what you like with your Kanakas once you've bought them for three years. They're not free to come and go, to change jobs or go back home if they don't like it—'

'They signed a contrract!' said Angus irritably. 'Thrree years at six pun per year.'

'You don't know what you're talking about, James,' said

Dougal with his mouth full of toast. He swallowed, and added, 'What about the Polynesian Labourers' Act which was passed to protect them?'

'Everyone ignores the Act, and you know it. You can feed the Kanakas as much or as little as your foreman thinks fit, and they have no rights. None of the white mill-workers would put up with the conditions they do.'

'What sort of radical talk is this?' cried Angus, outraged. 'God made the tropics for the black folk tae worrk in; white men were never meant to worrk ootside in the tropic sun. Do ye want to fly in the face of Proveedence, then?'

'Well, you may be in the confidence of the Almighty, Father, but I wish I could be so comfortably certain. It seems to me we exploit them for our own ends, and then justify the means by calling it "the Will of Providence".'

A dangerous light shone in Angus Johnstone's eye. He stared down at his son, daring him to utter another word.

Dougal said roughly, 'You talk like that nigger-loving editor in Brisbane. A lot of us think he should be tarred and feathered.'

'Some more tea, dear?' interposed Mrs Johnstone smoothly. 'James – coffee?' She never argued with the men, believing that it was not ladylike to do so. Helga was sunk in her own thoughts, her brow dark.

James shrugged and gave up the argument. He thought sometimes he would like to write, to inflame passions and champion causes with a pen mightier than the sword. But he had no flair for writing, nor indeed for anything but the book-keeping he did at the mill. And he enjoyed marshalling facts and figures, keeping neat columns of accounts, knowing where to find anything at a moment's notice in his complex filing system.

Yet on summer mornings like this he felt a divine discontent. He watched the parrots unthread themselves from the twig and go veering and shrieking through the trees in an explosion of green and crimson, yellow and blue. Free as the air! And surrounded by their own kind. Really, he had nothing in common with the rest of the family, or the other young men, sons of planters or professional men, whom he met socially. He had been born like a cuckoo in the nest, among birds of a different breed.

*

Helga was like a cuckoo in the nest, Mrs Johnstone was thinking as she checked the preparations for dinner. How did she come to have such a wilful, troublesome child when other daughters were dutiful and demure? Dougal was somewhat wild, but he would settle down all right when he had sown his wild oats.

She straightened a fork on the table and stood back to admire the effect: the lace cloth showing up against the sombre richness of the dark, embossed wallpaper of green and gold wreaths; the carved rosewood chairs with their green brocade upholstery, the mahogany sideboard with its load of silver dishes, looking as if it must have grown where it stood, for it was so solid and heavy that it could surely never be moved. Dinner was a serious occasion, even *en famille*. Tonight they were entertaining the editor of the local paper as well as Mr Lindsay, who was reputed to be very well-connected in England.

The silver candelabrum which made a centre-piece, standing with its base in the sea of red hibiscus blooms, reflected the light of the chandelier above. The flowers, lying on the cloth without stems, would not last beyond tomorrow even if set in a vase of water. They bloomed luxuriantly in the rich soil, but each flower faded at the end of the day. That was the trouble with all this semi-tropical exuberance: the trees dropped their profusion of flowers untidily at their feet, the jacarandas were ringed with blue, the coral-trees with red, the poincianas with orange and yellow. And luscious fruit, mango and paw-paw, quickly went soft and rotten. The plantation depended on a kind of monstrous grass that went mad and grew twelve feet high.

She stood back to admire the table. Yes, it would do. Harriet had folded the napkins into an intricate design of water-lilies; they were a credit to her.

Julia Johnstone prided herself on her taste. She would wish to turn out a daughter as finished as this long, stately room. Perhaps a young lady with smooth blond hair and pencil-fine brows, or like Miss Rose Lovelace, James's girl, with delicate hands skilled at needlework and watercolours. Helga played the piano well, and her other accomplishment was singing. But she was rather too tall, and her hands, though well-formed, were large and capable-looking. Perhaps it would have been better if she had been a boy.

2 The establishment

At dinner, Helga was placed next to young Mr Lindsay – well, not so young, he must be in his thirties, she decided – but he was quite a personable fellow if you liked that kind of solid, broad-shouldered, kindly-faced man who no doubt did not have a note of music in him. His hair was a dark blond, and he wore it rather long. She found herself strangely disturbed by the way it grew round the whorl of an ear. It was a strong, pink, well-shaped ear that lay close to his head, neatly, not like Dougal's ears which were large in proportion with the rest of him . . . but of course Mr Graham Lindsay did not interest her. She longed to meet great musicians like Verdi.

'Ye ha'e seen this nonsense in today's *Courier Mail*, nae doot, Lindsay?' said Mr Johnstone as the soup was served. His wife frowned slightly. She liked to keep away from controversial subjects, at least until they had reached the sweet course and the men had mellowed a little with the wine.

'Ah yes. You mean accusing the planters of being selfish capitalists who wish to increase their wealth by black slave labour?'

'Aye! What poppycock! The *Maryborough Chronicle* has aye pointed oot already that ony outrages are the worrk of Fiji traders; or, forbye, in nearly every case. Eh Woodyatt? Your leader in tomorrow's *Chronicle* will set them to rights.'

'Oh, absolutely; I have referred, among other things, to "this intolerable balderdash".'

'Mr Lindsay, you have lately sailed in one of the recruiting vessels, I believe?' put in Julia Johnstone smoothly. 'You will be able to tell us at first hand of the conditions, and that those described in the southern Press do not apply to Maryborough captains.'

(This had been the *Chronicle*'s theme all along, in spite of the setback caused by the unpleasant publicity of the *Jason* inquiry. For the tri-weekly paper's owners were also in the shipping trade, and the Editor knew he would not last long in his position unless he took the planters' viewpoint.)

Mr Lindsay knitted his fair brows. The question, in this company, was an awkward one. Yet he was glad of the diversion, for he had been intently aware of Helga's scrutiny. He blurted out, 'I'm afraid blackbirding is blackbirding, whatever the vessel's port of register.'

There was a brief, shocked silence.

Mr Woodyatt coughed. 'We don't use the term "blackbirding" here,' he said. ' "Recruiting", or "the Kanaka trade", or—'

'Yes, I've noticed,' said young Mr Lindsay drily.

'Hr'rmph. Some more wine?' Angus leaned forward to replenish the young man's glass with a hand that shook slightly. ' 'Tis a local wine, made by a Gairman fellow in South Australia, but it's a bonnie wee drop in my opeenion.'

His attempt at changing the subject fell flat. Helga had warmed towards Mr Lindsay as she saw her father's eyebrows begin to bristle with suppressed anger. Young Lindsay was a guest, and Angus was bound by the laws of hospitality, but he fidgeted in his chair as if sitting on hot coals.

'And coloured labour is absolutely essential to the survival of the sugar industry in Queensland; with its aid, Queensland will find itself the leading colony of Australia, rich beyond the dreams of avarice.' Mr Woodyatt was inclined to talk like one of his own leading articles.

'It's rather a question of whether the end justifies the means,' said Graham Lindsay.

'Pray tell us, Mr Lindsay,' said Helga, turning the full battery of her high-powered dark glance upon him, 'about your adventures on the trading schooner. What was her name? Did you like her captain? And were you the Government Agent on board? And where did you go? I should love to sail out into the Pacific Ocean.'

Lindsay looked flattered, but for a moment he did not reply; he could not. The effect of that sudden deep glance under her black brows had been like the thrust of a sword. He was pierced, shaken. He had thought her a quite attractive young lady with her brown curls and her rich colouring and a kind of controlled vigour or impatience which showed in the way she walked, or sat tapping a nervous foot.

He had seen her first a week ago, playing tennis on the Chindera grass court which was as smooth as green velvet from the attentions of the Kanaka gardener and his assistants. She threw herself into the game with a determination to win and concentration unusual in a girl. When he was introduced to her, though, he had thought her sullen. She scarcely spoke, and smiled not at all. Yet there was a certain magnetism about her.

Lindsay had been pleased to find that she was to be his dinner partner tonight. Her rich colouring was enhanced by the cool sea-green of her gown, worn with a simple necklace of fine seed pearls.

On his other side was Mrs Johnstone, presiding at the foot of the table, and opposite was James's fiancée, Rose Lovelace, a ravishing beauty but apparently without a word to say.

Graham Lindsay collected his wits for a reply. 'Well, I was s-sort of s-s-supercargo,' he said, stammering a little to his own disgust. 'There was this little brigantine, the *Bobtail Nag*—'

'But what an unromantic name for a ship!'

'Yes, well, she wasn't very romantic as it happened. She was the craziest, leakiest old tub, with cockroaches as big as mice, and—'

'Eek! Hateful creatures!'

'And we were loaded down with carbines and muskets for trade, all packed in crates manifested as containing axes. Though of course the Islanders will murder each other with axes almost as easily as with guns. A chap called Nixon was the GA, and he felt as badly as I did about some of the things we saw.'

'You mean the Kanakas *were* kidnapped then?'

'I don't know what else you would call it. Perhaps half of them understood their contract and came willingly; of the others, some were sold by their own chiefs, some were gulled by lying promises of what awaited them in Queensland; and at least ten per cent were taken by force, tipped from their canoes and pulled into the ship's boat. Those who had already been to Queensland, though, seemed ready enough to return. They said "Me gettin' no grub, no tobacco, longa own islan'. Mallybulla very good place." '

'That shows they know what's good for them,' said Angus. 'Forbye, they wouldna wish tae come back. And ye pay their chief relations, nae doot?'

'We carried plenty of trade goods: beads and nails and mouth-organs and so on. But part of the trade section, I found, was filled with thirty per cent over proof Jamaican rum! And the drunken wretch of a cook kept broaching it. Half the time we got no breakfast because of his morning-after head!'

'Delightful!'

He was talking directly to Helga, but he sensed that the whole table was listening. Exhilarated, he took a mouthful of wine and plunged on: 'And then at one of the islands the men collected some coconut-crabs for a meal, and left them in a box on deck. During the night they ate their way out (they have enormous claws, for cracking coconut shells), and they got all over the ship. They were in our bunks and in the galley. One of the crew nearly fell overboard when he met one half-way up the foremast. When they got into the captain's cabin he thought he was in the DTs, and started blasting away at them with his pistol . . . Oh, never a dull moment aboard the *Bobtail Nag*!'

He was pleased by the ripple of laughter round the table, caused partly perhaps by relief at such a safe subject as an invasion of monstrous crabs.

'But how did you come to sail in her, Mr Lindsay?' asked Julia Johnstone benignly.

'Well, you s-see, I was rather in need of a holiday, having been cooped up for years in the back-blocks. A cousin of my mother's has a sheep-station out West, and I went there as a jackaroo. I was sick of the smell of dust and sheep. So I came down to the coast, and this vessel happened to be in port, about to sail for the New Hebrides. I purchased a passage for a modest thirty guineas, and there I was – a sort of unpaid super-cargo.'

'It must have been an exciting voyage all the same,' said Helga, determinedly romantic about the vast Pacific.

'Not really, Miss Johnstone. It was rather monotonous once I'd got over being scared. But the weather moderated, and then we were stuck in an almost flat calm – an uncanny experience. The sea was like a huge glass marble, or rather a ball of quick-silver; you could see the earth was round. The most exciting thing, I suppose, was seeing my first coral cay, complete with coconut-palms, thatched huts, and a lagoon. Then the volcano on Tanna, reddening the clouds at night with bursts of flame...'

'And did you meet any cannibal chiefs?'

'Oh yes; though since the missionaries have been there they pretend not to know of such things. The first Islander I met on shore turned out to be an absolute savage – covered with coco-nut oil and very little else.'

(He forebore to mention that the 'little else' consisted of a coconut-shell codpiece which revealed more than it hid of the man's anatomy.) 'He could talk a sort of pidgin English, and told me "Me work big longa Mallybulla, longa that Misser Cran, my word, me plenty work longa soogar." ' This brought a laugh, for Crans owned one of the biggest plantations and mills in the town. 'He was a Tanna man, and they are fine, strong chaps, and they stand up and look you in the eye, even if they are only niggers.'

'They are men, after all,' said James quietly.

'Yes, but you'd hardly think so to hear them jabbering away like a lot of monkeys or parakeets.'

'What sounds like jabber to you is conversation to them. Just because you don't understand their language—'

'By Jove, that's true. I never thought of it like that. I suppose our whitefeller lingo sounds just as outlandish to them.'

'Exactly.'

The soup had been removed and Angus concentrated on

carving the duck. Julia heaved a small sigh of relief – small because her breathing was constricted by her stays, which had been laced a little too tightly by Harriet.

'As I understand it,' said the editor, 'the returns are always quite eager to sign up for another three years.'

'Some are, yes. But one of them said to me, "Captain he too much gammon me. Me go Queenslan', work all day, get notting, work like a horse. Boss in Queenslan' he killem me too much."'

'How could one be killed *too much*?' Helga laughed deeply.

'I think he meant he was beaten or knocked about by the overseer. And some of the older men don't want to leave their wives and children. Sometimes the wives or mothers would swim after our boat, calling and crying, or they'd try to hold the men back.'

'But that's the way of the world. "Men must work, and women must weep," as Mr Kingsley has said.'

'That is all very well, but if the trade goes on in its present proportions, the islands will be denuded of young men. Many never return to their own villages. And with the men away, few babies are being born to replace them.'

There was a strained silence, broken by the noise of knives and forks only. The implications of what he had just said struck poor Mr Lindsay forcibly. The ladies looked at their plates. Mrs Johnstone said in a chilly tone, 'Yes, I'm sure your island adventures have been most int'resting, Mr Lindsay,' and at once launched into a description of her plans for a grand ball to open the sugar season, to be held in the 'sugar room' at Chindera Mill.

Only Helga did not look down, and the healthy colour in her cheeks had not deepened. Perhaps she was too innocent to understand the relationship between men and new babies?

*

'Graham, tell us a bit about the black girls in the Islands,' urged Dougal as soon as the ladies had withdrawn after dinner. He passed the port and leaned confidentially towards Lindsay. 'Pretty good, eh? I hear they wear nothing but a few shells round their middles, or a grass skirt.'

His father tried to look disapproving, but failed to keep the interest out of his sharp blue eyes. Only James did not look up. He was staring at the candle-light through the red wine in his glass, slowly, slowly twirling the stem and thinking of his Rose.

'They're not bad,' admitted Graham Lindsay. 'Straight and slender as an arrow, and usually with a frangipani or hibiscus blossom tucked behind one ear, quite as effective as the most expensive diamond tiara. But they have such woolly hair, and they go off early. There was one old witch on Maré, in the Loyalties, she used to be a sort of priestess in the old days, and they say she was always given the left hand of every war victim to eat. The chief always got the right. Hands were considered a great delicacy.'

James looked up at last, in dismay. 'Real cannibals!'

'Oh yes. Fifty years ago they were all cannibals. If they had plenty of meat, say after a big war, they'd eat only the arms and legs. Sometimes when there'd been peace for a long time they'd get so meat-hungry that a party would wait for anyone walking along in the bush, and kill and eat him on the spot.'

'I've heard of them hunting Aborigines for meat, here in Australia,' said Dougal. 'They call them "man o' bush". They used to organize hunts on Sundays.'

'Aye, they're no ceevilized; fechs, they're scaircely human!' cried Angus. 'Did ye no hear aboot the overseer up country that fower o' them attacked with their pangas? They carved him up into wee pieces, he could no' have been recognized by his ain mither. Ye were takin' your life in your hands, Mr Lindsay, in gaeing among them.'

'Well, you can't really trust them. We always had the crowd covered with our carbines and the boat ready to row back to the ship. And once—' he shuddered, and took a sip of wine. 'I've seen things I'd rather not talk about at the dinner table.'

He thought of the time he had landed on the island of Mai, a young man enjoying the adventure and possible danger, when suddenly his party had come upon a tree at the entrance to a village, on which two blood-spotted sulus were hanging. At the foot of the tree grinned the two skulls and a pile of half-cleaned bones, the grisly remnants of the owners of the sulus.

'The remains of a cannibal feast, for instance ... A Sesac man told me there had been a "bigfeller fight" with the new guns the latest returns had brought back with them. Two men from a neighbouring village had been eaten; I saw what was left of them.'

'Grruesome!' said Angus Johnstone.

'Yes. And the two men eaten had come back from Maryborough just a few months before. The chap who told me was quite open about it. They all had Snider rifles and plenty of cartridges and were completely trigger-happy.'

'What a depressing conversation,' said James, pushing away the cheese he had taken on his plate, and tossing off his port. 'What do you say, Papa? Shall we join the ladies?'

'Aye, in a meenut. I have always maintained that recruiting was beneeficial to the Islanders in yon savage pairts, as well as to the planters. They see something of our worrld, and have a free trip and a box o' trade goods to returrn wi'. But guns! They should be proheebited.'

'Yes, and the recruiting of young boys under fifteen, who are not fit for the hard work,' put in James. 'We've had a number of deaths among youths in their first year.'

''Tis the cold winters we've had of late, they are not used to frosts. And the overseer tells me they will tak' their blankets into Maryborough on the week-ends and sell them for grog.'

'You mean McGriggen? He's a hard man, Father.'

'But efficient,' said Dougal. 'He doesn't let them put anything over him.'

'There's a Methodist mission working out at the Lagoon now, I hear,' said Mr Woodyatt. 'Or is it Presbyterian? And the Lutherans have started a Kanaka mission in the town, where they have hymns and so on. Think what a Christianizing influence these men will be when they return to their homes with the religion and the blessings of civilization!'

'I'm afraid they more often return with such "blessings of civilization" as a dose of the pox caught at the Japanese brothels, and a taste for gambling and opium fostered by the Chinese,' said Lindsay drily.

'Och, aye, 'tis a vexed question,' said Angus uneasily. 'Weel, what do ye say, gentlemen? Shall we adjourn to the drawing-room?'

James rose to his feet with alacrity, and the others followed more slowly. 'The mon's a bit of a radical,' murmured Angus in the editor's ear, 'but I like the cut of his jib. He doesn't mince worrds, I'll say that for him.'

*

When the men joined the ladies in the drawing-room, with its dark oil paintings in heavy gold frames and its grand piano draped with a shawl of Indian silk, Helga pursued her questions. Graham Lindsay found himself talking easily to her, as she drank in his words impatiently.

'And was the captain cruel to the natives?' she asked.

'Well, I did see him beat six of them for stealing biscuits, and he flogged pretty hard. He said their skins were thick, but one of them was ill for a week afterwards.'

'Oh!'

'And he used to amuse himself by throwing lighted crackers among them down in the hold. "Just watch them skip!" he'd call. He thought it terribly funny.'

'It was terrible, not funny,' said Helga tartly. 'Did you try to stop him?'

'The GA and I both remonstrated with him, but after all it was his ship. He was drunk a lot of the time, and quite capable of marooning us or chaining us up below. I can tell you I was glad to get back in one piece. We had the drunken cook to contend with as well, and he ran amok one day with the carving knife. What with the yells of the cook, and the Kanakas having their sing-sings, or wailing for their lost islands, it was never quiet and dull.'

'And did you meet any other Maryborough captains?'

'Yes, we saw the *Stormbird*, and were in port with the *Pacific*, Captain Woodcock.'

'Oh, I've heard of him,' said Helga innocently. 'Papa bought his last lot of Kanakas from him. The men call him Timber Dick, I believe. He must have been in the logging trade before.'

Dougal, who was in hearing, spluttered over his after-dinner coffee. Mr Lindsay kept a straight face.

Ah, if she had only been born a boy, Helga was thinking, she would have gone exploring before this, perhaps round the world on a windjammer, and to Europe to hear the great concert singers of the age . . .

Rose, James's girl, came over to sit with Helga and the tête-à-tête was broken. She had been silent at dinner because she was absorbed in pressing James's knee with her own, while their hands met beneath the cloth whenever they were not engaged with knife, fork or spoon.

She was all in rose-pink net, with a soft fichu from which her slender white neck and smooth fair head rose like a flower on its stem. Julia Johnstone regarded her as a dead loss at a dinner party as far as conversation went, but at least she was decorative. After all, you did not expect entertaining remarks from the floral centre-piece.

3 Maryborough

It had never occurred to Angus Johnstone that his wealth was built upon flesh and bones, human suffering. 'Why, they love the work,' he would say blandly. 'Mon, I have seen them gae laughin' and chafferin' tae the fields, and nigh helpless wi' laughter when a load of cane fell off the tram, though it was theirselves had tae put it back. They are like bairns, and dinna onderstand the value o' money; so whaur would be the sense in gi'eing them more?'

So the big plantation-owners justified themselves, and grew in power and wealth until they were running the whole of Queensland through their elected representatives in Parliament.

A sugar aristocracy had been built up in the coastal towns from Maryborough to Mackay; and for a while the leading sugar port was the town on the banks of the wide and beautiful Mary River.

White buildings, green palm-trees in the main street, a forest of masts beyond the wharf, a frieze of smoking chimneys, a wide sweep of tranquil river waters framed in the green slopes of public gardens – this was the port, twenty miles from the sea,

63

which was the new centre of sugar-growing in Queensland.

So far there was no bridge over the river, only a ferry.

The town had grown up because it marked the limit of navigation by ocean-going ships, and the river mouth was protected by the length of Fraser or Great Sandy Island. At first wool was exported from the back country, then the valuable native timbers: red cedar, swamp mahogany, blackbutt and cypress pine, and now sugar in its raw brown form.

The rich soils of the river flats had turned out to be excellent for growing sugar-cane. The climate, with its summer rainfall and dry ripening period in winter, was adequate except in very dry years; and the Government was willing to make Crown land available to settlers who would clear and plant it.

In the wide and busy streets with their imposing Colonial buildings decorated with pillars and balustrades – Customs House, Post Office, Immigration Office, Planters' Association; with its thirty hotels and five churches – it was hard to recall that only twenty-five years before the first settlers had carved the place out of paperbark swamp and vine-forest. Coloured labour had made places like Chindera and Yengarrie, Rosehill and Binburrum possible.

Ladies walked down the clean main street with their long skirts and parasols, accompanied on their shopping excursions by a woolly-haired, liveried servant to carry their parcels and books. The best families – that is, the wealthiest – also had a dark-complexioned Islander for coachman, who might double as a butler at home.

Only an occasional outbreak of bloody fighting between two Island factions wielding murderous cane-knives, or the deep-throated singing round the hut fires at night, would remind of more savage times and places.

In the sugar season (when the whole place reeked sickeningly of boiling syrup, and everyone moved in a sticky swamp of molasses) the Kanakas would sometimes hold a celebration. They stamped out with their bare feet the same all-pervading rhythm of the grinding, beating rollers in the mills and the chuffing of the big steam engines, continuing far into the night at the height of the crushing season.

Of the first inhabitants, the Aborigines, few were left. They were huddled on the railway station in rainy weather, begging from travellers, or sat listlessly in the sun while the flies crawled undisturbed over their eyes and mouths. At night they were rounded up like cattle and taken out to the Uloola Swamp or to their camp on the other side of the river. They were not allowed in the streets after five p.m.

From the first the Aborigines had refused to work in the canefields. They had never been an agricultural people, and could not see the sense of working all day in the heat, every day, for some vague reward in the future.

But the brown men from the Pacific, the Kanakas, found it not so very different from work in their own taro patches at home. They did not seem to mind the sticky heat in the airless channels between the ten-foot-high cane, where white men felt they could not breathe, let alone work.

Like the red soils of Jamaica, the bright red to chocolate-brown soils around Childers, Bundaberg and Maryborough were incredibly rich and deep. When the thick rain-forest had been removed, the sugar-cane flourished, sprouting in a mad growth of giant spears.

The Kanakas seemed strong and willing, yet it was true that a disconcerting number died in their first year. When the cold westerlies blew in winter they were miserable, and glad to get to work among the protecting walls of cane. At Chindera they broke up their neat huts of brick to get the timber framework for firewood; and they built themselves comfortable grass huts instead.

Joseph Efate, who used to be called Tula, was one who survived the critical first year. He was strong and well-muscled now, his skin gleaming with health. In the first difficult months he had been helped and protected by an older man. He had thought he would die at first. He was weak from the voyage, and after twelve hours in the fields he was terribly tired each night. If he was slow starting, the overseer would boot him in the behind, which hurt his dignity as well as his person. Some men smiled and pretended they did not mind, because they feared McGriggen with his bull-whip and pistols.

The work now was not so hard as at first: cultivating between the rows with their chipping-hoes, 'trashing' and burning and finally harvesting – it was not as bad as clearing the jungle. Felling a forest of paperbarks, standing calf-deep in swamps swarming with leeches and mosquitoes; or cutting thick brush, clawed at by cruel lawyer-canes or stung by the leaves of the stinging-tree, the gympie-gympie; his blood sucked by poisonous scrub-ticks; it was a wonder he had survived.

Now he had even acquired a taste for the rice and bread and tea of his daily ration, sweetened with molasses or brown sugar, or dressed up with corn and vegetables and occasionally a little meat. They cultivated a small patch of taro and ate the boiled greens cooked in coconut milk when they could find a few fallen nuts in the public gardens. It seemed to keep them healthy, for in his men's hut there were rarely any colds or influenza.

Dysentery troubled the new men most. He had seen young men getting weaker and weaker, so bad that the blood ran down their legs when they had to go outside to defecate. And then some of them would fling themselves down at the end of the cane-rows and drink from the stagnant, polluted water to quench their raging thirst. The bosses would not send water-carts into the fields, they said the men would waste too much time at them.

Now after six years they had their own group of sleeping huts built in Island fashion of bamboo and cane-grass; intricately woven; high-ceilinged and cool; and set high on stilts to catch the breeze. This idea had even caught on among the white masters, and now many Queensland homes were built of wood set on solid stumps with room for the air to circulate underneath, and a cool storage place in the shade beneath the floor.

Besides the community huts for men, the Islanders had quite a village of family huts where lived wives who had managed to follow their husbands to Australia, or runaway couples who had been recruited together, or Island men married to Aboriginal women.

Joseph's friend Zachariah was married to Eliza, who had a job in the big house, in the kitchen. Tombua, who had helped him during the first bad months when he used to fall exhausted to the ground after twelve hours' work in the fields, had been promoted to the big house at Chindera also, as coachman.

Zachariah was a Malaita man, superficially a Christian but deeply superstitious still: for a week before planting-time when he was engaged in putting out the setts of new cane in rows (for the 'rattoon' crop was good for only two years and had to be ploughed in and replaced), he kept away from his wife: he would not sleep with Eliza because it was a tradition on his island that to do so would affect the fertility of the crop: if a man went into the fields after breaking the rule of continence at planting time, the yams would be small and few that year.

Eliza had been longer in Australia than her husband, and affected to despise all such superstitions. She had been brought away from her home by the notorious Ross Lewin when she was only a child. She had been made much of by a white family until she grew up and became an embarrassment since she was neither a servant nor an equal, being coloured. So she had been 'lent' to the Chindera household, and there had met and married Zachariah.

Because he denied her at the time of planting, she would deliberately wear flowers in her hair and bathe herself in front of him; slowly; lifting the sponge with a graceful arm and letting the water trickle down the beautiful line of her back into the tin basin where she sat.

'Come, Zachari, wash my back,' she would coax, but he would fling out of the room and go over to one of the men's huts to sleep.

Eliza was the kitchen-maid and general help at Chindera. There was an Aboriginal girl in the kitchen too, but Eliza treated her like dirt to show that she herself was not just 'blackfeller rubbish'. She claimed to have been a princess in her Island home, or at least the daughter of a chief.

*

Somewhere between the two, Aboriginal and Islander, in the subtle hierarchy of colour from white to yellow to brown to black, stood the Chinese. There was a whole row of Chinese houses and shops in Adelaide Street, with Chinese characters painted outside the doors. They mostly kept to themselves, though sometimes an Islander married a Chinese girl.

Old Mother Kelly, a redoubtable Irishwoman, let the Chinamen drink freely at her Figtree Hotel as long as they were moderate; but she kept a solid shillelagh with which she quietened noisy drunks by knocking them over the head, whatever their race, colour or creed. Many Chinese prospectors had arrived lately from South Australia, some, who had been attracted by the gold of Gympie, drifting on to Maryborough and opening a shop or a gambling den.

On cold winter nights the Kanakas would gather under the boilers at Walker's Foundry for warmth, until caught and driven out by the nightwatchman. Then they might visit the Chinese fan-tan games or the Japanese and Afghan brothels; or they might light a big fire down by the river bank. If there was a birthday to be celebrated they might roast a whole pig in the village and have dancing and singing afterwards, to the old fierce Island rhythms.

On Sunday afternoons Tula and his friends liked to wander on the sloping lawns of the Botanic Gardens, with the river lying calm and blue beneath them. Tula would read out the names written on the trees, and the notice on the big bunya pine: 'At certain seasons of the year, fruit and nuts fall from this tree. Be warned, therefore, and do not loiter underneath.'

*

When Eliza became pregnant she went on working up to the last two months. At last the white cook noticed her condition and mentioned it to Mrs Johnstone, who insisted that Eliza should stay at home and rest. Eliza was bored at home all day and would rather have gone on working. The ladies of the house were very kind, often coming down to the village with little garments for the baby.

'What are you going to call it?' Helga asked.

'Mine tink might-be "Lorna" if she a girl,' said Eliza shyly. 'One-time I read book, this girl she name "Lorna".'

'*Lorna Doone*, I expect,' said the ladies. 'And "John" if it's a boy, eh?'

'I tink might-be "Albert",' said Eliza. She had a picture of

Queen Victoria and Prince Albert on a calendar on her kitchen wall.

'Isn't she sweet?' said the ladies, walking home beneath their frilled parasols, lifting their long skirts with one hand as they picked their way fastidiously among bits of sticky sugar-cane fallen from the trucks and the prickly burrs which lurked in the grass on each side of the narrow walking track.

Zachariah thought 'Lorna' was all right for a girl; but he didn't care for Albert or John either: 'Those names too hard,' he complained. 'Daniela more better, or Davita: somet'ing more like Island name.'

'We Australian peoples now,' said Eliza impatiently. 'What for you want Island name?'

'Me not forget,' said Zachariah. 'And you no forget either, you no have that baby under roof of house. Soon as you feel pains begin, you go out under t' sky. You know what happen bime-'by sposem you forget.'

'Ar, that all rubbish talk.' But Eliza spoke uneasily: she too came from Malaita, and in all these years she had not quite shaken off her dread of the Evil Eye. And she respected her husband's beliefs to the extent that she would not 'pass over him', that is her shadow must not fall across him, nor would she lean above him to place anything on the table at meals – for she insisted on a table, they did not eat from a mat on the floor – nor touch his head.

All-a-same, she was determined that her child should have a whitefeller name, like her own. She felt sure in her own mind that it would be a girl, and already she thought of her as 'Lorna'.

4 The Kanaka village

On Chindera plantation the annual hand-out of shirts, trousers and blankets was being made. Two hundred Kanakas, laughing and joking, were lined up along the fence which divided their village from the five-acre garden of the big house. There was some good-natured scuffling and horseplay as they waited.

Most of them wore nothing but a pair of stained work-trousers fraying at the cuffs, for they had lost both their shirts and their spare trousers at the Chinese fan-tan game in town.

They were happy because today was a special holiday; and holidays, like Sundays, were precious to men who worked six days a week. Also, as winter approached, they began to feel the cold, and looked forward to the issue of blankets. It was James who had persuaded his father that new blankets, of a cheap grey variety, should be added to the clothing issue at the beginning of each winter.

Samuel McGriggen, the overseer, swaggered up and down the line, a pistol stuck at an angle through his belt on one side, a long-handled whip on the other. He was followed by his pet bull-dog, better fed than the men in front of him, for it had meat every day. He called out.

'Orright, you black bastards: quick-time now, all boy catchim some-feller blanket, trouser, shirt.' His voice was loud and hectoring, but not angry. He used the term 'bastards' without malice, and 'black' was not meant to be derogatory either: after all they *were* black, weren't they, the poor heathen bastards?

Joseph Efate stood aloof. He did not join in the laughter and play. He was deeply aware of the casual contempt in the white man's voice and manner. Not for the first time he felt hatred instead of respect for this example of what he had early learned to regard as the 'white masters'.

McGriggen's hair was getting thin on his forehead, but his beard was black and luxuriant in growth. Beneath his black brows his eyes were a peculiar light blue, bleached-looking, with sharp dark pupils. He was a big man, bigger than most of the Islanders except the Tanna men. His hefty right foot encased in a hard leather boot often helped the slower workers on with a kick. Yet most of them bore the insult with a smile, expecting no less of the master.

He also had a habit of knocking them down with the butt-end of his whip 'just to remind them what's what', or if he fancied one of them looked at him cheekily.

'Orright,' he said, 'all boy e come, count-it own self. One, two, t'ree. All you savee count-it up to t'ree, aint-it? One boy, master give altogether t'ree tings: this-feller one, shirt. This-feller two' (a pair of denim trousers was held up), 'this-feller t'ree' (a folded grey blanket). 'Hey, you, get into line there.' He caught Joseph by the shoulder and roughly pulled him back into line; he had been leaning on the fence, watching. 'Now, number-one boy, e sing-out "One! Two! T'ree!"'

The line shuffled forward, each man self-consciously counting his goods aloud. Joseph rubbed his shoulder resentfully.

He resented not only the injury, but the insult of the talk in pidgin, which made them all like children or 'boys' as they were called, even fathers of families. He, Joseph, could talk proper English and understand it perfectly well. But if he talked back in English he was likely to get a kick or a punch to 'put him in his place'. It was 'cheeky-feller' to speak like a white man. He had to submit to being lumped in a faceless black mob. All the same, he made a point of enunciating the word 'three' clearly and correctly as he took the blanket from the pile.

Yet he had decided to stay on for another three years. He did not gamble, and he rarely visited the brothels; he was actually saving money out of his ten shillings a month. This meant, since he was already in his second term, that he would have been nine years away from his home when his time expired. He was now a proved, experienced worker, and was confident that he could demand and get a better salary when the time came for him to sign up again. Perhaps he would never return to Lifu. The memory of his island home was growing dim.

Sometimes they would strip off their clothes and dance round the camp-fire, singing the old songs full of the rhythm of waves and undulating seaweed; but Joseph preferred the Sunday School in town and the Church hymns which reminded him of the Duguids, who had been his friends although they were white. He remembered how he used to eat at table with Emily and Mrs Duguid, and how he quickly learned to use the knife and fork and spoon by watching them.

One Sunday he stopped in town for evening service in the Presbyterian Church, when it was announced that a new minister recently returned from mission work in the Pacific would address the congregation.

The grey-bearded, thin-faced, tall man with his fanatical deep-set eyes sat erect in the front row, his bony hands folded on his knees. It was only when he rose and went to the lectern to speak that Joseph recognized him. His heart leapt, seeming to hit his rib-cage a sudden blow that left him breathless. As in a dream he heard the announcement: 'And now I have the pleasure to introduce the Reverend Andrew Duguid, formerly of the New Hebridean Presbyterian Mission, now of Bundaberg.'

Mr Duguid walked up to the dais, spread his arms and rested a hand on each side of the lectern. He leaned forward in an impressive silence. Then Joseph, called Tula, heard the well-known Scottish accents as he began: 'Ladies and gentlemen, boys and gels of the Churrch . . .'

Joseph sat staring at the front row. There sat a lady in a bonnet which hid her face and hair, but he could see that she was rather gaunt and thin like the minister. And beside her a young girl whose fair, waving hair flowed down her back beneath her straw bonnet embroidered with raffia flowers. How her hair gleamed golden in the light of the candles, against the brown velvet of her dress! Could it be Emily, grown up already? And if so where was Jamus, her little brother? Joseph heard not a word of Mr Duguid's address, except the words 'Bundaberg', and 'Chinese dens of vice and iniquity', and something about a mission for Kanakas.

After the service, with his heart beating painfully, he made his way to the front. Thank goodness he was wearing shoes, the same as a white man, and the new 'ration' shirt issued the other day at Chindera! But he felt terribly shy. He had learned that this was a white man's country, and that the black man was kept firmly in his place, though that place was not so low for the Islander as for the native blackfellers of Australia. It helped the Islanders to keep their pride and identity, to feel that they were superior to someone, the idle, feckless Aborigine who refused to work in the cane for any money or inducement.

'Excuse me, Sir, excuse—' Joseph was plucking at the sleeve of the white preacher, but his soft voice was lost in the chatter of those who were competing to ask the visitor back to their homes for supper.

He was rescued by Mr Stewart, the Maryborough church minister. 'Mr Duguid, I'd like you to meet one of our congregation – also a trainee Sunday School teacher. He comes from the Islands which you know so well.'

Mr Duguid turned his deep, piercing blue eyes on Joseph and held out his bony hand. 'I'm delighted tae meet ye,' he said with a smile that transformed his long, dour face. 'I wonder do ye ken the Isle of Lifu where we were long stationed, and left three bairns buried there.'

'Three? You mean little Jamie as well?' cried Tula.

The minister's eyes flew wide; he grasped Tula's shoulder with his left hand. 'Joseph! Can it be Joseph Tula Efate? Is this whaur ye finished up? And what a fine mon ye've grown, that was but a boy when taken awa'!'

'I have long wanted, Sir, to tell you that I left not of my own free will,' said Joseph in the stilted English he assumed at church (for he had little other opportunity to speak correctly).

'Och, aye! Kidnapped with a' the young men. I wrote tae the Churrch, and the Australian Government, and they promised an inquiry, but did naething. A few o' the men came back, and we asked after ye; but they said ye'd been sent to a deeferent plantation. Your auld faither died soon after.'

Joseph bowed his head. 'And your Jamie?'

'Aye; the dysentery. It's why we left the Islands for good. Weel, come ower and meet Mrs Duguid and Emily. They'll be as pleased as I am masel'.'

Perhaps Mr Duguid did not expect the apparition of Joseph after so many years to have such an effect on his family. Mrs Duguid began to weep; her thin face, yellow from many tropical summers, crumpled up as she clung to Joseph's hand. 'You are one of the few wha remembers my little Johnnie and James,' she said. 'We had to leave them behind.'

'Och, Mither, they are with Jesus the noo. Ye should be happy they are safe in Heaven,' said Andrew reprovingly.

'I know it; I'm juist a wee bit upset,' and she took out a handkerchief and blew her nose briskly, and smiled wanly at

Joseph. He did not dare look at Emily. But suddenly he felt a touch, light as a butterfly-wing, soft as a moth, against his brown cheek. A strand of golden hair filled his mouth. Emily, standing on tip-toe, had kissed him.

Joseph was delirious with joy. He had hoped she might smile, and shake his hand perhaps in front of all these people. Instead she had kissed him.

'Dear Joseph,' she murmured, and looked down at the hymn-book in her mittened hands. She still wore skirts above the ankle and hair down to her waist, yet she looked grown up already. Her face was a delicate golden-brown from the sun (what trouble he'd had trying to make her keep her hat on when they went to the beach!) and her eyes were intensely blue, like the deep water of the Pacific away beyond the reefs. She was the most beautiful girl he had ever seen. He peeped under her bonnet, hoping for another glance from those eyes.

She looked up shyly. 'Do you remember how you used to give me piggy-back rides when I was tired? And I would beat you and tell you to go faster?'

'Yes—'

'Never mind that now, you were very small,' said Mrs Duguid, who had recovered her composure. 'Don't forget you are nearly fourteen, and a young lady almost.'

Emily looked abashed. The elder Duguids took it in turn to tell Joseph how they had come to Rockhampton and then to Bundaberg to work in an interdenominational mission church for the Kanaka population, which had been started by a Lutheran who was disgusted at the way the simple Islander was fleeced of his money and led into sinful ways.

'Men from Maré and Lifu are different,' said Mr Duguid. 'I am glad to say they are mostly Christians and, like you, can speak and understand good English. It is the wild men from the northern and western isles who are being bamboozled and seduced into fan-tan dens and worrse, and who go hame with a box of useless junk and no money at all after worrking harrd for three years. 'Tis a wicked shame!' He was launched once more into the substance of the talk he had just given. His wife nudged him gently.

'Andrew, these ladies are gey anxious to tak' us hame to supper, and they've hearrd you already this night.'

'Aye, one meenut, my dear. Joseph, I'd like fine for ye to come and talk at one of our Young Men's Pleasant Sunday Afternoons in Bundaberg. It's imporrtant worrk we are doing. Would they gi'e you leave for a few days, d'ye think? He could stay with us, Mither.'

Joseph's face lighted up with one of his huge grins. 'My three years is nearly up, Sir – my second three years. I could take a break before signing up again perhaps. How far would it be? I have fifteen pounds saved up.'

'Ha'e ye, indeed? Weel, it's only sixty miles, it's no distance at a', at a'! Tak' the coach, and I'll pay the fare at the ither end.'

It was left at that. Joseph went home in a daze of happiness. Emily had kissed him, and he might be going to Bundaberg and seeing her again!

He ran most of the way back to Chindera village and flung himself on to his bunk.

'Hey, 'Zekiela, what do you think? I'm going on a preaching trip to Bundaberg.'

'Eh?' Ezekiel grunted sleepily. 'What this you say? You going poaching?'

'Not poaching, you stupid coon, *preaching*. I'm goin' to address the Sunday School for Islanders there. *"I'm coming, I'm coming. For my head is bend-ing low . . ."* ' he sang.

'Ah, hit 'im on the head somebody, please do,' came another voice from the other side of the dim hut. Joseph lay down on his straw mattress and drew the grey blankets up to his chin, chuckling to himself.

Through the open side wall above his head he could see a huge star in the southern sky. It flared in bright alternating colours, now red, now blue, now red again. 'Bright Star of Eve,' he murmured to himself, some half-remembered song Mrs Duguid used to sing at the piano coming into his head. A great bubble of happiness rose in his throat and he wanted to laugh and shout. The stars seemed to twinkle and laugh back at him from the sky.

'Sorry we haven't any red coats,' said Dougal rather mockingly to the English visitor, 'but we can promise a good red fox, and a decent cross-country run.'

Five of them were going on a small hunting-party, including Claude Grant, an excessively tall and pink young man with a smooth face half-hidden by a luxuriant moustache who held himself as straight as a ramrod and had been in the Horse Guards. 'He can certainly sit a horse,' Dougal admitted, watching the firm way Claude dealt with the curvetting of the hunter, a lively roan, which had been lent to him from the Chindera stables.

Dougal had his new hunter, a massive grey, as a sign from his father that he was pleased with the year's operation at the mill. They had produced more than a thousand tons extra from the same acreage this year, on present estimates. An auspicious 'sugar season' was about to begin, with the thunder of the crushers and the smell of boiling syrup filling the air. Invitations had gone out for Julia Johnstone's beginning-of-season ball in the great sugar room at the mill, which would later be stacked to the roof with sparkling grains, and where now only a few handfuls remained in corners.

Dougal, who would be in the thick of the activity, working long into the night, was taking a last holiday. Helga, who loved riding, and Rose Lovelace, who was deceptively strong in the wrists and had a good seat on a horse, were both mounted on side-saddles, their long habits hiding all but one neatly booted foot.

Rose's habit was of green velveteen, and she wore a green hat with a plume nodding in it. Helga privately thought that this was putting on side. Rose looked bewitching, of course, but really—! They were only going to ride across the paddocks of a country town in Australia. Her own brown gabardine was workmanlike and comfortable. She had a gossamer scarf tied over her rebellious curls.

Claude's horse side-stepped skittishly, and his knee just

brushed against the folds of Rose's green skirt. Rose blushed, a pretty, pale-pink flush, 'Oh! Sorry,' murmured Claude respectfully. James, mounting his brown hack, frowned.

Helga noted the delicate change of colour. When *she* blushed (which was usually from containing her anger at some remark about women's voices being 'weak', or their musicianship inferior to men's), she turned a dusky unbecoming red to the roots of her hair, then abruptly white again as the blood drained from her healthy-looking cheeks. She suspected that Rose could turn that blush on whenever she liked, by holding her breath or something.

'Are we going along the river-bank?' she asked Dougal.

'On the way back. We're more likely to start a fox over near the Big Scrub. And by the way,' he said to Claude, 'look out for the gympie-gympie.'

'What's that? Some kind of snake?'

'No, the stinging-tree. If you get tossed in one you'll know all about it. Like a thousand giant stinging-nettles.'

'Thanks, old boy. But I don't allow myself to get tossed,' drawled Claude.

'Don't even brush against it. It has broad, flat leaves covered with little hairs which irritate for weeks.'

Claude Grant was staying at Chindera until the ball. Helga and Dougal found him rather a bore, and insufferably arrogant. Already they, the Colonial-born, were feeling their difference from the product of an older land, and his precise voice irritated them. James was rather jealous of him, though apart from the usual civilities he had shown himself indifferent to Rose's old-world charm or Helga's robust vigour.

'And by the way, it's not a "red" coat,' he said, looking down at his jacket and smoothing the sleeve. 'In the Old Country, we call it huntin' pink.'

'Looks bloody well red to me,' said Dougal indifferently.

They trotted along the edge of the road until they came to open country, then turned across a fallow cane-field and rode up a small, cleared hill. The 'hounds' were the two Johnstone dogs, Pebble and Lollipop, who were leading the way. Lollipop was an Irish setter, really a gun-dog, and Pebble a Border collie.

Their favourite pastime was swimming in the river, but they entered with enthusiasm into the idea of the hunt. Suddenly Lollipop uttered a strangled bark of excitement and they took off up the hill.

'There goes the little bugger!' cried Dougal, standing up in his stirrups for a better view of the fleeing fox.

'You say "view halloo!", don't you know, not "there goes the little – er – creature!" ' said Claude in a pained voice.

Helga dug her heel into her horse's flank, wishing she could ride astride like the men. In a moment she was out in front, flying after the dogs. James and Rose brought up the tail of the field. They were more interested in each other than in the hunt.

Claude and Dougal were making a race of it, both rather annoyed at having a girl leading the way. They leant forward in their saddles and took short cuts. Dougal had to admit the Englishman was game. He wanted to head the fox towards open country, where the cleared canefields would give little shelter. However, the fox bolted down the other side of the hill towards a small stream that flowed into the Mary River – no doubt hoping the dogs would lose his scent in the water. It held them in check for a while, but Helga had seen where he sneaked out the other side.

Recklessly galloping downhill, she put her mount at the stream, which was a little wider than he could manage. At the last moment he baulked, and she shot over his head. The thick lantana bushes on the bank broke her fall and prevented her going into the water. Her wrists were scratched where she had put her hands out to save herself from the prickly stems. She was breathless and furious, but not really hurt. 'Damn! Damn! Damn!' she muttered, gingerly twisting the foot that was bent under her to see if the ankle were broken.

The dogs had crossed the stream but were still aimlessly running up and down the far bank. Dougal reined in and called them back. Claude, who was nearest, dismounted and, leading his roan, stopped beside Helga.

Tall and straight, he did not bend towards her nor attempt to examine her ankle to see if it might be sprained or broken.

'I say, you're all right, aren't you?' he asked in his impeccable accent.

'Perfectly, thank you.' Helga suppressed a snort of laughter. Her shock and anger had worn off, and she was aware that she smelled strongly of lantana, and that the skirt of her habit had been displaced. Poor Mr Grant was embarrassed at the sight of her knickers.

She managed to make herself respectable as Dougal, having caught her horse, came crashing down the bank and gave her a hand to rise. 'Nothing broken?' he asked cheerfully. He was hatless and the sun shone on his orange curls. 'That was a stupid thing to do, wasn't it?' he added without sympathy. 'Lucky you didn't land in a gympie-gympie.'

'I'll smell of lantana for a week,' she moaned.

'You do pong a bit, old girl.'

James and Rose came up and dismounted, Rose looking quite concerned. 'You poor girl, are you all right?' she exclaimed, embracing Helga, then stepping back hastily as she caught the strong lantana smell. Helga warmed towards her. She was human after all, which was more than could be said for that stuffed-shirt of an Englishman. He had been, like Graham Lindsay, on a recruiting voyage, but was reticent about his adventures. She could not imagine him ever getting his hands dirty nor his hair ruffled.

They decided to give up hunting for the day – the fox would be safely in his burrow by now – and instead go for a ride along the bridle-track through the Big Scrub, the last patch left of the original vine-forest.

'Oh, isn't it beautiful?' said Rose, gazing up at huge mossy trunks, twined with creepers and vines as thick as serpents, to the gleam of sunlight on leaves far overhead. 'And so quiet! You can scarcely hear the horses' hoofs.'

As if to contradict her, a whip-bird called in the forest, a loud, ringing cry ending in a sound like the crack of a stock-whip. A cat-bird meowed. Somewhere in a clearing, a kooka-burra laughed maniacally.

'Birds!' said Claude. 'Amazin'!'

At last they came to the clearing where sunlight fell directly on to grass, on to an old grey weathered paintless timber house, perched drunkenly on wooden stumps. Helga was relieved. She had found the forest oppressive, too green, too teeming with life, the silent, terrible struggle of plants towards the sun, the strangler fig slowly encircling its host in a death-grip.

They were all thirsty by this time. They decided to ask at the wreck of a house for a drink from the outside tank of rusty iron. 'Probably got a drowned possum in it, but still – it's water,' said Dougal for Claude's benefit. He climbed the rickety stairs to the white-ant-eaten verandah.

At the top of the steps a loaded and cocked Snider carbine was propped against the railing.

About half a dozen dogs inside the house started barking. An old man came to the door. He wore a grey flannel shirt and old, baggy trousers, and he was drinking tea from a rusty jam-tin with the mark of the tin-opener still visible round the edges. He seemed to use his tobacco-stained moustache as a strainer for tea-leaves.

'Wot d'yer want?' he asked.

'Oh, er, we—' Dougal indicated the group still on their horses below the steps, 'we wondered if we could get a drink from your tank.'

'Rainwater? 'Course yer can. But waddabout a cuppatea? I got the iron kettle on.'

Dougal peered round the single living-room. An indescribable smell hit him in the face. There were no cups visible, just empty tins. 'No, no – just water'll be fine, thanks,' he said. He turned to descend, avoided a hole in the verandah, and nearly tripped over the gun.

'Why do you keep that in such a dangerous place?' he complained. 'And loaded, too.'

'Well yer see, the goats've all gorn off somewhere and I'm clean out of meat. I'm waitin' to pot a crow for supper. LAY DOWN, you mongrels!' he added to his dogs.

After drinking from their cupped hands, careful not to waste the old man's supply in the dry winter season, the little party remounted and rode on in single file. Claude was getting impatient with the slow progress through the shadowy scrub with its lawyer-cane and wait-a-while.

Claude set off at a swift canter on the wider track (which followed the general direction of the river back to the town, but eliminated some of the bends). Coming to a fork in the track he took the right-hand branch, a wide and well-marked trail. In a few minutes, as the others reached the parting of the ways, there came a loud cry ending in a long wail of horror and a splash.

'My God! He's gone down the chute!' said James.

The chute, or 'shoot' as local spelling had it, was a steep slippery slope which led straight into the river. Timber jinkers would come along the track to tip giant logs into the chute, which had first been wetted with mud to make it slippery. Down would go the great logs to be floated by river to Maryborough and the saw-mills of Wilson, Hart & Co.

The track ended abruptly in the chute, which had been used recently and was still in a very slithery state. Claude and his horse had been too late to stop.

The others stood on the bank above, trying not to smile at what they saw; but the contrast with the cool, correct, elegant figure of a few minutes before was too comical. The horse was thrashing about and trying to climb the steep bank. Claude, with his pomaded hair lank and streaming with mud and water, clung to a rock out in the stream. Then they saw with horror that his hands were streaming with blood.

'Wait – hold on – I'll come in and help you,' cried Dougal, heroically preparing to go down the chute also.

'Nonsense. I can swim,' came the reply. 'Just – just gettin' my breath back, don't you know.'

Fortunately there was a shallow reedy bank downstream from the chute where the horse had already managed to make dry land, but it looked a likely place for deadly taipans, or at least red-bellied black snakes. Claude let go of his rock and swam to this bank, but the trouble was to get up to road level again. To negotiate the chute in any but one direction – down – was obviously impossible.

'Wait there, and I'll see if there's a break in the bank further along,' called James, and he and Dougal rode back to the main road and watched for another track leading to the river bank. They soon found one with a cleared slope, not too steep, leading to the water where cattle evidently crossed. James stayed there to help the unfortunate man out of the water while Dougal went back to direct him to float down to the next bend, where he'd get up easily.

'D'you think you can make the horse go with you?'

'I can do anything with a horse,' said Claude coolly. His teeth were chattering slightly from cold, shock and immersion. He took off his 'pink' coat, now a dark, saturated red, and tied it to the horse's saddle.

'Keep your boots on!' warned Dougal. 'Oyster rock!'

'Is *that* what you call it?' He looked from his bleeding fingers to his shins, where his riding-trousers had been ripped in places as by a tiger's claws. 'I thought it might be crocodiles' teeth.'

'James is waiting to help you out downstream, on this side. No rock there.'

'Right-ho.' He looped the horse's bridle over his arm and coaxed the unwilling animal into the water. He swam beside it, keeping close to the bank. The current was about four knots and they were soon out of sight.

'Well!' said Helga. 'He's a cool customer. His poor hands! But what wouldn't I have given to see him go down the chute.'

'Horse, hunting-jacket and all,' grinned Dougal.

'The poor man!' said Rose softly.

And indeed he was a mess when they got to him. He had insisted that he could ride and there was no need to send for the carriage. Both hands, where he had grasped the rock, and one leg from shin to ankle had strips of flesh removed by the knife-sharp oyster shells which attach themselves in angular clusters to any underwater rock. He had been able to hold the reins only by wrapping his hands in two handkerchiefs, and even then it must have been agony.

Julia Johnstone mixed him a hot punch with her own hands – 'to counteract any chill from your immersion' – of fresh limes, honey, brandy and water, and he was bandaged and packed off to bed. Dougal dined out on the story for weeks.

3 Reaping the whirlwind

1 Revenge

'I'd like to go back to the Islands just once more,' said Captain John Coath, spitting a loquat-stone over the rail of his verandah.

'Then why don't you?' said his young wife. 'You still have the *Cerberus*.' He looked at Tina with pleasure, as always. He had married late in life and now, with retirement from active trading, had become a model husband and father.

'Because I don't like leaving you.' He wound his hard fingers in her long black hair and pulled her close. She had some admixture, Chinese or Malay, in her blood which made her exotically attractive, with that faint slant to her eyes, that beautifully formed mouth. 'It's not that I don't trust you,' he added, laughing, 'but I don't trust my fellow men. I know what they're like when it comes to a woman left alone.'

'Yes, from personal experience. And how many Island girls did you have before you met me?'

'Not one!'

'No, I bet it wasn't. More like half a dozen.'

He smiled reminiscently, but prudently said nothing. When he smiled, his weather-hardened face folded into rows of brown creases that seemed carved from old wood. He had shaved off his beard at Tina's insistence, and looked years younger. 'You know, I could fence the decks so the kids couldn't fall overboard, and we could all go,' he said. 'Sail to the New Hebrides, or say to the Marquesas and back.'

He thought of the Marquesas, those improbable islands of pink and blue rock rising like giants' teeth suddenly out of the Pacific. 'No cyclones this time of the year – weather should be good—'

'But what about their schooling? And little Marcia might get sick.'

'What, sea-sick? No child of mine could be a bad sailor. And never mind them missing a few months o' schooling. The voyage'll teach them things they'll never learn in a classroom: real geography, f'r instance. I bet you'd never even heard of the Marquesas.'

'No-o.' She smiled unwillingly. Tina never denied him anything, and she gave in now, though not without misgivings. She knew John was a good navigator and an experienced seaman, but the *Cerberus* was so small – less than fifty feet long, though she was completely decked over so that she could not be swamped unless a hatch was left open.

There was a tiny forepeak where the native crew lived, and a roomy cabin which would hold the skipper and his wife and four children, the youngest only three.

*

They sailed out into the deep blue Pacific, the little schooner and her crew of three Kanaka boys, one of whom would double as cook. She would not make more than a hundred miles a day on average, but they were in no hurry. Coath had a contempt for the Islanders as people, but he preferred them to a white crew. There would be none of the troubles that might arise with a young woman in close proximity on a long voyage.

Look what had happened to Bully Hayes – clubbed by a crewman and tipped overboard, and all over a woman, the owner's wife that Hayes had run off with. He himself meant to enjoy his retirement. He had made a come-back after the scandal of the *Jason* case, and since he was one skipper who did not drink all he made, he now had investments in several trading vessels besides owning the *Cerberus*.

His wife Tina lay relaxed on the small after-deck, which had been completely fenced to keep the youngsters safe. The sea was tranquil under a cerulean sky, the water blue and clear as sapphires, with a tinge of wine-purple in the wave troughs from the reflections of great towering clouds which hung motionless on the horizon. There was just enough breeze to drive them through the water with both fore and aft sails set.

The Kanaka crew, happy at sailing towards their old home in the New Hebrides, were singing some island song in the bows. John Coath was steering, an expression of content on his weather-beaten face, his eyes half-closed against the morning sun towards which they sailed.

They were keeping a steady nor'-easterly course, more east than north. No fleck of white showed anywhere save for the crisp bow-wave. Flying-fish scattered from this in silver trails. As they moved, the horizon's unbroken ring enclosed them in an endless circle of blue. On, on, on! As they pitched the rail slowly rose, and slowly dipped in a graceful curtsying to the long swell of ocean far from land. Sapphires and wine, she thought drowsily, half asleep.

She knew that John had once been in trouble over black-birding; she did not know he had made his money by being completely ruthless. She did not know, for instance, about the little boy he had kidnapped with his uncles in a canoe, who, being too small to be worth anything on the market in Mary-borough, had been put over the side two miles from shore with a pair of coconuts tied beneath his arms. In the surf he had slipped from the coconuts and been drowned before the eyes of his family, though his father had swum out in vain.

Nor did she know of the young girl, no more than twelve or thirteen, that he had kept in the cabin for his own use on the way back to Queensland, and then sold to the Japanese brothel keepers in Bundaberg.

They reached Malekula in the northern Hebrides a month after sailing. It was one of the happiest months of Tina's life. John seemed different, younger, when he was at sea, and she loved the long blue days.

They anchored on the sheltered side, off Bushman Bay, which John Coath remembered as the site of a most successful blackbirding operation. But he was retired now, he was not after men, though he wouldn't mind trading for some fresh coconuts and yams to add to the salt beef and the occasional roast chicken when they killed one of the birds Tina had brought in the hope of getting fresh eggs. He wanted to replenish the water supply, too.

He did not expect any danger. He had been lulled by living among 'tame' Kanakas in Queensland, it was years since he'd been to the Islands. And of course it was all changed these days, with the civilized 'boys' coming back as returns. Still, he took his Snider rifle with him just in case, and with a loaded pistol in his belt he got two of the Kanakas to row him ashore. There was no welcoming party of natives on the beach, no canoe putting out with fresh fruit and yams.

Leaving the men in the boat, with orders to wait for him and to be ready to pick him up and row for the ship at once if they heard a shot, he walked up the white coral sand path towards the village.

Before he came to the first bend, he heard a cry of terror from the beach. He spun round, and there as on a picture-postcard he saw the brilliant beach framed in coconut-palms, the boat drawn up on the white sand, the blue sea beyond, and the blood that was beginning to stain it red. The crew was gone.

He turned to run into the jungle to hide. In the line of his vision, straight ahead of his boot as he looked down, was a black, splay-toed, naked foot. He looked up into the cruelly smiling face of a man holding an axe. Behind him stood another holding a war club.

Desperately he looked over his shoulder. Two more savages guarded the path to the sea. One swung a tomahawk with a good metal blade imported from Australia. The other held a musket aimed at his head.

He knew there was no use in running or in trying to shoot it out. At best he could kill one before they got him. He tried parley.

'Look, you feller want-it new gun, pistol? I give you. Here.' He held out the rifle.

With one stroke the man, still smiling, cut off his forearm.

Coath gave a strangled cry, and stared unbelievingly at the stump from which his life's blood was spouting. He pulled a handkerchief from his pocket and with the aid of his teeth tied a tourniquet above the elbow. He felt no pain, only a sort of numbing shock and weakness. They picked up the fallen rifle and removed the loaded pistol from his belt.

The man with the club prodded him from behind. He began to stumble along the path towards the village. It was only then he realized his mistake in not letting himself bleed to death. But

Tina—! She would be waiting for his return, with only four children and one Kanaka to protect her, not knowing what had happened. He must get a message to her somehow, to get away at once.

In the village the ovens were heating, the stones beginning to glow. Someone went and brought the bodies of the two Kanakas from the beach in two baskets. They were already dissected for cooking.

'Fresh meat,' the men who had captured him said in their language, mocking him. And then in pidgin, 'Whitefeller, him good-feller kai too.'

He tried to run, but they caught and trussed him like a chicken. His severed arm was put in the oven, covered with earth and left to cook. When it was done it was passed to what seemed to be the chief priest, with elaborate leaf arrangements in his hair and round his arms, and incongruously a panama hat on his head.

Almost swooning, Coath saw the grisly object served on a plate of banana leaf. The skin had split to let the brownish cooked flesh protrude. The fingernails had curled up and back, so that his hand looked like a five-legged octopus, hideous.

Grinning, sitting straight in front of him so that he could not help but see, the man began to eat. John Coath closed his eyes. He clenched his teeth, willing himself not to vomit.

'For God's sake!' he cried, almost weeping. 'For God's sake!' He remembered how the mate had begged him in vain for the mercy of death.

He was to be more fortunate. An axe descended on his neck as he bowed his face in his hands, almost severing his head. He died still mouthing appeals, and was cooked and eaten along with his two crew members who had never been asked to sit down at table with the white man. All men were made equal at the cannibal feast.

Vengeance had been done. The Islanders could scarcely credit their good fortune when they found their old enemy delivered into their hands. Did he think they would have forgotten him, him and his devil-ship?

On board the *Cerberus,* Tina felt vaguely uneasy. Yet all was silent and peaceful. A white-breasted sea-eagle, russet-winged, swept out over the water, then swooped for some floating carrion.

The children were getting restless. The boys wanted to go ashore and look for Papa.

'No, I want you to stay with me. It will soon be dark. And anyway the boat hasn't come back and you couldn't swim all that way, there might be sharks. If he hasn't come back for supper – and I'm sure he will – you can wade ashore at low tide tomorrow.'

'Boss, e come back quick-time, along sun-e-set?' she asked the remaining Kanaka, who was beginning to roll his eyes uneasily. The boat had been hidden by a point of land and he did not know what had happened, but he thought he had heard the echo of a cry.

'Boss, e come,' he said, reassuring himself.

'*When* will he come? I'm hungry,' wailed the youngest boy.

'Papa's going to bring some fresh yams and taro for us, and Tommy will kill the last chicken. It's stopped laying,' she said.

The deck-hand hung the protesting fowl by its feet from the rigging and neatly chopped off its head in the middle of a squawk. Blood dripped on the deck.

Sun left the golden curve of beach. The sand turned grey-white and cold. The green of palms darkened against the sky. Still no sign of John, nor of the boat from round that wooded point . . . No sound of a shot had reached her. If anything had gone wrong he would never have given in without a fight.

But Tina shivered. She had seen the look in Tommy Tanna's eyes. 'They must be going to stay in the village for the night,' she said at last. 'The chief is entertaining Papa, so we will have our meal and go to bed. He will come in the morning.'

It was a subdued little party which ate the chicken under the awning on deck by the light of a hurricane lamp. There was no moon, but the lagoon was dancing with stars.

Tina put the younger children to bed. The older ones went at last, protesting. For a long time she paced the deck alone: Tommy was curled in the forepeak, apparently asleep. She could see a glow, it must be the fires of the village, above the trees. Why didn't John send one of the Kanakas back with the boat with a message, or one of the canoes? There must be plenty in the village ... They could have killed John and the two Kanakas, and be even now preparing to come out to the ship in force, and—!

She shuddered and went below, carefully bolting the hatch from inside. They were safe enough here. One of the children whimpered in his sleep. She sat tense, listening. Was that bare feet moving on deck? 'Tommy, is that you?' she called sharply.

No reply. There came a yell and a splash, then silence. A noise of hammering overhead? What could they be doing? And who were they? She climbed into her bunk and took the second pistol from under the pillow. It was loaded. She checked again to make sure. Then she stepped on to the floor and went up to her ankles in sea-water.

'Nick! Marcia! Wake up, darlings. The boat is filling. I think we're sinking!'

She grabbed warm wraps for the children. Please God the tide was low enough for them to wade ashore. She went up the companionway, undid the bolts, and pushed. The hatch cover would not move. It was battened down from above.

That hammering! They had nailed bamboo or wooden slats across, perhaps with iron nails which they had received as trade long ago from Queensland ...

The water rose steadily. The porthole! She was too big to get through, but she tore at the bolt, skinning her knuckles. The youngest might escape; if Tommy was still alive he would rescue her somehow.

The open porthole made the end a little quicker. The Malekulans had cut a hole in the hull just below water level. The captain's wife and children went down with the ship, all but little Marcia; tied to a small wooden cabinet-drawer to make her float, her mother managed to push her through the porthole.

Next morning she was washed ashore, drowned. The Islanders, their meat-hunger satisfied for the present, did not eat her since they preferred meat they had killed themselves. They left her for the sand-crabs and the sea-eagles.

2 Sugar town

'One lump or two?'

While the ladies of Maryborough, Sydney, and London poised their sugar-tongs over the steaming bohea or Ceylon tea, while silver spoons tinkled against translucent china and gay young blades in cutaway coats lounged against the grand piano, stirring the delicate cups, did they once think of the social significance of that bowl of white, compressed crystals? The human misery of the slave trade, the ruin of West Africa, the depopulation of the Pacific Islands, the wealth of the plantation economies in America, Fiji and now Queensland?

> Roses are red,
> Violets are blue,
> Sugar is sweet
> And so are you,

wrote young men in the autograph albums of young ladies, using a pink, white or green scented page.

They ate jams and preserves, condensed sweetened milk, chutneys, pickles and sauces, syrups and cordials of every kind which contained sugar as a main ingredient, apart from all the sweets, chocolates, cakes, biscuits, éclairs, marzipans and tarts consumed all over the civilized world. How did people ever exist without it?

The demand seemed never-ending, from the old swaggie who dropped half a handful of sugar into his billy of tea, to the tray brought to Queen Victoria at tea-time at Windsor Castle. Sugar, unknown in Europe before the fifteenth century when Portuguese voyagers introduced it, had become an essential of life.

Out of this need fortunes were being made. In Queensland alone, ten thousand tons of sugar were being produced every year. With the world price up to forty pounds a ton and hundreds of thousands of pounds invested in the industry, the voices of protest at the way it was carried on were soon suppressed.

Only in London, where the British still had a bad conscience over the slave trade from Africa to Mauritius, the West Indies and the Americas, did *The Times* thunder against Queensland and Fijian planters with cries of 'A nation of slave-holders! A blot on the Empire!' The Colonists were hurt and amazed at the nasty things said about them – after all this was indentured labour, and the men were paid – and at the unnecessary zeal of British gun-boats which occasionally arrested the Australian captain of a trading schooner.

But the 'Wide Bay Farmers' and Planters' Association', representing Maryborough and Bundaberg districts on the Mary and Burnett rivers, formed a strong lobby in Parliament. The Premier, Thomas McIlwraith, was a big, bluff Scot who himself did a roaring trade in shipping and recruiting, and was busy as well buying up cattle stations in the north, with British capital, and cutting them up into cane-fields.

The anti-Kanaka lobby, led by humanitarians and retired missionaries from the Pacific, had little hope of being heard, it seemed.

Chindera was now a large plantation, though smaller than the thousand acres first taken up, with 450 acres cleared and planted. This meant, first, clearing the thick vine scrub from the rich soil, with its leeches and scrub-ticks, stinging-trees and snakes; then burning off the dry, felled timber, clearing the land of stumps, ploughing and hoeing. Finally, 500 holes had to be dug in every acre, and two setts of cane planted in each hole. Then, it was not a question of sitting back and waiting for the cane to grow; weeds sprang up to choke the young cane, and teams had to go out with their chipping-hoes to cultivate between the plants.

The wages bill on Chindera was nearly £10,000 a year, and of this the Kanakas got less than a quarter. The hundred white men employed around the office and the mill, and as foreman, overseer and so on, accounted for the rest of it. There were also half a dozen Chinese.

The whole place was a model of efficiency and energetic administration; and a certain Scottish carefulness over expenditure tended to keep overheads down and profits steadily rising. The obvious place for a careful manager to save money was on rations for the Kanakas; so meat was a rare treat, and rice and maize meal helped to fill even if it did not satisfy men working in the field from 6.00 a.m. to 6.00 p.m. with two breaks for breakfast and lunch. The tea was what is known in the bush as 'clover-leaf tea' – three leaves to the pot – and might as well have been plain hot water.

The only food there was plenty of was sugar: sticky brown 'ration' sugar, and molasses, the black, bitter-sweet syrup left from the first spin-off. There were fifteen sugar-mills scattered about Maryborough, which produced about 180,000 gallons of molasses between them. It was fed to horses, mixed with their dry feed, and builders even mixed it with mortar to make a kind of cement.

Excitement was in the air as the beginning of the harvest and crushing season came close. The Islanders were reminded of the harvest festivals at home when the yam-houses were bursting with gathered food.

Although tired from work, they would stay up half the night dancing and singing, stamping out the same urgent rhythm as the thump of the engines and the rollers in the mill. With matched drums made from hollow lengths of giant bamboo, which grew here just as it did at home, they would beat out a hollow tattoo to an accompaniment of Island songs. They threw away their juice-stained European trousers and wore a cloth sulu wrapped round their loins. Some put flowers in their hair.

And this year Mr Johnstone had promised them a feast of two whole roast pigs to mark the opening of the season.

Looking from the balcony on the first floor at Chindera House, Helga was reminded of the patchwork quilt on her old doll's bed.

Quilted in patchwork colours over the undulating plains beside the river, the cane-fields stretched under the winter sun as far as she could see: squares of solid green or yellow alternating with the deep red loam of fallow land. Some of the cane was already blackened with trash fires, ready for harvesting. Some was 'spearing' with pale flower-pannicles, giving a misted mauve colour to the fields.

She could remember the quilt that had been given her for a needlework task one summer, when she was only eight or nine. She remembered the still, suffocating heat in the nursery, and her little fingers, sticky with sweat, trying to push the needle through the stiff material. One of the squares was a bright yellow brocade, terribly difficult to pierce.

Rebelliously she had sat at her task, hearing through the window the shouts of her brothers swimming and skylarking in the river. It wasn't fair! She would much rather have been born a boy.

She gazed now across the winter fields, spread under a sky of unbroken blue. Like ants among the roots of a giant lawn, black men worked in the airless channels between the rows. They wore blue denim trousers, wide felt hats, and a variety of bright scarves as sweat-rags. Set in the midst of all the greenery was the small clearing of the Kanaka village.

*

In her grass-walled, thatched cottage Eliza felt her time drawing near. She didn't want to miss all the fun of the harvest this year because of the taboos referring to pregnant women which Zachari insisted she should observe: she must not go anywhere alone, she must not eat with her left hand, nor look at the new moon, and so on. He feared the Evil Eye.

She had not told him, but she had in fact seen the new moon through the window last month, by accident. She had shut her eyes quickly and had not looked again. Besides, she was 'all-a-same whitefeller' now, and was beginning to doubt all that stuff about the evil spirits. She was not on the Island now, anyway, and how would they find her here in Queensland?

She was tired of waiting, of being heavy and ungainly. They had told her she need not work in the kitchen any more until after the birth, and she was bored. Now Zachari had this crazy idea that she must have the baby out in the fields, not under a roof.

Mrs Johnstone had brought her the prettiest little garments for 'Lorna', and Miss Helga had given her a shawl to wrap the baby in. Eliza did not want to have it outside on the ground, like an animal.

Helga, glancing across at the cottages, decided to go down and visit Eliza, and take her some fruit from the garden. She fetched her parasol and went downstairs, and taking up the basket of fruit imperiously summoned Claude Grant to carry it for her, since he was idling in the morning-room.

They would call at the mill on the way back, and see the preparations for the grand ball going on in the sugar room.

Claude came with alacrity. He walked behind Helga on the narrow foot-track to the village: what a picture she made in her pale, frilled gown between the great walls of green cane! He was watching the back of her neck, the skin white and fine as silk beneath its cluster of dark curls. Yes, she disturbed him. He did not understand her, with her moodiness and her music, he was not, certainly thinking of proposing to her; but for some reason her shape, her colouring, even the rich, deep tones of her speaking voice, held a fascination for him. It was this that kept him lingering in Maryborough when he should be seeing some more of the country.

Helga had told him only that she was taking fruit to a village woman 'because of her health', without going into details. But Eliza was sitting at the open louvres of her house and her condition was obvious. A little embarrassed, Helga left the fruit and led the way briskly to the complex of mill buildings, including the great sugar store.

'You mean this room will be filled to the roof with raw sugar?' asked Claude, staring at the ceiling and dim, distant corners. Men were sweeping up little heaps of golden, transparent grains left from the year before, and scattering chips of wax candles for polish.

'Completely filled, at least once. Then it is bagged and sent away for further refining. My father thinks we should do the whole process here in Maryborough, right to the First White grade.'

'What do you take it to now?'

'The Second Yellow – like the grains you see on the floor. Shall we go back and take morning tea, then?'

'Yes, thank you; but I won't take any sugar in it,' he laughed.

'After breathing sugar, and walking on sugar, I don't fancy it somehow.'

Helga smiled. 'You get used to it. Wait till you smell the sickliness of the air in the crushing season.' She showed him the little trams which would carry continuous loads of cane to the crushers. To her, Joseph, bending to clear one of the tracks of last year's cane debris, was just another black man employed by her father. But he looked at her under his brows and thought, A young lady like you has kissed me! That would surprise you, wouldn't it? Just then a familiar voice sounded on his ears:

'I say, what would they say back in England to my having walked over a pound of sugar before morning tea?'

Joseph looked up, staring. That tall young man with the pink face and the yellow moustache – he could almost see the cup of coffee in his hand, and hear his 'I say, what would they say at home to my shooting a dozen niggers before breakfast?' He would never forget it.

Trembling, he bent again to his task while the two white people walked away, crossing to the driveway of the house, soon swallowed in the shade of the huge mango trees.

3 The ball

The sugar house at Chindera Mill was lit outside with burning braziers and torches in iron stanchions. Inside, the sugar room with a few odd crystals left on the floor gleaming like yellow diamonds in the light of the carbide lamps, was filled with a crowd of women in light-coloured silks, men in formal black, all moving with a rustling chatter about the flower-decked room.

The brilliant white glow of the lamps lit up real diamonds sparkling in the hair or corsages of wealthy matrons, the sugar aristocracy of Maryborough; and above it all, stars glittered like blue diamonds in the frosty sky.

Everyone who was anyone in the town was invited: the newspaper editor, the biggest shipowner (who also owned half the newspaper) the owners of timber-mills and plantations, the two doctors, the Church of England minister and his wife. (Methodists and Presbyterians, those interfering busybodies with their missions to the Islands, were conspicuously absent.) The Chief Immigration Officer was present, and the Polynesian Inspector, of course. It was as well to be friendly with *them*.

The PI was not a popular man. His duty was to supervise recruiting vessels, to protect Islanders, and to protect the Australian worker from the encroachment of Kanakas in other domains than sugar-growing. He visited plantations, settled disputes, and was supposed to enforce all contracts after the regular three-year indentures were finished.

An orchestra of piano, two fiddles and a bassoon was tuning up on a raised platform resting on molasses-barrels at one end of the high-ceilinged room.

Claude Grant surveyed this scene with a certain amusement. Really, these Colonials were quite surprising. Here they were, on the edge of a vast continent full of howling deserts and unsubdued savages, having evicted the original savages from this bit of the coast – how long? only forty or fifty years ago – and putting on a grand ball as though they were in London at the height of the season.

The ladies were, if anything, over-dressed, with much silk and satin, jewelled embroidery and feather head-dresses. Miss Johnstone, on the other hand – he swept his monocle to his right eye to survey her better – looked charming in simple white muslin with a pink sash, and a diamond brooch twinkling among the folds of the fichu where it crossed her full, rounded bosom. She wore nothing in her hair but a white satin ribbon, and her rather wild profusion of dark curls had been dressed in Grecian style.

Hm, he would ask her for the first dance.

'May I have your programme, Miss Johnstone?'

She had been searching the crowd with her eyes for young Mr Lindsay, and had not heard his approach. She turned a little impatiently and thrust the silver-printed card at him, with its tiny pencil attached by a thread of lilac silk.

'Oh, pray call me "Helga", Claude. All this formality! You always call Dougal and James by their first names.'

He bowed. 'Well, yes. But it is a little different, don't you know. I was waiting for your permission. It is an unusual name.'

'It's a record of one of my parents' tours to Europe. Mamma was fascinated by the Nordic countries.'

Helga was glad her mother had insisted on this rather exotic name, whereas her father had wanted to call her Janet. But she wished her second name had been something more like Paderewski. Perhaps one day she would marry an illustrious name ... somewhere in Europe, or America. She knew with absolute certainty that her life would not be lived out in this provincial town at the bottom of the world. She meant to go abroad.

'Miss Johnstone! I've been looking for you everywhere.'

That deep, manly voice – she felt it vibrate along her nerves, it affected her as Claude's bleating, correct tones could never do. She turned with a dazzling smile which made young Lindsay blink as if he had looked at the rising sun. Her dark eyes – were they grey or brown? – intensified the brilliant colour in her cheeks, which he would swear was all her own.

'I wanted to ask you for the first dance,' he said.

'I am afraid it is taken ... Mr Claude Grant, may I present Mr Graham Lindsay? ... but you may have the last.'

Before he shook hands, Claude rapidly wrote his name opposite both the supper dance and the last.

'Sorry old boy. Miss Johnstone gave me *carte blanche*, don't you know, and the last is taken.' He handed the card back to Helga with a self-satisfied flourish.

Helga frowned. 'I did no such thing!'

'That's quite all right,' said Lindsay coolly. 'I'll take all the rest, if I may.'

'No, you may not, Sir!' said Helga, smiling. 'You may have – let me see – three. That is fair, is it not? I always keep one for my brother James, who is an indifferent dancer but feels he should make an appearance on the floor; and Mr Grant has three.'

'I don't see that it's fair at all. He has you for the whole of supper, and has three dances as well!'

'Four then. But that is absolutely all. It leaves me only one to spare, unless there are any extras.'

Unexpectedly, she had begun to enjoy herself. Usually she had to dance with old men, friends of her father's, whose paunches got in the way in the waltzes. The square dances were different, she didn't mind who partnered her for the lancers or the Alberts, it was fun just to be on the floor.

*

In the cleared space in the middle of the Kanaka village, between the ring of community huts and the married quarters, another dance was going on under the sky. Men in sulus and bare feet, with bracelets and armlets of green leaves and hibiscus blooms stuck in their tight black curls, were stamping and dancing round the fire where the whole pigs were roasting. Someone had got hold of some illicit rum, distilled from molasses.

Already the dances were becoming wilder. The hollow bamboo drums tapped out the rhythm which was taken up by hundreds of clapping hands.

On her straw palliasse, Eliza moaned and turned restlessly. A young girl sat beside her, not an Islander but a part-Aboriginal belonging to the cook's family. Eliza was not allowed to be left alone, but the child resented having to stay indoors when so much was going on. Suddenly Eliza gave a scream 'Quicktime!' she gasped. 'You go find Zachari. He dancing, along other boy. He carry me outside place.'

Eliza dreaded his wrath if she did not obey, yet she would rather have stayed in her bed. Indeed, if he did not come she would have the baby here, for it was coming quickly, the pains close together.

The girl ran, delighted to get away. Halfway to the dance she paused where the women were dishing out baked taro and bananas from the underground ovens. They smelt delicious. Her mouth watered.

'Here, Leila, you want some kai-kai?' A woman held out a steaming heap on a banana leaf. 'Him smell good, eh?' and she rubbed her belly and laughed.

Leila hesitated, was lost. She crammed handfuls of the

savoury yet sweet vegetable into her mouth, muttering to salve her conscience, 'Eliza, her time bin come. You bin see that feller Zachari?'

'Ho, Zachari! He bin drink plenty rum, plenty palm wine. Mine tink he go asleep, close-up.'

Zachari, at last told by young Leila that his wife was in labour, had quaffed another cup of palm wine and gone bounding off towards his home. There, to his horror, he found Eliza had already given birth. Weak and trembling, she held the baby on her arm, still unwashed. The mess of the afterbirth lay on the bed.

'I bin bite the cord,' she gasped. 'Bin tie him off orright.'

With a wild cry Zachari snatched the baby from her and held it close to the lamp. The child's face was blue, it did not seem to be breathing. He held it upside down, striving to remove whatever was blocking its windpipe.

'You know, O woman, what you have done!' he cried in a terrible voice in their own tongue. 'You have brought down the curse of the Evil Eye upon our child. Why did you not wait? Why did you not send for me earlier? The place was prepared where my son would have been born beneath the stars. Now he will die, unless blood is let at once.' He thrust the baby back at her, and after gazing wildly round, snatched his cane-knife from the wall.

'Zachari! What you do? I not—' But he was gone. Eliza rocked the apparently lifeless child and moaned.

Young Leila, having brought the old woman who attended births, fled from the smell of blood. The native midwife held the tiny male form by the feet and slapped it hard. It began to cough and cry.

*

Lindsay and Helga were dancing the schottische, a lively galloping dance rather like a polka. Helga's cheeks were glowing; her curls had come a little out of place, which Lindsay found enchanting. Breathing heavily, they stopped at the end of the number in the shade of a potted palm. Helga fanned herself with a dainty handkerchief.

She liked tall men, she decided, they made her feel small and fragile when she knew she was rather sturdily built. He was still holding her hand as though he had forgotten to give it up.

'May I get you a cool drink? An ice?'

'Oh, a lemonade I think.'

The moment he had gone Claude Grant appeared beside her. He was even taller than Mr Lindsay, or perhaps he just held himself straighter – his back was like a ramrod. But he was a very good dancer. She had enjoyed her dances with him.

'By Jove, it's warm in here!' he said.

'It is after dancing the schottische, I assure you.'

'I say, would you, er, care to go outside into the cool? The night is quite clear.'

'Oh! I'm sorry, but I'm waiting for Mr Lindsay to bring me some lemonade.'

'No doubt he will find you.'

He put a hand under her elbow in masterful fashion, and began propelling her towards the door. Helga stopped like a baulky horse.

'I am sorry!' she said icily. 'I am waiting for Mr Lindsay to return.'

'Quite!' It was Grant's turn to be icy. With a magnificent bow he left her, turning and striding out of the open doors into the night.

'What's biting him?' asked Lindsay cheerfully, arriving with two glasses of lemonade.

'Oh dear! I'm afraid he's used to having his own way.'

'Was he annoying you?' He sounded quite fierce.

'No. He just wanted me to leave you in the lurch.'

'And you wouldn't? Good girl!'

'I don't like being bullied, even in the most gentlemanly way.'

'I should say not . . . Listen! I say, those Kanakas are having quite a shindig.'

Now that the orchestra had ceased, over the chatter in the big room could be heard the strange rhythm of bamboo drums struck against the ground, a hollow *whumph! whumph!*, the clapping of hands and men's voices blending in some Island song, ending in a wild shout.

'Strange how you forget when you're back here in Queensland that they are less than a generation removed from the cannibal savage,' said Lindsay. 'Or not at all removed. Some of course have been Christianized, but others go back to their old practices as soon as they return. And being armed with guns they have more victims.'

'But not – not cannibalism, surely?'

'Yes, indeed. I myself have seen it, and among "boys" not long returned from Maryborough.'

'I can't believe it! Why, when I was growing up we had a houseboy, Tolu, who used to make me spinning-tops and strings of beads. He was the kindest man, dear fuzzy-haired Tolu. He—'

'My God! What was that?'

They had moved closer to the door with their drinks, to get the benefit of the cooler air outside. Suddenly a terrible yell went up, followed by a choking cry.

'Wait here!' For once Helga did as she was bid, while Graham Lindsay rushed outside with a crowd of young men who were near the door.

They stumbled over Claude Grant lying in a pool of blood beyond the light of the flaring torches in their brackets. He was half-way along the lane that led to the Kanaka village from the mill – perhaps he'd been on his way to have a look at what the Islanders were up to – when he had met Zachari running through the darkness, bent on letting blood and attacking the first person to get in his way.

Half-stupid with grief and half-crazed with drink, he had slashed out savagely; then pausing only to make sure that ritual blood was flowing, had sped back to his hut. There he found the baby alive and breathing, miraculously saved from the Evil Eye. Eliza was asleep. He ran on, afraid now of what he had done.

Claude was carried along to the anteroom of the sugar house. The leading local doctor was called from among the guests. The tall Englishman was now of a ghastly pallor, his face looking strangely pure and young with all the blood drained from it. The doctor felt his feeble, thready pulse.

'Loss of blood,' he murmured, while bystanders tore up their evening handkerchiefs to staunch the flow. 'He's far gone, poor fellow.' He listened to the bubbling sounds from the man's chest, noted the pink froth on his lips. 'Internal injuries – knife must have pierced the lung.'

'Feller – went for me – no reason . . .' said Claude faintly.

'Yes, yes. Don't try to talk.'

Claude was put on an improvised stretcher and taken to the hospital, but died as soon as he was admitted.

Rumours flew about the sugar room, the supper room. The band began to play again, but nobody danced. Then news came back that Claude Grant was dead. Angus Johnstone got up on the dais to announce that the ball was over.

'It is my painful duty to tell ye,' he said in a voice charged with emotion, 'that our guest and fellow-man has been foully murdered.' His blue eyes glittered under their beetling brows. 'Aye, and done to death here in the grounds of Chindera, and apairently by ain o' the plantation Kanakas. Mr Grant knew none o' the labourers, the mon must ha' been oot of his mind; but we feel it best for all tae gang to their hames, and stay there the nicht. The murderer will be brought to book.'

A great babble of talk broke out, alarm and consternation showed in the faces of the women, anger in the men's.

'He should be lynched!' was one furious comment. 'We won't be safe in our beds if these black devils start breaking out.'

'He must be made an example of, whoever he is!'

'Hanging is too good. Should be drawn and quartered – towed behind a cart – and all the Kanakas mustered to watch. Put the fear of God into 'em.'

'But why did he do it?' asked Helga, feeling sick and faint, as she rested a trembling hand on Graham Lindsay's arm. 'You know something of these men in their Island homes. Here they have always seemed such happy, laughing people.'

'Well, as I said, they've had only a generation or less to change. Judging by the noise out there tonight they were working themselves up, and one of them was overcome by a primitive blood-lust. Poor old Grant just happened to be in the way.'

'I feel it's my fault. He was angry with me when he left.'

'Nonsense, it might as easily have happened to anyone.'

'They have always held dances at the beginning and end of the sugar season, and nothing like this has ever happened before.'

'What – no fights? No bloodshed? I would be surprised—'

'Yes, but not—' She stopped.

'Not a European, eh? It makes a difference, doesn't it? Do you realize that if white labourers, a collection of young men, died at the rate the Kanakas die in Maryborough – I believe it is more than ten per cent – there would be a huge outcry?'

'Surely not! Not on Chindera.'

'I'm afraid so, Miss Johnstone. I was talking to a doctor who has been signing death certificates for years. He says there will have to be an inquiry, the Polynesian Inspector will demand it. Things can't go on like this.'

'Indeed no! Yet I can't believe it . . .'

'Helga! There you are, my dear! The carriage is coming, we must not consider walking across to the house!' It was Mrs Johnstone, her face pale, her eyes glittering. She clasped Helga to her large bosom for a moment, and the girl felt her trembling. Then she realized that her mother was in a towering rage.

'To think my ball should have ended in such fashion!' cried Mrs Johnstone. 'And my guest – poor Claude – I shall never hold my head up again,' she said, unconsciously lifting her determined chin and strong aquiline nose. 'The worst thing is, they seem to think it was one of the Chindera boys.'

'Never mind, Mamma. It will go down in history.'

Mrs Johnstone held her at arms' length and looked at her suspiciously. However, she merely said, 'It seems that Zachari is missing, and his wife is hysterical—'

'Eliza! Has the baby arrived, then?'

'I really couldn't say . . . Come, my dear, perhaps Mr Lindsay will be good enough to hand us into the carriage?'

The coachman was Tombua, who had unwillingly got into his uniform, for it was nearly midnight. Mrs Johnstone looked at his dark, impassive face above the smart frogged jacket she had designed. 'I can never feel the same towards them again,' she said, and shuddered.

4 Zachariah

Sermons were preached in most of the Maryborough churches that Sunday on the theme of murder and retribution, for the tragedy at the ball was uppermost in everyone's mind. At the Presbyterian Church the text was, 'He that soweth the wind, reapeth the whirlwind.'

The Minister suggested that such incidents, and the one which had happened up-country when an overseer on a station had been cut to pieces by four Kanakas not long ago, were inevitable while coloured men were brought into the country without equality, not educated to take their place in the white community except as serfs.

'Too few of them are given a Christian education, or taught to put aside their heathen ways and enter the love of Christ,' said Mr Stewart. 'Too many of them come to this great Christian country for three or six years, and return knowing no more than when they came – except how to gamble, and drink, and fornicate, which they have learnt in their sojourn here.

'This unfortunate man, Zachariah, who was given his Christian name by missionaries on his island, may have been crazed with grief when he committed this crime. It seems he thought his child was dead. We know he had been drinking, aided and abetted by the overseer. There had been no attempt to check the wild orgy among the Kanakas while their employers were indulging in the questionable amusement of ballroom dancing!

'Many are calling for his blood in retribution. Yet think, brothers and sisters! Are we not all to blame for this tragedy? All of us who depend on sugar for our livelihood, directly or indirectly, and that is a large portion of the people of Maryborough. For the whole system of indenting coloured labour is wrong, is an iniquity before the Lord.

'Therefore let us pray for Zachariah of Malaita, as well as for the soul of his unfortunate victim. Let us pray that he be sent back to his island, together with his wife and new baby, that they may take with them a message of the spirit of Christ: "Father, forgive them, for they know not what they do." '

The congregation was silent after this sermon, though many did not agree and thought a public hanging was called for.

Many other sermons were full of fire and brimstone: 'Vengeance is Mine; I will repay, saith the Lord.'

White men gathered on street corners, muttering. Dark people kept discreetly off the streets and out of sight. Most of them were just as shocked as the whites, but they knew what it was to suffer guilt by association. Poor Eliza turned her face to the wall and would not look at the baby decked out in the pretty new clothes the Chindera ladies had given her. She kept calling for Zachari. This terrible thing that had happened was all her fault, and she wanted to tell him she was sorry and beg him to forgive her.

Joseph had come to see her and explained that Zachari could not come, he was being held at the police station.

'What for? What he done? I tell 'im and tell 'im, don't get into no trouble, we got the baby comin' . . . It's all my fault, he like a wild man las' night.'

'It wasn't your fault, Liza.'

'Well, what he done? Why he not come?' He looked at her silently, and she nodded slowly. 'He done kill someone, for sure! He take the cane-knife with 'im las' night. He not come back.'

Joseph could see only the whites of her eyes in the dimness of the grass hut. The baby was asleep in a basket beside the mat where Eliza lay. 'You mustn't worry,' he said. 'He'll be all right, you'll see.'

But Eliza knew better. She believed now in the Evil Eye which had nearly destroyed their child. She just wanted to tell him, and beg him to forgive her. 'Who he bin kill? Nobody done tell me nothin'. He killem 'nother-feller Kanaka? Might-be his people come after me now.'

'No, Eliza. He – he didn't mean to kill 'im – he hurt a man who got in his way – one of the white bosses.'

'Ai-ee-ee!' Eliza began to wail, on a high-pitched note. 'Him finish properly now. Zachariah dead-feller bime-by.' She turned her face to the wall, keening on a long note of misery. Joseph crept away. He would have liked to tell her that the white man was a cold-blooded murderer who had shot many Islanders on board the *Jason*; but what good would that do?

He was the only person who knew. And no one but Eliza knew that the killing of Claude Grant had been a ritual act to save their child. Nobody asked her; and Zachariah said not a word in his own defence. Rumours and counter-rumours flew round the town.

'Of course, it was jealousy. The Englishman liked a bit of "black velvet" on the side, and this chap had caught him going to his wife's hut—'

'They say she gave birth to a half-caste, a yeller-feller, and this Kanaka went berserk and tried to kill the child and then went for Claude Grant because he thought he was the father—'

'He was rushing along to the overseer's place with this big cane-knife to carve up Sam McGriggen, they say. This chap Grant tried to stop him . . .'

*

For the last two days they had been erecting a gibbet on the Green, the town's public common, in a loop of the river. The wood had been ordered from Hyne's saw-mills before the trial was even begun or the death sentence passed; so certain was the outcome where a black man had clearly murdered a white.

Good, tough Queensland timber went into the construction, good Walkers Bros nails held it together. The rope was best Manila, guaranteed not to break under the strain of holding the tall, well-made body of Zachariah by the neck until he was dead.

The trial was finished; Zachariah had made no attempt to deny his guilt; and he was duly sentenced to death. Wednesday morning at eight o'clock was set down for the hanging. Children were kept back from school so that they could be taken to the Green to witness the event, and have impressed on their young minds the evils of wrong-doing and its consequences.

Wednesday dawned bright and clear, a perfect late-winter morning with a breath of spring in the air. A few soft white clouds sailed rapidly across the sky of brilliant blue. The river in its rippled surface reflected this colour more intensely than on a day of absolute calm.

The crowds on the Green had almost a festive, picnic air. Friends greeted each other, children were held up so that they could see. Only one section of the crowd, the group of several hundreds of Kanakas brought from the different plantations, was silent. They had been brought by their foremen to see the white man's justice meted out.

Most of them accepted that Zachari would have to die. They understood the law of retribution all right. But they stared with awe and horror at the contraption which would end his life. Even on the Islands where they once used to strangle a chief's widows as a matter of custom, it had been done with a certain ceremony and dignity. The widow would dress in her best, and six leading men of the village pulled on each end of a valuable tapa rope until she fell senseless.

Even when men in the prime of life had to die, perhaps so that the pillars of a chief's house would stand strongly, there was no unseemly struggle against their fate. Each would get down into the post-hole, and sitting down and embracing the post with his arms with a last 'Farewell!', would wait for the earth to be shovelled in and trampled down.

Yes, they were familiar with death, but this was different, obscene. This was the white man's calculated revenge for breaking his law. They stood silent, eyes cast down, and waited for the hanging to begin.

The 'time gun' which used to fire at one o'clock each day in the public gardens, now went off to mark the stroke of eight. There was a stir in the crowd. An open cart drawn by a black horse drove up to the gallows bringing the condemned man, in denim trousers and work-shirt, his feet and head bare, his hands tied behind him. With him was the chief constable, a minister of religion and the executioner.

Zachariah was pushed forward till he stood beneath the loop of rope. Every Kanaka there shrank a little as the shirt was folded back and the rope put round his neck. The minister murmured a prayer, and Zachariah was asked if there was anything he wished to say. His face worked with terror; he seemed unable to speak. Then a hoarse cry burst from his lips: 'Liza, I sorry!'

The mask was drawn over his face, the trap was pulled, and Zachariah was dancing on air.

A little girl sat on her father's shoulder and stared and stared. She felt sick, but she could not look away. Oh! The poor man had wet himself, all over the front of his clothes. Now he was swinging, first to the left, then to the right . . . One more convulsive movement and he hung limp. She struggled out of her father's grasp and ran blindly through the crowd, pushing against trouser'd legs and long skirts, wanting only to get away. Once she had seen a hanging in a Punch and Judy show, but this was a real man, though he hung like a puppet, an obscene, lifeless *thing*.

As the struggles ceased, a deep-throated wail went up from the watching Islanders, a spontaneous 'Aie-aah!' of grief. They were hustled off in different directions by their overseers – all armed – before there could be any incidents.

The random, pointless death of Claude Grant had been suitably avenged. The white townspeople repaired to the pubs to discuss the event, determined to make a holiday of it.

*

Helga forced herself to go down to the village to see Eliza and the baby. Eliza sat by the uprights of the hut in the sunlight, peeling potatoes with an old, sharp knife. The cook had sent down a bucket of them to peel, as she had asked for some work to keep her occupied.

Eliza looked up with a dead, expressionless face, then dropped her glance to the half-peeled potato turning in her hands.

'Eliza! I came to say how – how sorry I am about Zachariah and – and everything.' This was going to be harder than she expected. Eliza said nothing, but firmly removed two eye-specks from the potato with the point of the knife. 'Is there – is there anything you need, anything I can get for the baby? Are you all right?'

Oh God, how stupid, thought Helga; but what on earth do you say to a woman whose husband has just been hanged?

Eliza nodded silently, finished the potato, dropped it into a bowl of clean water and took up another. Helga noticed for the first time how pale the palms of her hands, the tips of her fingers were – as though she were a white person who had merely darkened on those surfaces turned towards the sun. There was pink colour in her fingers and in her lips. Somehow this was surprising, as if she, Helga, had imagined dark people had dark-coloured blood. Whereas the colouring was only skin-deep.

Suddenly Eliza spoke, still intent on her task. 'Milk belong-me bin dry up,' she said. She clasped her arms across her breasts, the knife still in one hand, the potato in the other. ' 'Nother Mary, she take baby an' nurse him.'

'You poor girl! But at least you'll always have him, even if—' She stopped. Even if his father is dead, she had meant to say. She was smitten with a feeling of helpless guilt, as though she personally had been responsible for the tragedy. And after all, if her father had not imported coloured labour from the Islands, Claude would not have died, nor Zachariah have been hung . . . but that was fanciful.

'—Even if you can't feed him at present. And later I'll send you down some milk in-a-tin, and you can mix it up and feed him yourself from a bottle when he's a bit older.'

She smiled brightly, relieved that there was something practical she could do. 'Here's some fruit and some cold chicken, you must keep your strength up.'

She put a parcel on a shelf by the back door, taking it from the basket she carried, and made her escape. No word had been said of Zachariah's end; what could be said? It did not bear speaking of, now or ever.

4 The loves of the parallels

1 Helga

Since the night of the ball Helga had warmed towards Graham Lindsay. They had shared that moment of shock together; she still felt the firmness of the hand he had placed over hers where it trembled on his arm. She remembered the horror and disbelief with which she had recalled that the hand now cold in death had so lately been warm upon her elbow.

She was pleased to hear that Mr Lindsay had not gone to the public hanging. James too had stayed away, and so earned his father's displeasure.

The next time Mr Lindsay came to dinner she asked him to play the accompaniment for her while she sang. Rather to her surprise he agreed, readily if rather diffidently. Certainly he was not a brilliant performer, but he had feeling, and she was relieved that at least he could read music.

As she sang, Helga's white, well-formed breast under its frills of muslin expanded and threw forth the notes as purely as the butcher-birds singing in the dew of a Queensland morning: those black-and-white birds who pumped their wings and flung back their heads with all the panache of a concert performer.

She sang Elena's aria from *Martha*, better known to the company as 'The Last Rose of Summer' than as part of Flotow's opera. Her voice was too strong for a drawing-room, even the large, high-ceilinged room at Chindera. She made the glasses ring, the window-panes vibrate with her top notes.

Her mother, sitting with a fixed, approving smile on her strong-boned face, thought that Helga's singing was scarcely ladylike, though fortunately she was not a contralto with one of those deep, masculine-sounding voices, but a coloratura soprano who reached top C with ease.

As soon as he could get young Lindsay away from the piano,

'Angus Johnstone edged him into a corner and talked sugar-cane. He had a proposition to make and not being versed in diplomacy, he came straight out with it.

'Helga's a fine-looking gel,' he said suddenly, veering from the subject of the good overseas price for sugar and the new areas being opened up at Childers, Bundaberg and even as far north as Mackay, where the Johnstone mill had interests.

'Oh – er – yes!' Graham Lindsay, who had in fact been staring across the room at her curly dark head bent above a sheet of music, coloured slightly.

'But not getting any younger. Ought to be thinkin' aboot settling doon and stairting a family. But she's got this music nonsense in her heid. She's wishing to study abroad, and all that rubbish.'

'I'm sure she is talented,' said Lindsay. 'Her voice is pure and true. But what a loss to us in Australia!'

Angus shot him a considering look from under his unruly eyebrows. 'Ever thocht o' setting up as a planter yeself?' he asked, apparently reverting to his first subject. 'There are opportunities for a guid man in the north.'

'Oh! Well, not actually. I doubt if I have the capital for the sort of enterprise that seems to be needed nowadays.'

'That could be arranged; but furrst ye must have experience. I was lookin' for a manager, noo, of ain of our new plantations oot o' Mackay. What would ye think of the idea? And perhaps a pairtnership later on.'

Lindsay was both surprised and pleased that Mr Johnstone should think so well of him. 'If you think I could do it, Sir—'

'And why for not? Ye've had experience with Kanakas on board a labour vessel. Onyways, ye could get an overseer who's used to handling them. As for cane-growing, it's juist common sense and keeping proper bukes; and James can ground ye in the paper worrk – tallies and wages bukes and a' the rest. How-somever,' and Angus shot him another of those piercing blue looks, 'ye'd find it lonesome away up north on your ain; ye'd be needin' a wife, I'm thinking.'

Startled, Graham Lindsay looked up and saw the shrewd old eyes fixed on him, with a twinkle in their depths. Angus had studied the young man and had not missed the way he followed Helga with his eyes. 'Well, lad,' he rose and clapped him on the shoulder, 'I thocht I'd juist let ye know whaur the land lay. Ye'd ha'e ma blessing on whatever enterprise ye embarrk on.'

He crossed the room to speak to another guest, leaving Lindsay's head buzzing with speculation, astonishment and a growing exhilaration.

*

The moon, just past full, was rising over the Mary River, lifting slowly in a halo of honeyed light. On the smooth broad expanse of water it painted a wide golden track flecked with transverse shadows. Helga and Graham Lindsay were on the upstairs balcony after dinner, watching the moonrise. They leant companionably on the balustrade.

A silent army of flying foxes passed overhead to their nightly feeding-places. Like cut-outs of black paper against the sky, they followed as if along an invisible track. As each one reached the big jacaranda at the corner of the drive, it changed direction slightly, and the silent wings gave out a leathery flap as of dry parchment.

'You could never mistake them for birds,' Helga was saying. 'They are weird creatures – have you seen one close up? Dougal shot one and showed it to me. Head like a red-brown fox, sharp furry ears, and the wings of a bat. But altogether more like a dog than a bat. I hate bats, I have a horror of one getting tangled in my hair.'

'Some ladies have a horror of mice.'

'Oh, I don't mind them, I used to keep white mice once.'

Graham spoke absently, his mind was revolving round the problem of how to lead up to a proposal of marriage. It was pleasant just leaning here and talking inconsequentially, but though the setting was romantic their conversation was not. If he had been madly in love with her it would have been easier.

He thought Helga a lovely girl and as the only daughter of old Johnstone she was obviously a good catch, without the bait dangled by Angus. But he had expected love to be something more than this, a sort of divine madness in the blood. He admired Helga, he found her disturbingly attractive, but she intimidated him rather.

In desperation, he laid his hand on top of hers where it rested on the balustrade. Helga's voice faltered in mid-sentence. She caught her breath.

'Miss Johnstone! Helga!' Instinctively Graham took the right action: he appealed directly to her senses. Without another word he swept her into his arms in a masterful kiss; then, carried away by his own reaction, prolonged it beyond the bounds of decorum.

'Oh!' When at last she was released, Helga leaned back against the balustrade and stared at him with wide eyes. Her hair was a shadowy mass against the increasingly moonlit garden. Her breast heaved. She was shaken to the depths. No man had done more than brush her lips or the back of her hand with a whiskery mouth. Graham's kiss had wakened some sleeping thing she had not known existed.

'I'm – I'm sorry. I shouldn't have d-done that. But you looked so lovely in that white dress – what is it? It feels like moonbeams.' He felt her puffed sleeves, delicately, between his fingers.

She laughed. 'Nothing so romantic as moonbeams, I assure you. It is white chiffon.'

'My dear Helga ... Pray do not think ...' He stopped. It sounded like the opening line of a letter. Perhaps it would be easier to write to her. He tried again. 'I mean, don't think that I don't respect you; I was a bit carried away. But I want you to be my wife. May I ask your father's permission?'

Helga frowned quickly. 'I don't intend to marry. You know that I plan to go to Europe to further my career. Singing is more important to me than anything on earth. And besides, how could I ever settle in Queensland, it is so *provincial*!'

'Perhaps we could go abroad later. I have a doting aunt in England, she has a place in the country and a house in London that they rarely use. Meanwhile I have the offer of a managership on a plantation in Mackay.'

'Mackay! Preserve us! That is even further in the bush than Maryborough.'

'But you would probably find some congenial friends among the planters' wives. And it would not be for ever. Couldn't you – wouldn't you try to put up with it for a while, till I get the mill established? We'll have a delayed honeymoon – get to England in time for the spring, the daffodils in Hyde Park, the cherry blossom . . . I will show you—'

All the time he was speaking he was gently caressing her forearm, just above the wrist, with sensitive finger-tips. Helga listened with only half her mind; she heard the blood singing in her ears, pulsing in the veins of her wrist. She wanted him to kiss her again, to stop her from thinking.

'Perhaps . . .' she said faintly.

'My dearest girl, I promise to make you happy.'

Seeing her so quiet and shaken, he was overcome by a rush of feeling. Once more she was crushed into his arms, willingly mastered, for the first time in her life, by someone stronger than herself.

The flywire door from the upstairs hall banged, and they hastily moved apart.

'Oh, I didn't know you two were out here,' said Dougal cheerfully. And then, noticing a certain stiffness in their shadowy figures, he added, 'I say, I'm not interrupting anything, am I?'

'Not at all. We were just going in,' said Helga coolly. She was in control of her feelings once more as Graham held the wire door for her to pass inside. He gave Dougal a glare which was lost in the dimness. In another minute, he'd swear, Helga would have accepted him.

2 Dougal

All these romances going on around him made Dougal restless. There were Jamie and Rose, always mooning in corners, and now he'd lay a pound to a penny that something was on between Helga and Lindsay – good luck to him! He wouldn't like to take on anyone with Helga's temperament, but there was no accounting for tastes.

Dougal played tennis and went on moonlight picnics on the river with a succession of girls, but he was wary. He didn't want to get married yet, and every Mamma in Maryborough with an eligible daughter had her eye on him. James was already engaged, and Dougal was the obvious inheritor of the plantation and its wealth. He might be the younger brother, but he was the driving force in the family business of the mill, while his father ran the plantation.

Dammit! He was hungry again, he would go down to the kitchen and get something before he turned in; it would help him to sleep. It was late, the servants had probably all gone home.

In the kitchen the cook and kitchen-maid had finished; the washing-up was all done and put away. Only Estelle was there, warming her row of Mrs Potts irons on the wood range, and pressing shirts. She had been away sick last week and had a lot of laundry to catch up.

'Hullo, Estelle! Any tucker about?'

'Aw, I dunno, Mitter Dougal. There some fruit-cake in th' tin.'

Dougal opened the knife-drawer, found a knife and hacked himself a chunk of cake. For a moment the knife made him think of Zachariah and the death of Claude. He shook off the thought and leant back against the sink while he ate, watching her as she ironed with firm thumps and expert turnings of the wrist.

'That one of my shirts you're ironing?'

'Might-be. I dunno.'

'Yes, it is. That's my striped cambric. Hold it up and let me see.'

She finished the second sleeve and held up the warm, smoothed shirt with its smell of heated cotton and the air and sun which had dried it. Dougal came and stood behind the shirt, spreading his arms under the sleeves. 'There! Don't you think it suits me?'

His white teeth gleamed in the light of the oil lamp. There was something sharp, foxy about his smile under the pale gingery moustache. Estelle shivered slightly, but it was a pleasurable fear. She put the shirt down on the table and started folding it.

'I'm still hungry, blast it! Isn't there any real food in the place?'

'There some cold tongue in the safe, down th' cellar. You want me get-it for you?'

'That'd be good-oh. I'll get myself a slice of bread and butter to go with it.'

Estelle took a candle and opened the little picket-gate that shut off the steep stone steps down to the cellar. Dougal looked appreciatively at her trim waist with the striped apron tied round it, her brown arm holding up the candle so that its light fell on her tight frizz of hair, the line of her brown cheek.

She left the gate open and descended. Suddenly the light disappeared and he heard a shriek. She had slipped on the narrow steps where they turned and, grabbing the wall for support, had let the hot wax drip on her wrist. She dropped the candlestick with a clatter.

Dougal took the lamp and crossed the kitchen. 'What's up?' he called.

'Ah dear, I bin drop the can'le, burn arm belong-me.' She caught her breath in a sob.

'There, there. Are you all in the dark?' He balanced the lamp carefully on the corner-post of the cellar gate, and went down the steps. There was room for only one on the narrow stair. He put out his arms and encountered a soft bosom.

'Oh!' An indrawn breath.

'Where does it hurt?' he asked caressingly.

'Me – me wrist – him not hurting much.'

He slid his hand down the length of her arm and raised her wrist to his lips. 'There! I've kissed it better now.'

Walking her in front of him, his strong arms holding her nearly off the floor, he proceeded down into the dark, musty-smelling cellar.

'Me get that cold tongue now, Mitter Dougal. Please—'

'Never mind the old tongue. I'd rather have *you*, Estelle. Estelle? Come on, be nice to me now, you know you want to. Come on. Ain't I the master here? All right, you be a good girl and do what I want. Otherwise, might-be trouble.'

His mouth closed on her protests, his warm tongue slid between her lips and began searching her mouth. He swung her round against the stone wall, fumbling urgently under her long skirts which only inflamed him the more with their resistance. She was begging and crying, but suddenly she went soft and limp. Her mouth opened unresistingly.

There was a heap of old sugar bags in one corner, smelling strongly of jute. In the dim light from the lamp upstairs he found this and flung her down, himself on top of her. It was all over in a few minutes, a hasty coupling which yet gave him intense pleasure. He was ever afterwards to find that the carpet-smell of jute in furniture shops, or in sheds full of sugar-bags or wool bales, recalled for him that high point of his youth before custom and marriage had staled an act which should, he vaguely felt, be wild and free.

He was quite without conscience in the matter, and scarcely gave the girl another thought.

3 Emily and Joseph

If guilt-by-association oppressed the Kanaka community for a time, and whites who had regarded them as fun-loving children began to look at them with suspicion and even overt dislike, the effect did not last for long.

Basically the attitudes had never changed. The white man felt himself superior to 'the savage'; the dark man felt conscious of this, and confronted with the enormous material advantages of the white population could not help feeling that it was justified, even though he resented it.

A particularly brutal murder in the country outside Maryborough, when a man, his wife and child were all mutilated with a tomahawk, set the town ringing with alarm again. It seemed that people were no longer safe in their beds. For the time being the antipathies between the two races were more obvious.

Poor Joseph, lately so set up by his meeting with the Duguids and his invitation to preach in Bundaberg, was very cast down.

Not only had Zachariah been a friend of his, but every Islander on Chindera plantation was under the shadow of the murder. He wished he could have told Zachari that he, Joseph, had once vowed to kill that particular white man – he was sure it was the same – and that the murder had been no more than just retribution for the many lives cold-bloodedly taken in the hold of the *Jason* years ago. He had thought of asking to give evidence for the defence, but in the prevailing mood of the town he would not have been believed.

However, Mr Duguid wrote to him reassuringly:

'We are all distressed over this unfortunate happening, for which there was no doubt some reason if we knew all. God works in a mysterious way. Do not let it delay your coming to us. This is the very time when, by showing that you (an Islander born and bred) are also an educated Christian, you can help to counteract the prejudice and distrust in people's minds . . .

'Let me know, and I will arrange a date for you to address our congregation.'

Joseph decided to ask for a month's leave before signing up again for his next three years. He had already re-contracted for a second term at a much better salary, for 'old hands' were more valuable than new recruits.

When his second term was nearly expired, Joseph went to the foreman and put his request. He spoke in pidgin English, knowing that McGriggen hated to hear a 'flash nigger' trying to 'talk-talk all-a-same whitefeller'.

Samuel McGriggen narrowed his eyes and contemplated him morosely. Many of the Kanakas were unsettled by the cautionary display on the Green, and anxious to go back home. Since Joseph was a steady worker he would be glad to keep him on; but it would never do to admit it.

'How I know you come back, for sure, no gammon?' he asked. 'Sposim you get job longa Bundaberg, no come back to Chindera, if I let you go?'

'No-more! Me come back, I speak you true. Mister Stewart, he tellem you—'

'I don't need the parson to tell me! Sposim you no come

back, I come Bundaberg and beat you to a jelly. Killem you prop'ly. Savee?'

'Yessir. Me come back.'

McGriggen was in an evil mood because he had found some of the white mill-workers chuckling over an inscription on one of the boiler-room walls:

> Samuel McGriggen
> Wants bloody-well friggin'
> And shovin' up Chindera's arse.

The men had melted away quickly when he arrived. He read it, and his brow became thunderous. He'd made one of them paint it over, but there were still sly grins. He couldn't pick out who had done it; it wasn't the work of a Kanaka, that was for sure, though it might have been one of those bloody Chinamen, they were too clever by half ...

'Orright. One month,' he said now to Joseph. 'And that means four – weeks – only. You savee?'

'Yessir.'

*

Joseph sat in the coach for Bundaberg, half-fainting with excitement. It was the first time he had travelled any distance in Australia since arriving in the ship six years ago, though he had gone down the coast, fishing, with his work-mates.

Now he was alone. There was a white boy, about twelve years old, sitting in the seat next to him; his parents were on the other side. Joseph had paid his fare the same as everyone else, but he had learnt certain things. He made himself as small as possible so as not to touch the boy at any point or give him any cause for annoyance.

He smiled continually, unable to contain his joy. The coach rattled over the rutted, deep-red earth road. The fresh horses cantered in great style.

Half-way through the journey, the family party started on their lunch. Joseph had brought nothing but an apple, which he had already eaten. His stomach rumbled with emptiness as he watched the boy begin on a huge meat sandwich.

Just then he felt a touch on his knee. The woman had leant forward and was offering, with a smile, an identical sandwich to him. In his shyness he refused, shaking his head, saying 'No, thank you' very politely, but the boy said 'Go on, they're good!' and Joseph's hand went out almost of its own volition and took the thick slices of bread. It was the nicest food he had ever tasted. He ate every crumb, and when he had finished he took out a clean handkerchief to wipe his fingers.

The boy regarded him curiously. Joseph knew that an Australian Aborigine, a 'man o' bush' as the Islanders rather contemptuously called them, would never have been allowed to ride inside the coach, or been offered food by a white woman.

It gave him a tiny thrill of superiority and pride.

He was no 'blackfeller', he was a Pacific Islander, and proud of it. He pressed his face to the window to watch the scenery. Here was some of the big vine-scrub not yet cleared from the Childers district: tall Pacific palms, karri and bunya pine, red cedar and swamp mahogany. The green creepers and climbing lianas twining through the forest reminded him of the island where he was born.

Not tired but refreshed by the journey, he watched the beginning of the Bundaberg plantations appear. Skirting the headwaters of the Burrum Creek, the Isis and the Gregory, they had driven through the lush Upper Burnett valley. Bundaberg was on the lower reaches of the river. Here were miles of tall green cane, the deep, rich red loam of the fallow fields.

Mr Duguid was waiting at the coach terminal. Joseph was aware that his stock had gone up at having a white man, and a minister at that, to meet him. The lady passenger gave him a warm smile when he thanked her and said goodbye. He suddenly felt travelled, knowledgeable and assured. Compared with the ignorant boy who had been Emily's nursemaid on the island, he had indeed come a long way.

*

'Some more soup, Joseph?'

'No, thank you, Ma'am.' Joseph had laid down his spoon with relief. It was a shallow soup spoon worn thin at the edges, and most of the soup had seemed to pour back into the plate before he could get it to his mouth. He had not forgotten the knack of a knife and fork; all the same his first meal with the Duguids was something of an ordeal.

The third course was a home-made fruit cake with plenty of nuts, cherries and dried raisins. It was delicious, and after hesitating to see what the others did, Joseph realized he could pick it up in his fingers, though Mrs Duguid and Emily cut theirs into two smaller pieces. He did not refuse a second serving.

'Joseph appreciates your cooking, Emily,' said her mother with a smile on her thin face.

'Did *you* make it?' asked Joseph, his mouth half-full. 'It's a very good cake.'

'Oh – I just mixed in the eggs. Mamma did it all, really.'

'Nonsense. She's an excellent cake-maker.'

'Yes; it is an ex-cell-ent cake,' he said precisely, storing the word in his retentive memory.

Emily sat next to him, on his left. Once, as he was struggling with knife and fork at a tough piece of meat, his left elbow just touched her right. It sent a shock through his system as though he had touched a sting-ray's spine. After that he tucked his elbow in nearer to his side.

Now he saw her without a hat she seemed even prettier than in the Maryborough church. Her hair was a rich gold, almost straight with the slightest ripple as it fell over her shoulders. Yet her brows were dark, fine and well-marked above her blue eyes. And he thought he had never seen anything so delicate as her hands with their transparent, blue-veined skin.

After supper he and the Reverend went into the 'study', a tiny room at the back lined with religious works, and with a deal table for a desk.

'Ha'e ye thocht what your subject will be for tomorrow?' asked Mr Duguid, removing some papers from a chair so that Joseph could sit down.

'Well, yes, I thought of preaching on "Lighten our darkness, we beseech thee oh Lord", and referring to the need for missions back in the Islands, some of which are still in heathen darkness after all these years—'

'Aye, verra guid, verra guid. Though ye don't know the most

recent worrk that's been done over there, by some of your ain people who have gone back and started missions; aye, and have been successful, too.'

'Yes, but the light seems to come in waves, and fade again. In the early days, you know, there were Polynesian missionaries on Lifu, like Ta'unga of Samoa; then later there was the London Missionary Society and yourself; but in between the people were as backsliding as ever.'

'Aye, it's true. What's needed is tae get the men to churrch whiles they're here in Australia, and they'll carry Christian principles back with them. We had a mon here from the Murray River in Victoria, who's training Aborigines to be missionaries to their ain people.'

However, it was disappointing to see, the next afternoon in church, so few dark brown faces and fuzzy heads among those gathered to hear him speak. Vanity came into it a little; he wanted his own people to see him addressing a congregation. All the same, he felt a thrill of pride to think that so many white people had come to hear him.

Mr Duguid introduced him in his brief, dry Scots manner; then Joseph, pulling nervously at the bottom of the dark jacket which Mrs Duguid had given him, rose to speak. It was from Andrew's wardrobe, and was a little tight on Joseph's muscular chest, but he left the buttons undone in front over his best shirt.

He took a deep breath, opened his mouth, and looked up. A hundred and fifty pairs of eyes were fixed upon him, a hundred and fifty pairs of ears waited to hear his first word. Nothing came forth. Joseph felt his heart pound, his head begin to swell. Where had his voice gone? What had happened? His palms began to sweat with panic.

Sweeping bewildered eyes over the audience which had so paralysed him, he saw in the first row an embroidered raffia bonnet, straight fair hair, a pair of blue eyes smiling encouragement.

He took another deep breath, and began to speak. He preached directly to Emily Duguid, warming to her little nods of comprehension, to her eyes fixed on his face.

Even when one of the congregation, who had had too much

Sunday dinner, began to snore gently, and there were a few suppressed giggles at this, he did not falter. He sat down amid a round of applause in which he saw Mrs Duguid and Emily join enthusiastically. It was the proudest moment of his life.

*

The year of 1875 was unusually wet. The Mary River came down in a flood which swept away part of the wharf. One of the casualties of the flood was the local Polynesian Inspector, who had been one of the most vocal of the lobby calling for a Government inquiry into conditions for Kanakas in Maryborough, where new recruits continued to die quietly.

One dark wet night when the Inspector was checking a sugar-barge moored to the wharf, the barge somehow became untied and drifted away on the floodwaters. It was turning helplessly and floating fast, far out in the stream, when first seen. No one realized there was a man on board.

Later, away downstream near the mouth, someone saw a figure waving and calling through the rain; but by the time a boat was launched the barge had gone – out to sea, or more likely overturned and sunk on the bar. The Inspector was never seen again. Once more there were dark rumours among the anti-planter faction. Murder was hinted at, and there was renewed clamour for an inquiry into the whole industry of sugar-growing in the district.

To top all, there was an outbreak of rust in the cane, and only those who had planted the 'Rose Bamboo' variety, resistant to the disease, escaped severe losses. Angus Johnstone congratulated himself on his foresight for he had lately replanted with this type.

What worried him most was the shortage of new recruits. A large proportion of deaths among workers had not mattered when new men could be found easily at £6 a head (and that figure had now doubled). There had always seemed to be an unlimited supply of Kanakas in the Islands. Now the recruiters found that men were not so keen to 'go along Queensland' voluntarily, and they had become too wary to be kidnapped easily.

Relations between recruiting vessels and Islanders had

deteriorated. One group just returned from a bankrupt plantation in North Queensland without pay, guns or 'trade boxes' were so incensed that they attacked the next vessel to arrive and massacred the whole crew.

These troubles made 'regulars' like Joseph and his friends more valuable. They had twice agreed to stay on for another three-year term at better wages, and he now got £18 a year instead of £6. He often thought of getting married.

He looked at some of the Aboriginal girls, the only ones available to him, but he did not fancy one as a wife. Many of them worked in town in the Japanese brothels. It was against his Christian principles to visit them there, but what was a man to do? He resolved each time not to go again. Island women who were unattached were rare. Zachariah's widow had already remarried.

Joseph thought often of Emily Duguid, who had pressed his hand after his talk at the Pleasant Sunday Afternoon in Bundaberg, and who had kissed him goodbye when he left to catch the coach back again. He hoped to see her again one day; but beyond that he did not allow his thoughts to wander.

Then, one Sunday morning – he had been tempted to go swimming in the river instead, but had stood firm against his companions' jeers and had gone to church – there she was, with Mrs Stewart, come down for a visit. She had grown surprisingly in less than a year. No longer a child, she did not greet him with a kiss after the service, but primly extended her gloved hand.

The Stewarts asked him home for Sunday dinner. Once more he sat beside her at table, careful to keep his elbows close to his sides. Emily was, if possible, more beautiful than ever in her new maturity, with her young bosom swelling above a tiny waist. (For ladies were admitted to have a shape on top, that is above the hips; but layers of skirts disguised anything below, so that they might have glided on wheels rather than on anything so unmentionable as legs.)

Joseph, who knew quite well what white mysteries those long garments concealed, resolutely kept his imagination in check. Mr Stewart went to his study to compose his sermon, and Mrs

Stewart to her room to lie down after dinner. Emily was left to entertain Joseph in the parlour. (The Stewart boys, both younger than her, were away at school in Brisbane.)

They played noughts and crosses for a while, and then fell to talking of the old days, with 'Do you remember—?' until Mrs Stewart came in with afternoon tea.

'It is so nice to have you, Joseph dear. The house is so quiet with the boys away,' said kind Mrs Stewart. 'And of course we'd like Emily to stay as long as she can.'

'Dear Mamma has not been very well. I can only stay a week, I'm afraid, for she needs me.'

'Well, if your mother needs you, I understand. But I wish I could return with you, I don't like your making that long coach journey by yourself.'

'It's not far, really. And a kind lady looked after me all the way down. She was going on further, to Gympie.'

'We are to have a railway service to Gympie in the near future. Perhaps to Bundaberg, too. Won't that be exciting?'

'Oh yes! I have never been in a steam train. Have you, Joseph?'

'Never. But I will come to see you in Bundaberg when the new line is opened.'

'Will you? But that may be a long time – two years!'

'We will see each other before that,' he said.

'I hope so.' Their eyes met, and spoke without need of words.

The following week-end he went into town to see her off. There was an empty seat beside her, and Mrs Stewart was admonishing Emily to keep her reticule on the seat. Some man might try to sit beside her.

There came a loud whistle and a hoarse 'Giddap! Clk, clk,' and the coach started with a bound. The coachman, with an oath, sprang to the horses' heads, for he was still on the ground helping to load boxes on board. He turned on a black-and-white bird which was hopping about his feet.

'Get to hell out of this, Charlie, you damned interferin' bird!' he cried. For Charlie had learnt to speak around Cobb & Co's stables, and delighted to start the horses. His language, it was said, 'would make a bullocky blush'.

'Get to hell out of it, you bloody old bastard,' he replied in a harsh squawk.

The coachman threw a stone at him, but he skipped nimbly away. One of his wings was clipped so that he could not fly.

Mrs Stewart looked scandalized, but Emily caught Joseph's eye and laughed. The coach was nearly ready to leave. Suddenly he was seized with a wild idea.

'Excuse me a moment,' he said, and dashed into the coach office. He had money in his pocket, for Friday was pay-day. He bought a return ticket to Bundaberg.

'I will go with Emily,' he announced calmly, though his heart was beating fast. It meant he would be late for work on Monday and would have to face the wrath of the overseer, but he didn't care.

'Oh, Joseph!' said Emily, her eyes shining. 'But can you afford it?'

'Of course!' he said scornfully, as if he had not just spent most of his fortnight's pay.

The coachman climbed up and clicked to the horses. The magpie called 'Giddap!' and they started with a bound. Emily waved her handkerchief out of the window to Mrs Stewart, with Joseph smiling broadly beside her. He felt big and protective. Once more he was looking after his charge, little Em'ly.

There were only three other passengers, all men. Two of the men, travelling together, looked askance at this dark fellow squiring a white girl, but they said nothing. The third slept most of the way with his mouth open. He would begin to snore, then a jolt of the coach would wake him, and he would lift his head and close his mouth. Then he would begin to nod again, his mouth would fall open, and soon he would be snoring. Emily and Joseph found this vastly amusing, and giggled together each time he dozed.

There was only one change of horses, but during the afternoon there was another unscheduled stop. The coachman got down and looked carefully at one of the back wheels. The axle was running hot. 'I'll have to let it cool off a bit,' he said, putting his head inside the coach. 'Youse might as well get down and stretch your legs, we'll be stopped 'alf an hour.'

The two wakeful passengers got down and lit their pipes, walking up and down in a companionable silence. Joseph helped Emily down – such a small, fragile hand was enveloped in his great dark fist! – and somehow they remained hand in hand as they walked.

Wandering along the winding track between walls of greenery, they became aware of the heat and stillness of the bush, with the stridulant cry of cicadas underlining the silence which became complete when the cicadas ceased their song.

They rounded a bend in the road, and might have been alone in the Garden of Eden. Tree orchids, brown and yellow, grew high on the trees that towered over their heads. Great buttress roots surrounded the trunks with ferns and mosses growing in their clefts.

'It's like the jungle on Lifu!' cried Emily. 'You know, I can remember it so sharply – the clear water in the lagoon, the feel of the coarse white sand under my nails, the path up to the house through the forest, the dusty smell of the mosquito net over my bed; and Jamie—'

Her brow clouded. 'I have no brothers left. You will have to be my brother, Joseph.' She turned to him and with the utmost naturalness rested her forehead against his shoulder.

Joseph's heart beat violently. He thought she must hear its thunder and be startled. He put his cheek down on her soft, shining hair – for her bonnet had fallen back and was hanging by its ribbons from her shoulders.

'The only trouble with that is—' His voice was too husky to go on. She looked up inquiringly into his face. He stared into her blue eyes, dazed and dazzled. 'The only trouble, little Em'ly, is that you're grown up now. And I'm not your brother, you know. I'm a man, and I have the feelings of a normal man, and – oh, Jehosaphat!' (which was the nearest he dared come to swearing before her) 'you make it very hard for me.'

He pulled his hand away and began walking back the way they had come.

Emily stared after his sturdy, retreating figure while the colour mounted steadily in her cheeks.

'Joseph!'

He did not turn or answer.

'Joseph! Wait for me this instant!' He had always been her slave. He stopped in his tracks, and she began to run after him. She slipped her hand into his again. His fingers closed tightly round hers. 'I'm sorry,' she said in a small voice. And then, 'I – I didn't think.'

'It's all right. It's not your fault. You think of me still as your faithful servant, and yourself as the little missie who liked to boss me around. But I have changed, and you have grown into a beautiful young lady. I shouldn't have come.'

'I'm glad you did.'

Suddenly embarrassed, she dropped his hand, making the excuse of picking a dainty white orchid growing on some rotting wood beside the road. They walked back to the coach in silence. He looked at the flower, so delicate and white, tucked into her bodice, and sighed deeply.

Up the steep pinch called 'Gentle Annie' the brake was still binding a little on one wheel, which creaked and protested. They had to stop again, and the result was that they did not reach Bundaberg till well after dark. Emily was asleep with her head on Joseph's shoulder. To him it was torment and happiness; he wanted the journey to go on for ever, her eyelids closed and shadowed with weariness, her soft mouth relaxed in sleep. He wished there were no other passengers, that he might kiss her while she slept.

As the coach wheels rattled on the metal roads of town, Emily's eyes flew open and fixed themselves on his face as he gazed down at her tenderly.

'Oh, Joseph! I was dreaming about you – about us. We were back on Lifu, yet we were grown up. And—' She stopped, bit her lip, and smiled. She sat up straight, putting on her bonnet. 'Do you know, I don't believe I think of you as a brother after all!'

'Emily—!'

They were coming into the coaching station, and there was Mr Duguid looking anxious at the late arrival of his daughter.

Emily gave Joseph's hand a quick squeeze. 'I will write to you, dear Joseph.'

The Duguids asked him home for the night. He would have to be up early to catch the morning coach – but even then he would not be at work till Tuesday, and there would be trouble with the overseer. But he did not care.

Nothing mattered but the touch of Emily's hand, the promise in her blue eyes.

Mr Duguid, most unworldly of men, saw nothing odd in Joseph's having accompanied Emily home. At dinner he was full of the mission school for Kanakas started by Miss Young on Fairymead plantation – the school was held in the evening in the men's community hut and already the literacy rate was high. She also taught them hymns like 'There is a green hill far away', and they were forming a Polynesian Choir.

Joseph slept heavily and had to be called, though he was used to being at work by six. Andrew Duguid drove him down to the coach, and he did not see Emily again. But he had her promise: 'I will write to you, dear Joseph'. Somehow the intimacy of their night journey, of her sleeping with her head on his shoulder, had resolved all shyness and distance between them. He felt they had an understanding.

4 James

'When are we going to get married, James?'

This was the question he had been dreading, the direct demand from his gentle Rose, to whom it was no longer possible to make evasive replies. Of course he wanted to marry her; but there was something delightful too about the state of being engaged. They were allowed a certain freedom, could go boating on the river alone and arrive home late, saying they had waited to see the moon rise. They could go walking off together from a picnic party without causing gossip.

James, being a romantic, feared perhaps that the magic would evaporate once he entered the sober state of matrimony. His parents were married, and who could imagine anything romantic about that admirable arrangement? He was blissfully happy now. Was it possible that there could be anything but a decline from this high peak once he had Rose there every night, whenever he wanted her, in his own bed?

He had been close to achieving the ultimate centre of bliss on more than one occasion, indeed Rose was always making excuses for them to be alone together and he believed she would not have stopped him. Under her pink and white, flowerlike and fragile charm she was a warm-blooded, passionate girl. It was he who had drawn back, wanting her, but wanting her too to be a virgin on their wedding-day, dressed all in symbolic white.

'We've been engaged for nearly a year now,' she went on. 'Mamma keeps asking me for the date, and when will she start ordering the invitations to be printed. What may I tell her?'

He was lying with his head in her lap, while she twisted his silky side-whiskers round her slim fingers. 'Um? What shall I tell her?' She gave a painful tweak to the whiskers.

'Ow! Tell her – tell her I never get married in a month with an R in it ... Ouch! So that rules out September, October, November, December ... let me see – January, February, March, April ... good heavens, we can't get married till May of next year!'

'James, be serious. Anyway, August doesn't have an R in it.'

'What! Next month! You couldn't be ready by then, my sweet'

'Oh, you'd be surprised. Sometimes I think you don't love me as much as I love you.'

He gazed up at her tenderly, at her fine skin like rose-tinted porcelain, her long green eyes, her strands of golden hair the colour of the stamens at the heart of a pink rose. He pressed her hand against his mouth.

'I love you more than anything, but – but – I can't explain it, but I enjoy knowing that you will be mine. But we must make a definite date. September would be a good time, I think. The harvest will be finished, and it will still not be too hot for travelling. Would you like to go to Tasmania?'

'I should like that above everything! To see Hobart Town, and Mount Wellington, and the apple blossom in spring ... And to travel in a ship. I have never been to an island.'

'The whole of Australia is just a big island, really.'

'Dearest James! I shall go home at once and order the material for my dress from Brisbane. And you aren't allowed to see it before our wedding, it would be unlucky.'

'Am I allowed to know the material? You will look lovely even if you wear an old sugar-bag.'

'Tut! A sugar-bag! I shall order yards and yards of *gauze de Chambrey*, with a pink *crêpe-de-chine* underlay, and a long train; and my going-away bonnet will be of bronze-coloured velvet with black piping—'

'Spare me! You have it all worked out, I see.'

'Dear James! I do love you.' She bent over him and pressed her soft mouth to his. His heart beat fast, he buried his face in her skirts and felt with urgent hands for the outline of her thighs beneath the layers of petticoats. Rose moaned and swayed above him. 'I can't wait till September!' she cried.

'The very first week in September, then. We will announce the date tomorrow. I do want you, Rose. I'm like a little boy who keeps a sweetmeat in a box, and looks at it and tastes it, but can't bear to eat it up too quickly. You're so sweet, and lovely and desirable and adorable, and I promise to love you for ever and ever, amen.'

'Till death us do part?'

'Till death us do part.'

She shivered, and laughed. 'Someone walking over my grave.'

'Don't let's talk about death and graves. We are going to be happy. I promise not to get tired of you for twenty years.'

'Twen-ty ye-ars! Goodness, I shall be an old thing of forty!'

'Thirty years, I mean.' They both laughed at the idea of such a ridiculously long time. Life stretched in front of them, endless and golden.

By the middle of August the invitations had been sent out, and Rose's favourite dressmaker had made up the white gauze dress.

One afternoon James left his office early and went to call on Rose at her home. Usually he came in for a drink just before dinner, if they were not dining out together. Today it was the housemaid's day off and the cook was busy in the kitchen. No-one answered his knock at the heavy cedar front door.

With the familiarity of long acquaintance and his future membership of the family James let himself in; for the door was standing open and only the mesh fly-screen door was closed.

'Rose!' he called up the stairs. He stood in the hall, looking up the curving stair. A door opened. It was Rose, who was trying on her wedding finery for the first time.

'You look ravishing!' he said sincerely.

She stared down at him with wide, frightened eyes.

'James! What are you doing here at this hour? Who let you in?'

'Why? Aren't you glad to see me, dearest?'

'Of course I am, I mean I would be, but you shouldn't have seen my gown! Especially with me in it. Oh!' And with a wail she disappeared into her bedroom. The door closed with a bang. Her mother, plump and fair (her complexion had once been like her daughter's, but her cheeks were now breaking into a network of tiny veins), was woken from her nap. She came and smiled indulgently down at James.

'Go into the drawing-room,' she said. 'She'll be down in a minute. It's just nerves, you know. She's a bit upset.'

'You mean that superstitious nonsense about my not seeing the dress before the wedding?'

'Just a girl's fancy. She will get over it.'

*

Helga had rather ungraciously consented to be bridesmaid, since like herself Rose had no sisters. She thought fashionable weddings a lot of nonsense, but she was a girl who loved dressing up and she soon began to take an interest in the details of what she was to wear.

She also began to get on better with her future sister-in-law as they had something of joint interest to talk about, and the usually silent Rose became more animated as the date of the wedding drew near. Several times she rode over to Chindera on her sleek chestnut mare, Vilette.

Though not a sturdy, outdoor type, Rose was rather addicted

to riding. She knew that she made a picture in her green riding-habit and feathered hat on the gleaming chestnut mare.

Also she had discovered that when she trotted, lift-saddling with an easy motion, a delightful sensation began and spread throughout her body. Poor Rose, roused by James's caresses and left unsatisfied, did not understand the restless ache which was relieved sometimes in dreams and, as she had found, by the rhythmic movements of the sturdy mare beneath her. She rode side-saddle, of course, one knee held firm by the pommel, the left foot down in the stirrup – an awkward way to ride, but ladies were not supposed to have legs, so obviously they could not bestride a horse.

One afternoon, leaving Chindera's drive, she felt this sensation beginning, and instinctively turned away from the public road, skirted the river bank, and plunged into the Big Scrub where they had ridden with Claude on the day of the fox-hunt. She had always wanted to go back alone to that green, shadowed track among the ferns and mosses, the vine-entangled trees, the silence of the forest.

Slowly she felt that languorous sensation creeping over her again. Almost fainting, she closed her eyes and gave herself up to it, not watching the track. Vilette shook her head and whinnied. She came to a division in the track, but received no guidance from her rider. She pricked her ears and whinnied again, then chose the descending, right-hand track.

Rose opened her eyes at the sound of cantering hoofs and voices ahead. She gathered up the slack reins and prepared to make room for the other travellers. As she saw them come round a bend she caught her breath.

There were three mounted men, young, flashily dressed, and black. Rose had been taught not to fear the Kanakas, but these were different. They were Aborigines, and not the sort she had been used to seeing about the town: shy, quiet men who shuffled past with eyes lowered, seeming to pretend that they were not there. These men sat their horses with careless grace, and stared at her cheekily.

She realized that the horse had taken a wrong turning while she was not watching. She kept her back straight and tried not to show by the faintest flicker in her eyes that she was afraid. As they came abreast she said rather haughtily, 'Could you please tell me the way back to the river road, and Chindera Plantation?'

She knew them now; they were the notorious Queensland Native Police trained in Victoria and brought up here to hunt down their fellow Aborigines in the northern Colony. Each of them carried a carbine slung over his shoulder.

They did not reply at once, but their eyes slid over her appraisingly. They looked at each other; then one of them said, 'Yairs, Missis – bes' way, you go 'long this track, till it begin to climb again. Firs' turn right, keep bearin' right, you come out on t' river road.'

'Thank you! Goodbye.' Keeping her back very straight, she cantered on past them. Behind her she heard a low-voiced remark, and a burst of laughter. Her cheeks flamed. Whatever had made her do such a mad thing as to come into the Scrub without telling anyone where she was going?

Here was another fork in the road. She guided the mare to the right. The track was stony and rough, and still seemed to be going downhill. In fact it led down into a gulley where there was a little creek choked with lantana and fern. The track did not cross the creek. It seemed to end there, as though it had been used for fetching water to some farm back on the ridge – perhaps by the old 'hatter' they had seen in the clearing when his tank ran dry in bad seasons.

Rose sat staring at the wall of green beyond the creek. She was trying to think. If she went back the way she had come, and kept turning left . . .? They must have mis-directed her. She decided to turn and let Vilette find her own way out of the Scrub. The horse would know best.

Just as she pulled at the reins to bring Vilette's head up from where she had begun cropping the grass bordering the creek, she heard the jingle of a bit, the sound of a stone dislodged by a horse's hoof. A hand seemed to clutch her heart in an icy grip. Her blood froze. She looked round. The three native police were riding in single file on her track. There was no other way out of the gully.

'Kindly allow me to pass.'

Rose had reined in her mare, holding her golden head high with its green hat and nodding plume.

The three men sat carelessly in their saddles, one behind the other. Did they sense something wild and unsatisfied in her blood, with some subtle perception unknown to more civilized men? Was it revenge for the slights of a lifetime, for the look of disdain from 'white Marys' who had passed them by like dirt?

The leading man leant forward and knocked the feathered hat from her head. Rose screamed.

Vilette, frightened, reared suddenly and Rose pitched off into the green of lantanas and vines. As she tried to rise, a booted foot came down across her throat. It pressed and pressed, stopping her breath, hurting unbearably. She clawed at it more and more feebly, then slipped into blessed unconsciousness, with a roaring in her ears and coloured lights behind her eyes.

5 Amelia and Andrew

'You know, my dear, your faither and I are no' getting ony younger,' said Amelia Duguid as she darned a woollen sock, sitting by the window to get a good light on her work. Her eyes were failing. They had a fine network of wrinkles round them from being screwed up in the effort to read the small print of the Bible, which she did every day.

'Neither am I, Mamma; none of us gets any younger,' said Emily.

'That isna what I mean, of coorse. I meant . . . your faither and I would like fine tae see ye settled doon and marrit. Is there nae young man in the offing? When we gang to our lang hame, we wouldna wish to leave ye a' alone.'

'There's plenty of time, Mamma.'

'I wouldna be so sairtin aboot that. I'm gey worrit by Andrew's health o'late. Ye ken how little he eats – and he's losing weight, thin as he is already.'

'Yes, he doesn't look well.'

'He hasna been the same since we left the Islands. He

preaches a guid sermon still, mind ye, and he worrks hard for the kirk, and the mission; but och! he's homesick for Scotland, aye, perhaps even for Lifu, a place I wish never mair to see! Forbye my bonnie bairns lie buried there . . .'

Emily noticed how under the stress of emotion, which she rarely showed, her mother fell into a rhythmical turn of speech.

She said, 'Perhaps he will be better in the summer. You know how he hates the cold.'

'Aye. He was complaining aboot it last nicht. And here it is late spring, nigh on summer already.'

Indeed, Andrew had whimpered like a child, most unlike himself, and suggested he should come into her bed and get warm. It was not the first time he had made the suggestion since Amelia had banished him to a single bed in her room. But she was firm. Soon she would be past the age for bearing infants, praise the Lord! She was determined to have no more.

It had been as a sort of penance for herself, rather than for him, that she had given up the comforts of the marriage bed. It had seemed to her after Jamie died, that the Lord did not wish her to have more bairns, nor to bring a son to maturity. She was being punished for her carnal sins, perhaps, in having those which were born to her taken away.

Deeply troubled, she had gone to the Bible for guidance, and on opening it at random her eyes lighted on a verse of Paul's 'Epistle to the Galatians', at the bottom of a page:

This I say then, Walk in the Spirit, and ye shall not fulfil the lusts of the flesh . . .

She turned the page.

. . . But the fruit of the Spirit is love, joy, peace, long-suffering, gentleness, goodness, faith,

Meekness, temperance: against such there is no law.

And they that are Christ's have crucified the flesh with the affections and the lusts.

Yes, the message was clear. She had showed the passage to Andrew, who at the time had seemed to agree. But it was not long before he began backsliding, and one night she found him creeping quietly in beside her.

'Andrew!'

'Amelia, dearest, I am lonely for you, and besides it is cold in the wee sma' bed. Let me – just for tonicht?'

'Once we gi'e in to the flesh, the Spirit will be conquered. Andrew, I want for ye to get dressed, and gae ootside and contemplate the stars. We must crucify the flesh.'

'But, Amelia!'

'Please, Andrew. It is harrd for me too, my dear, dinna think it's no' a sacrifeece. But I couldna face the Lord if we began anither bairn. Gae and put some warm things over your nightshirt. It is a braw nicht and the stars will calm your mind. Ye know what Saint Paul saith.'

Grumbling, he had pulled on an overcoat and warm slippers, and she'd heard him walking up and down outside muttering a prayer for help and guidance. She thought of what St Paul had said earlier in the same passage: 'I would they were even cut off that trouble you.' No doubt it was harder for men. Their sex was there in front of them all the time, demanding to be noticed. She sighed. How she would like to yield! But she had thought again of those lonely little graves on distant Lifu, and hardened her resolve.

'Mamma! Did you hear a word I said?'

Emily was looking at her impatiently. She had been far away.
'Forgi'e me, my dear. I was thinking o' the past.'

'And I was speaking of my future. You might as well know, Mamma. I intend to marry Joseph.'

'Marry Joseph?' Amelia stared uncomprehendingly for a moment; her hand rose to her throat. She had been mentally back on Lifu, with Joseph as the sturdy playmate and guardian of her little ones – Joseph Tula, who was only a child himself.

'Yes, Joseph. He is a Christian, and I love him!'

'But Emily! A – a Kanaka? A coloured labourer? Ye canna mean it.'

'I do mean it. He hasn't asked me yet, he's too shy, but I know he wants to. And haven't you always said that there is no colour bar in the sight of the Lord: "For ye are all the children of God by faith in Jesus Christ ... there is neither Jew nor Greek, bond nor free."[2]

'Aye, but your faither—'

'I have it all planned, Mamma. We'll start a mission to the Kanakas on Chindera Plantation, with the Church's help, like the one started by Miss Young here. I will train as a teacher first, and will be able to take classes. And we will ask for subscriptions from the public.'

'A life of poverty! I had thocht of something better.'

'And have you ever had riches, Mamma? And isn't it better to have "treasure in heaven, where neither moth nor rust doth corrupt, nor thieves break through and steal"?' Emily, brought up on the Bible, could always confute arguments with an apt quotation. 'And the most important thing is that we love each other. "Better a narrow house, where love, is, than—" '

'A'richt! A'richt! I ken the quotation. But ha'e ye given thocht to the bairns ye may have? They'll be neither black nor white, but half o'each. Is it fair to them?'

Emily looked uncertain for the first time. 'They will be given love, and a good home, which is more than some white children have.'

'I canna think; I've a heidache,' and Amelia went and lay down in her room. Emily prepared to meet her father's wrath.

*

Andrew Duguid plucked agitatedly at his beard, which had now turned from sandy to silver-grey. 'Ye cannot be serious, my gel! Joseph is a God-fearin', Christian young man, I grant ye, but – but I'm aginst the mixture o' races. It flies in the face of Proveedence.'

'Where does it say so in the Bible?'

'I dinna ken that it says so preecisely. But black and white were no' meant to marry, of that I'm sairtin. And your bairns will a' have his fuzzy hair and darrk complexion. My grandchildren, the descendants o' cannibals!'

'Ah! It's your grandchildren you're thinking of, not my happiness.'

'Ye'll not be happy, child. It will end in disaster, I tell ye.'

'I am willing to take that risk, Papa.' Emily, who had always

138

been obstinate like her mother ('pig-headed', Andrew called it in his disenchanted moments), was strengthened in her resolve by her father's opposition. Her blue eyes hardened to a sapphire glint. 'Anyway, it is no use talking, my mind is made up.'

'And to think I ha'e nourished that Joseph like a viper in my bosom! And he wanting to take my only bairn.'

'We love each other, Papa.'

He went to his room, muttering in his beard, but turned at the door to point a trembling finger at Emily.

'I forbid it! I absolutely forbid it, onderstand that!'

At least, thought Emily, he had not flown into one of his towering rages. He was milder lately, not like himself. No wonder her mother was worried about him.

*

Joseph, returning to Chindera a day late, had to face the bullying overseer on Tuesday morning.

'So we're taking holidays without leave now, are we?' McGriggen was deceptively silky and calm. 'And where the hell have you been?' he roared suddenly. 'You weren't in your hut yesterday, I checked. Were you?' Remembering he was addressing a Kanaka, he lapsed into pidgin. 'Where you-feller bin? Why you not come along work? You talk-talk, quick-time, or me give-em you clip along ear, see?'

Joseph nearly replied, 'I bin longa Bundaberg, Boss.' But something, a vision of Emily with her head on his shoulder, gave him confidence.

'I was in Bundaberg for the week-end, and I missed the coach,' he said in perfect English, standing straight and looking unflinchingly into the bloodshot blue eyes in the red-meat face.

'So! "I was in Bundaberg", was I? You black bastard! Don't try to talk whitefeller fashion with me. So you bin longa Bundaberg, longa bus. Whaffor?'

'I was there on Church business, at the invitation of the Reverend Mr Duguid of St Andrew's.'

A stinging blow in the face sent him reeling back, holding a bleeding nose.

'Well, you on plantation business now. Sposim you want-it keep-im job belong you, get into line quick-time ... Right!

Somepella all got mattock? Now we-all start chipping between th' rows longa new cane.'

Laughing, racing each other to the end of the drive, the men set off for the cane full of their usual high spirits. Only one or two were distressed on Joseph's account; most of them accepted it, were used to such treatment, to playful flicks from the overseer's long whip, or his boot helping them on from behind. They had learnt to laugh at such manifestations of the white man's impatience. 'Boss, him prop'ly angry!' they told each other, grinning.

Ezekiel handed Joseph the rough cotton kerchief from round his neck, which he held against his nose till the bleeding stopped. In his heart was a seething rage against Samuel McGriggen. He told himself he was a Christian, and supposed to turn the other cheek. Instead he indulged in a fantasy of bashing in that meaty face with a rock.

If only he hadn't signed up again, he'd leave and find a job somewhere else.

5 Developments

1 Rose

Rose Lovelace's brother Robert rode over to Chindera that evening to escort her home, since she had not returned in daylight. He found Helga sitting on the terrace watching the last glow of sunset reflected in the tranquil waters of the Mary.

'Where's Rose?' he demanded. 'She's supposed to be doing the flowers for Mamma's dinner tonight. Has she forgotten?'

'Rose?' Helga turned a startled face. 'Why she left here hours ago, on Vilette. I thought she was going straight home. About half past three it would have been.'

'Did she have a groom with her? One of those damned Kanakas?'

'Now, Robert! We have a "damned Kanaka" for a coachman, and he's a most trustworthy, excellent fellow. He's Estelle's husband you know, our laundry-maid.' She frowned slightly, remembering that Tombua had been rather surly and uncommunicative of late, while Estelle on the other hand was rather pert, full of secret smiles, while she came to work rather more smartly dressed than usual, often with a flower tucked in her dark woolly hair. Helga said, 'No, Rose was alone.'

'Is there anyone else she might have called on?'

'Perhaps the dressmaker in town who's making her going-away costume. But I wouldn't think she'd ride into town, she would have taken the carriage, or walked.'

'I don't like it. Where's James?'

'He's working late, doing the sugar returns.'

'Damn! He ought to look after her better,' said Robert unreasonably, for James did not even know Rose had been at the house.

She knew he was busy and had not called at the mill, as he was expected later to dinner at their place.

Robert rode over the mill buildings and strode into the office, which always smelled slightly of warm sugar, without knocking. James looked up from his columns of figures.

'Where's Rose? Do you know where she is?'

'I assure you she's not hidden under my desk,' said James lightly. 'Why, where should she be?'

'This is no time for joking. She left Chindera house before four o'clock, on Vilette. It's now six-thirty, nearly seven, and she's not home.'

James leapt to his feet, scattering pens and paper.

'We must begin searching at once. She may have been thrown, knocked unconscious – be lying somewhere—' He was distractedly pulling on his jacket over the white cambric shirt he worked in now the days were getting warmer. 'Have you got your horse outside? Come over to the stables while I saddle up.'

By the time it was dark a posse of men had been gathered to help in the search. There was a full moon, and by its brilliant light in that clear atmosphere they could see each pebble in the road. But they would have to wait for morning to get the black trackers with their uncanny skill to follow her tracks.

Luckily, thought James, there was a contingent of Black Police in town, on their way out west to track down the murderer of an outlying settler who had been found killed and mutilated with a tomahawk – what looked like the work of Kanakas.

'It certainly looked like niggers done it,' the bar-room gossips opined. With the Chindera murder fresh in their minds, there was a certain hostility towards the coloured workers on the part of the townspeople.

Riding back to Chindera homestead after midnight, with the white moon now sailing, a cold, flat disc overhead, James thought he heard the sound of hoofbeats on the dusty road. His horse pricked up its ears and whinnied.

Then he saw Vilette, reins trailing and broken, the moonlight glinting in the whites of her eyes. He caught the mare and led her back to the stables. He knew now that Rose had fallen, was perhaps lying injured somewhere, or, or even dead—! How could he sleep? Dougal came trotting up, and dismounted to unsaddle his horse.

'I have her mare,' said James, grim-faced. 'She came from along the river road. Do you think Rose could have gone down the chute – you know, where Claude fell in? God! I don't know. She could be anywhere. We'll get them to drag the river tomorrow. Meanwhile I must keep looking.'

'Listen, old chap, there's nothing you can do until daylight. We'll ride straight up the river tomorrow, and probably find her safe and well, with the help of the trackers. She won't die of thirst or exposure in a single night—'

'I can't sleep! To think she might be alone – frightened – injured!'

He would not utter the worst dread that was at the back of his mind. If only the damned horse could speak!

'Come and I'll get you a stiff whisky. You must lie down and rest for a couple of hours, or you won't be fit for the search. Come on. Come on, your horse needs a rest too.'

James, too tired and numb to resist, went with him like a child. Dougal, with unusual tenderness, got his brother a whisky with hot water and lemon, helped him to bed fully clothed, only pulling off his riding-boots and jacket, and tucked a blanket round him.

'Try to sleep, old man,' he said.

To his surprise James did sleep, and woke to find the window growing light. An uneasy feeling at the back of his brain troubled him. Then remembrance hit him like a blow. *Rose!* He leapt from his bed, cursing.

At the Town Square he and Dougal met young Lovelace and his father, who was also a planter, with several of his friends and three members of the Queensland Black Police. They were smartly turned out in flashy green uniforms and high-heeled boots. They had keen dark eyes and nervous, white-toothed smiles.

James explained where he had found Vilette, coming from beyond Chindera, so they rode out that way along the river. The mounted police spread out ahead, walking for once, and studying the ground. One pointed to a hoof-mark, then another. They called to each other in dialect. The white men followed impatiently behind.

At the entrance to the Big Scrub the trackers searched around, shook their heads, shrugged their shoulders, and said something to old Mr Lovelace.

'What is it? What do they say?' cried James.

'They say there are no tracks leading to the river, but that there are too many tracks on top of each other just here, they can't tell if she went into the Scrub.'

'Well, we'll go in there for a bit and see if they can pick up anything ... Why, I could do it myself! Look, there are clear hoof-marks in that soft patch ... going both ways, but then Vilette could have come back again without her rider. Quick-time, you feller look for track all-about, big-feller money sposim you find Missie!'

The men looked obstinate or sheepish, James thought. They reluctantly led the way along the winding track under the huge trees. They walked casually, but their eyes darted quickly from side to side, noting and observing.

At last they stopped. 'No-more,' they said. 'No more track Missie's horse. Might-be she walk, bin lose way.'

'You mean she did come into the Big Scrub on her horse? And she didn't come out again, you think? How far could she have walked in a night?'

'Might be, little-bit long way.'

'Oh God! They're hopeless,' said James to Dougal. 'Let's you and I and Robert keep on, and follow every side-track just on the chance she's in here somewhere. The others might as well go back, we can only ride single file anyway.'

'At least we know she's not in the river.'

'Do we?' said Dougal. 'I don't trust those bastards, somehow. I know they're supposed to be brilliant trackers, but they haven't made much of a showing this morning.'

*

They found her four days later: Robert, Dougal and James, red-eyed with lack of sleep, unshaven, saddle-weary from hours on horseback.

It was James who noticed the hoof-marks leading into the little-used track to the dead-end gully. They had been down the branch-track several times without noticing them. By then the

Black Police had moved on, but they had proved fairly useless anyway. The three men dismounted and, leading their horses, followed the vague marks on the stony track to the gully. They came to the little stream, the wall of green that had stopped Rose. They tied up their horses and searched up and down separately.

It was James again who came upon her hat under a bush, its feather crushed and broken. He gave a hoarse cry and pressed it to him with both hands. He was sure now that she was dead.

Under a log they found the rest of her clothing, some of it torn and muddied, with traces of blood. The hideous suspicion which had been growing in their minds flared up into their eyes; still they said nothing of it to each other . . .

Dougal, searching along the bank of the stream, came on a shallow grave scooped in its verge, which held what remained of Rose Lovelace. Perhaps the murderers had thought the next flood would disperse her bones and remove the evidence.

Dougal turned away and was quietly sick among the ferns, before calling to the others.

'Don't look!' he said sternly to James. 'You are not to look, Jamie. But – I have found her. She is—' He shook his head and blinked hard, as if trying to erase the horrible picture from behind his eyes.

'Rose! Rose!' James started forward, but Dougal brought him down with a football tackle. James struggled.

'Don't be a fool! Remember her as she was – as you last saw her. It can do no good. We must leave her undisturbed till the police come. That is most important, isn't it Robert?'

'Yes; he's right.' Young Robert, looking rather green in the face, agreed. There was a smell on the air which he remembered from when he used to leave the rabbits too long in his traps. He did not want to look.

They somehow got James on his horse and drove him ahead of them up the steep slope, for he kept trying to go back. Bundled in his arms he held some frilled white underthings, torn and bloodstained, and the hat with the broken feather. Dougal had taken the green riding-habit of which she had been so proud, and gently covered her remains from the sun and the crows.

2 Joseph

The *Maryborough Chronicle* thundered in a leader: 'Our women and children not safe in the streets ... This dastardly crime ... Must be punished with the full rigour of the Law!'

Relations between the races had never been so strained in Maryborough. The hanging of Zachariah had frightened and disgusted the Islanders and the Aborigines; it seemed such an undignified way to kill a man. The white people, shaken by the murder at Chindera and the brutal, unsolved killing at an out-station, now jumped to the conclusion that Kanakas were responsible for the murder and rape of Rose Lovelace, and the mutilation of her remains. It was thought that more than one person was involved.

Yet most of the Kanakas in the district would have been at work on the day of the murder. Who had been wandering freely round the countryside lately? Samuel McGriggen, still angry at the manly way Joseph had stood up to him, remembered that he had been away from work. When? Last Monday, the day Rose had gone riding and had never come back!

McGriggen went to the police with his story.

That night, as Joseph lay on his sleeping-mat looking at the bright chinks of moonlight through the woven walls, there was a sudden commotion outside. Dogs barking, men asking the way to the hut with rough voices, women calling out in excitement and alarm.

A loose wooden door was wedged in the only opening to the hut at night, to keep out bats, flying foxes, and evil spirits that walked in the dark. This was roughly pulled aside. Two dark figures towered over Joseph on the floor.

'Joseph Tula Efate?'

'Yes. What is it?'

'I arrest you in the name of the Queen—'

'But what for? What have I done?'

'On suspicion of Wilful Murder—'

In a daze, Joseph stumbled into his clothes. It was like a nightmare from which he couldn't wake up. They jostled him out into the moonlight. Ezekiel gripped his hand, told him not to worry, that he would go and tell young Mr Johnstone and they'd have him home again in no time. It must be a mistake.

'Go to Mr Stewart!' said Joseph. 'Tell Mr Stewart at the Manse, and ask him to come.'

In the police station it might have been the middle of the day. Everyone was wide awake, brisk, hurried. Someone came with a sheaf of papers and set them on a big desk. Joseph was taken to a small room. Three big policemen crowded round him.

'Thought you'd got away with it, eh?' One of them shoved him heavily in the chest. He staggered back against the wall. Another grabbed him by the shirt and pulled him forward.

'What's this on your shirt-front? Blood! So you did kill her. Go on, admit it, you might as well. Who else was with you, eh? Or did you do it on your own?'

'My – my nose bled. At work the other morning.'

'Where'd you learn to talk so la-di-da, nigger?'

'At the mission, on Lifu. If you would ask the Reverend Mr Stewart, he—'

'Ah, a mission boy! They're always the worst. Get above themselves, think they're as good as the whites.'

'So you thought you'd like a white Mary for a change.' The biggest policeman pushed his face up close. 'Did you follow her into the Big Scrub?'

'I don't understand.'

'He's playing dumb. Miss Lovelace, did you follow her from Chindera? And then rape her and strangle her? Or did you strangle her first?'

'Where you bin last Monday? What for you bin late for work?'

'I bin go longa Bundaberg, longa coach.' Hating himself, Joseph heard the humble pidgin come from his lips. He was scared, sweating. He thought of Zachariah dancing on air, eyes protruding, face darkening. They would do the same with him. If only he had washed his shirt after his nose bled! But there was no time before work in the mornings, and he was tired at night. They used to do all their washing together in the little creek on Saturday, if they were free, or Sunday mornings, and spread their things on the grass to dry.

'S'pose you go longa Bundaberg Monday, you no get back to work Tuesday. You gammon me.'

'No gammon, I tell you true. I bin go longa Sunday bus, come back Monday night. You ask Mister Stewart, he tell you.'

'He's as guilty as hell,' said the biggest policeman contemptuously. 'Strip off, nigger.'

'What?'

The big man grabbed at his shirt, tearing off the buttons. 'Get your clothes off.'

Shaking, Joseph obeyed. He was beginning to feel guilty. He had heard rumours that Miss Lovelace of Rosehill was lost, that there was a search party with black trackers out after her. How could they think that he had anything to do with it? Yet it looked bad. He hadn't told any of the others that he was going to Bundaberg, it had been on the spur of the moment. But Emily, the Duguids, the Stewarts – they would say that he was there. He felt helpless, trapped.

He stood naked before three pairs of cold, curious eyes.

'H'm, no scratches. Still, he could 'ave done it, he's got the equipment.' There was a dry laugh. They looked at his genitals consideringly. Joseph felt his member shrink with shame.

'Are you going to make a confession, you black bastard? Or do you want to be beaten up first?'

They pushed him into the room with the desk. One of the policemen sat down, picked up a pen. He wrote, then read aloud: 'I, Joseph Tula Efate, Polynesian labourer, of Chindera Plantation, Maryborough, do hereby confess that on the afternoon of Monday, August 14th—'

'I didn't – it wasn't me!'

'You better admit it, you feller Joseph, or by God you be properly sorry.'

Naked, defenceless, Joseph stood with his back to the wall and looked at his tormentors. 'Please, it all a mistake. You ask Mister Stewart, he tell you—'

'Quit lying, you know you did it.' A booted foot flashed out and kicked him in the groin. A flame of agony went through him. He doubled up, groaning.

'Stand up when I talk to you, blast you.' The policeman

grabbed him by his fuzz of hair and banged his head back against the wall. 'Now, you've only got to admit the charge, and you can go lie down. Just say, "Yes, me-feller guilty" or "I done it, boss", and you can go. Quick-time, now. What you got to say?'

At each sentence his head was banged against the wall.

'I didn't – I never—'

'Ar, let the bastard stew till tomorrow. He'll be more reasonable after a night to think about it.'

'We ought to beat the stuffing out of him.'

'Leave it.'

They frogmarched him to a cell, threw him in, and flung his clothes after him. Before they went away with the lamp, he saw a bench in the corner with a grey blanket on it. It was like the shelf he had slept on in the *Jason*.

Ah, why had he ever left his island? He felt the white men's hatred and contempt through all his bones. It seemed to shrivel his self-esteem. He fell on the hard bench in a stupor of misery and fear.

*

Julia Johnstone was flattened by this new blow to her social prestige. It was bad enough to be connected with such an unsavoury case through poor James – and now the murder looked like being the work of one of the Chindera boys. Again! And an inquiry was pending on the high mortality among their Kanakas, malnutrition and meanness would be hinted at. Really, she would have to go to Brisbane on a long vacation; but how would they get Helga married then?

And James worried her, so pale and grim and silent, with dry, red, burning eyes. He looked like a madman, almost. He would never rest until the murderer was punished. So in one way she was glad someone had been arrested.

From the inquest nothing emerged except that Rose had died on Monday afternoon, murdered by a person or persons unknown. There was evidence of sexual assault, probably involving more than one assailant. The evidence was horrifying, but it put up the sales of the paper.

Then came the news that Joseph Efate had been released. The blood on his shirt was from a nose-bleed, as he had claimed, and was his own. The Reverend Allan Stewart had testified that he had seen him on to the Bundaberg coach; the bus-driver remembered him coming back late on Monday night. He had not been formally charged, and was soon free.

Inquiries went on. It was now thought that two or more horsemen had been involved, but as the three searchers who found the body had all been mounted, the confusion of hoof-prints was difficult to decipher; and the black trackers had now moved on to another district. Also it had rained heavily since.

Time passed, the pathetic remains of Rose were buried, and James was left with only the lock of her golden hair that he had asked for. He buried a piece of it in the garden beneath his window, and planted a bower of roses there. He began to train the climbers over a lattice. When they flowered for the first time there would be a mass of pink and yellow roses.

James had prided himself on being tolerant, without preju-dice, though in fact he had little to do with the coloured people except the servants at home. There were, of course, no Islanders or Aborigines working in the office; such an idea would have been laughable.

Even after the murder of Claude Grant he felt sympathy rather than hatred for the pathetic Zachariah. But now – now he could not bear to see Harriet's dark hands serving the veg-etables at dinner, and when he used the coach, accompanying the family to church, he turned his eyes away from the back of Tombua's frizzy head, his hands on the reins. What colour was his – his – that thing which had violated poor, pretty, golden Rose? James could scarcely keep from gnashing his teeth and groaning aloud at his thoughts. It was this that haunted him, the endless question: Had she died first, or afterwards? How much had she suffered in fear, and pain, and disgust, before the mercy of death? And to think how he, James, had held back, had forborne to take what had then been grossly forced – by how many, oh God? Oh, if he could kill just one of them with his bare hands!

The only peace of mind he knew was in cultivating the rose bower, training the climbers, pruning the standards. One day he surprised a little dark boy stealing the first of the Golden

Emblem roses. He probably belonged to the plantation village, one of Estelle's school-age kids perhaps. James saw red. He chased the boy with angry cries, pelting him with clods.

He began to ride about the countryside, sometimes in company with young Robert Lovelace, seeking clues. The police had not closed the case, but they seemed to have given up hope of solving it. However, they did solve the other murder. A white man was caught trying to sell some of the goods stolen from the outstation earlier. He confessed to the murder, and that he had used a tomahawk on purpose to make people think that Islanders had done it. He was hung quietly one morning at the town gaol.

Joseph, released from prison, found his position worse than before he was arrested. McGriggen picked on him continually, trying to make him lose his temper, to answer back, to give him an excuse for a beating-up.

In despair, Joseph went to Mr Stewart.

'It is providential that you should have come to me just now,' said the minister kindly. 'I was about to advertise for a verger for the church, since old Simon is retiring, and the congregation is growing so that I need a younger man. Indeed, he has not been strong enough to dig a grave for some time. You would not mind that work, Joseph?'

A twinge of old Island superstition went through him. He did not like graveyards. Of course the spirits of Christians went straight to heaven, and only their mortal remains were buried, which no-one need fear. He said no, he would not mind, he would do anything.

The cemetery was a little way out of the town, near a swamp. It would be his duty to look after the Presbyterian section, to keep the grass down on the graves and to dig new ones as required. His church duties would include ringing the bell for service, sweeping out the vestry, and putting out hymn-books in the pews. It would, he realized, be lonely work, though easy compared with his work in the cane-fields. He who had always worked among a group of his mates, his own people, would now be isolated. There was even a cottage available, which went with the job. What he needed was a wife.

Mr Stewart went to Dougal Johnstone and asked for his release from the new contract. He grumbled, but gave in, and Joseph had the job.

Now he had a home of his own, there was nothing to stop him getting married. He decided to write to Emily, whose promised letter had filled him with wild hopes. He did not doubt her reply; what he dreaded was facing the Reverend Andrew Duguid and asking for her hand. He hoped her mother would be on his side.

3 The Black Police

Graham Lindsay had formally proposed to Helga, had asked her father for her hand, and was accepted as her fiancé. It had come out in conversation – and how little value Lindsay placed upon the fact showed in his not mentioning it earlier – that the aunt in England had a title; in fact she was the wife of a baronet, and her name was Lady Lindsay.

In the new young democratic Australia, newspapers like the Sydney *Bulletin* affected to despise a title, and would never refer to a knight as 'Sir' anybody. But the fact remained that the Colonials in their raw new cities, the oldest of them just a hundred years old, loved nothing better than a lord or a knight, unless it was a prince. The visit of the young Princes, Albert and George, was to set Sydney in a flutter in 1881.

When Julia Johnstone heard of Graham's titled relatives she became convinced of his desirability as a match for her daughter. To be able to refer to 'dear Graham's aunt, Lady Lindsay of Surrey' would help to counteract the unfortunate publicity over the terrible affairs of Claude and Rose.

She had been too subtle to press the match upon Helga, whose obstinacy she knew all too well, and she advised Angus too to show restraint in this matter; but she managed, by careful arrangement, to throw the young people together constantly, and to leave them alone when possible.

Helga, seeing a visit 'Home' for a honeymoon as a way of at last getting to Europe, had decided to accept him after all.

She found him intensely attractive. He was a virile and personable young man with a mind of his own; not classically handsome but good-looking, besides being tall and well-built. He was the only person on earth who could make her feel fragile and delicate.

For Helga's chest, to her distress, continued to increase in size; perhaps the singing lessons she had been taking from a retired Italian tenor in Maryborough helped to develop her bust, she thought. She practised hard every day, starting her scales early in the morning when the butcher-birds were at their matins outside her window.

Ah-ah-ah-ah-ah-ah-ah-ah! she sang, rising effortlessly up the scale, and Ah-ah-ah-ah-ah-ah-ah-ah! down again.

The two butcher-birds sang in chorus, one sang 'Ah-ah-ah!' and the other 'Ee-ee-ay!', throwing back their heads and opening their beaks wide. They put everything they had into the performance, pumping their wings and swelling their throats. Helga imitated them, in a voice clear as a bird's. She had always known she had talent, and that one day she would be famous; perhaps, she had once thought, as a concert pianist. Now Signor Moi had given her new hope and encouragement in her singing.

'If you will work hard, and if you are careful not to strain the *magnifico*, the superb eenstrument which *il dio buono* has given you, you will sing at La Scala and at Covent Garden in London. You will see!' he said.

And she *had* worked. Already her breathing was more controlled, her voice was becoming an instrument on which she could play at will. At times it seemed there was something magical about it. She took a breath, opened her lips, and the notes fell out like pearls from the lips of the princess in a fairy story she had read. They were clear, rounded, effortless; yet her voice lacked, she knew, something ... a maturity and richness which she would need if she were ever to sing the greatest roles in Grand Opera, like the great singers Marie Malibran and Adelina Patti. Helga knew that nothing less would satisfy her ambition.

She knew also that she had the physical strength and stamina for a singing career; she had never felt more vigorous and alive. Yet that something which Signor Moi had hinted was lacking – depth? – emotion? Only experience of life could give it to her, and the experience of marriage, of becoming fully a woman, could only help her voice.

She loved life, enjoyed food, good talk, exercise, sunshine, and above all, music. She found that she enjoyed Graham's kisses as he became more daring. Did she love him? Perhaps she was just in love with love. Yet romantic novels, with their swooning heroines in Gothic settings, bored her.

But then to be free, to have her own home! Her mother was irritating, with her social preoccupations; and Dougal with his coarse manners and jeering voice drove her mad. James, when he was home, was a dead loss socially: brooding, with a white, set face which never relaxed in a smile. The office work at the mill was neglected.

She got on best with her father these days. They were too much alike in some ways, but they respected each other. He was delighted at the engagement and promised her a dowry.

*

James was rarely at home. Sometimes he rode off alone, sometimes with young Robert Lovelace. One day, riding through the Big Scrub, he came on the clearing and stopped to talk to the old man. The hatter had heard about the murder, remembered the time well. They sat on the step to talk. 'It was the time the Black Police company was through 'ere,' he said. 'I mind they come in to water their 'orses, and arsked the way out of the Scrub.'

'You mean after the murder, when they were helping us with the tracking?'

'No; oh no, this'd be the day before, the Sunday. They was goin' to camp in the bush and borrered some tea and sugar orf me. Didn't never pay it back, neither.'

James jumped up and pressed a note into the old man's hand. 'Here, buy yourself some more tea. You've given me an idea.' He got on his horse and rode off, filled with new purpose.

Robert and James rode westward, away from the coast, on the trail the Black Police had followed in going after their man.

When they were well beyond Gayndah they came upon an Aboriginal camp, or rather shanty-town built of packing-cases, sheets of old iron and other rubbish.

They made their usual inquiries, saying they were investigating the death of a 'white Mary' at the coast, near Maryborough. The Aboriginal men did not meet their eyes; they looked down, shuffled their feet in the dust, looked away. The small bush-flies crawled unheeded on their faces.

'No, boss, we don't know nuttin',' they murmured. This was the usual reaction, so James thought nothing of it at first; yet he had a feeling that this time they were hiding something.

'Let's stop here another day,' he said to Robert. They camped not far away, hobbling their horses and making a fire to boil their billy of tea and bake their damper.

The Aborigines, dispirited and mostly old, did not pose any threat, but the two white men slept with their pistols handy and a loaded rifle between them, just in case. They had asked the old men where all the women had gone, for there were only two old gins in the whole settlement.

'Tumble down, Boss,' they said. They were all dead; and there was not one young woman in the camp to produce new life, so the whole tribal remnant must soon perish.

James, who found it hard to sleep these days, woke from one of his recurring dreams of Rose, Rose mutilated and crying for help. He woke groaning, and became aware of a dark figure squatting beside him.

Instinctively he reached for his pistol, but the figure put out a skinny hand and touched his arm. It was one of the two old gins. She pulled at his shoulder urgently.

'Boss! Me tell-em you true. That one white Mary—'

'Yes! What-name?' he hissed, sitting up wide awake.

She looked fearfully over her shoulder.

'Them Queenslan' Black P'lice – they bin come here one night, plenty grog, plenty playabout, they bin talk how they catch-im this feller white Mary. Plenty drunk, they is. She ride-em horse, got lost, bime-by they come up, killem dead-feller an'— you know . . . They prop'ly show-offs,' she added scornfully. ' "They never catch we," this feller say.'

'What name belong-im?'

'Peter. Two other P'lice and him. They done it.'

'Thank you, old woman. Berry good, budgery-you for tell-em me.' He thrust a packet of tobacco into her skinny hands.

She crept away. James, feverish with excitement, could not wait till morning. He stirred up the fire, put on the billy, and woke Robert. They left before dawn, making in stages for the headquarters of the Black Police at Rockhampton, two hundred miles to the north.

There they put their case to the major in charge. The men who'd been in Maryborough at the time of the murder were out on patrol. James recounted how they had been reluctant to penetrate the Scrub, how they had been 'unable' to find any clear tracks, how the old man said he had seen them in the area the day before the crime. It all fitted together.

Vengeance was swift, as soon as their guilt became clear. The three men were apprehended by white police. One of them, Peter, desperately trying to shoot it out rather than be arrested, was shot in the stomach and died in agony. The other two were 'shot trying to escape' while being brought back to Maryborough for trial. It saved a protracted court case with all its painful attendant publicity.

James seemed to relax, to become more reconciled, once the murderers were dead. He dreamed of Rose, vivid dreams in which she was no longer hurt and terrified, but appeared to him young, fresh and perfect as in the early days of their courtship. He had become a recluse, spent long hours in the bower of roses, and began to 'hear things', such as ghostly hoofbeats crossing the Chindera fields on nights of full moon.

Others, among them the part-Aboriginal cook, Bella, claimed to have heard them too. Bella even swore that she had seen a lady riding by on a pale horse, in a riding-habit and a hat trimmed with a drooping plume. She would not go outside on nights of full moon after that, and if she had to work late would sleep in the little room off the kitchen instead of going home.

Sometimes Estelle spent the night there too, when she had a lot of ironing to finish, claiming that she too was 'too much fright' to go home. At such times Dougal would often happen to come down to the kitchen for a late supper, and find his way into the narrow single bed with her.

For, remembering the sweetness of that encounter in the cellar, he had waylaid her in the laundry and asked her to meet him again. It was not long before he tumbled her once more, among the cane-rows not far from the house, with the tall green stalks meeting overhead and rustling secretly in the wind.

The solving of the mystery of Rose's attackers led to some soul-searching over the use of native police in Queensland. They had earned a reputation for ruthlessness, and it was known that the Snider carbines they wore each carried a number of notches to show the tally of Aborigines they had shot.

Now that the local natives were decimated, driven away from the centres of business and thoroughly cowed and demoralized, there was a swing of sympathy towards them in the cities.

The *Queenslander* even devoted a leader to the subject;

When the blacks, stung to retaliation by outrages committed against their tribe, have shed white blood or speared stock, the native police have been sent to disperse them.

What 'disperse' means is well known. The word is a convenient euphemism for wholesale massacre ... The natives, hunted from places where they were used to find food, driven into the barren ranges, are shot like wild dogs on sight. Murder and counter murder, outrage repaid by violence ... till at last the blacks, starved, cowed and broken-hearted, their numbers thinned, submit to their fate; and disease and liquor finish the work we pay our native police to begin ...

James, reading this, felt that it was fair enough. He remembered the quiet, cowed group with the two old women of whom one had given him the clue he had sought.

Around Maryborough the unequal war between spears and carbines was long over. The Queensland Government had brought these reprobates from the southern Colonies to hunt their northern brothers. No wonder they were hardened and brutalized by their occupation.

Sometimes, fancifully, he felt that Rose had forgiven her murderers. There was a sense of peace now in the rose bower, as though her unhappy ghost had at last found rest. Yet still there would come reports of someone hearing the ghostly hoofbeats passing over the paddocks on nights of full moon.

4 Burnt sugar

'Neath a ragged palmetto an old planter sat,
A-twisting the brim of his cabbage-tree hat,
And to relieve his mind of a load
He chanted the words of the following ode:

'Oh for a cocktail, and oh! for a nip,
Oh! for a pistol, and oh! for a whip,
Oh! for a captain, and oh! for a ship,
And oh! for a cargo of niggers every trip . . .'

The Melbourne *Argus* printed this rather satirical verse as the southern newspapers continued to lambast the planters in the north, and to call for the abolishment of 'the slave trade'.

But the Planters' Associations in the sugar-towns were vocal too, and the local press supported them. Mr Woodyatt of the *Maryborough Chronicle* – soon to become a daily instead of a tri-weekly – insisted that 'a serious loss would accrue' if coloured labour was banned, and 'this vigorous young Colony – which now produces 20,000 tons of sugar a year – would be brought to its knees'.

He did not add that one of the reasons why white labour would be uneconomic was that white Australians would never put up with the conditions and the diet that Kanakas were expected to survive on. But suddenly the truth exploded like a bombshell in Maryborough.

Following a report from the Polynesian Inspector on the alarming mortality among Kanakas on the bigger plantations, a Government inquiry into conditions was begun in 1878. In 1879, the two doctors making the inquiry reported, deaths among new arrivals had reached 180 per thousand. The average for the Maryborough district was 74 per thousand, or less than 10 per cent, but on the plantations of Yengarrie, Yarra Yarra and Chindera it was 107 per thousand.

At Yengarrie and Chindera the water-supply came from stagnant water-holes which were found to be teeming with bacteria. Poor feeding, over-work and lack of proper care for the sick were the other main causes of death. Dysentery accounted for many.

This was something which could not be swallowed easily, a bitter pill for the proud land-owners who were told that their own meanness was the cause of all this suffering, that they found it cheaper to import more labourers than to look after the health of those they already had.

It caused quite a scandal in the town, and there was much soul-searching in the columns of the *Chronicle*. It was discomfiting to be told that the new wealth and progress of which they were so proud was based on exploitation and death. They had been able, on the whole, to turn a blind eye to the iniquities of the blackbirding trade, but these latest revelations came too near home to be ignored, were too shattering to their self-esteem.

Angus Johnstone had been deeply mortified by the report and the publicity which followed it. Other big plantation owners could say they didn't know what their managers were doing, but Chindera was a family concern, where his manager and book-keeper were his own sons.

It was not just the threat of having to spend a lot more on rations that worried him. It was getting harder to find new labourers, for recruiting vessels were coming back empty, or quietly returning with the same men they were supposed to have delivered to their homes.

'Most of the deaths can be traced to the determination of the managers to save money,' said the report. When a labourer fell sick, usually with dysentery, there was no proper medical care beyond 'a dose of castor oil and a kick in the behind', as one overseer had told the inquiry.

Julia Johnstone was horrified at 'the disgrace', especially the charge of meanness, as Scottish people had a reputation for being careful with their money.

'And I have always been so kind to the sick,' she cried indignantly. 'Why, we visited that poor girl, what was her name, Eliza, every week before her baby was born. And Estelle, I am sure, is just like one of the family.'

Dougal choked on his food, and began to cough.

'And as for the mill, Dougal, I am sure you are not such a hard master. Though I don't know about that man McGriggen who supervises the field workers. He looks a bully to me.'

'He is a bully, but he gets results. The Kanakas are scared to report sick unless there's something really wrong with them, they know they'll just get a kick for malingering otherwise.'

'But how can he tell if they're really ill? And does he really give them castor oil?' Helga asked. She made a face. 'D'you remember how Mamma used to put it in a "sandwich" of orange juice for us when we were little? It didn't help, just made the orange drink taste revolting.'

'Yes, castor oil and sulphur-and-treacle are his only medicines.'

James was silent. He pushed his plate away from him, feeling guilty as he always did now, at sitting down to three good meals a day when the Kanakas in their employ were living, or failing to live, on a daily diet of rice and cornmeal. He had known, of course, that the food bills were ridiculously low for two hundred men who worked a sixty-six-hour week at hard labour in the fields.

'We'll aye be ruined!' cried Angus Johnstone, finishing a big plate of roast beef with vegetables and Yorkshire pudding. 'If this new Pacific Island Labourers' Bill goes through, we'll ha'e to keep them at the Maryborough Hospital when they tak' sick. Ay, and the rations: a pound o' beef or mutton, or *twa pounds* o' fish! Five ounces o' sugar – that's a'richt, we wouldna grudge them that; a pound o' bread, or flour to mak' it; fower ounces o' rice; and of course tea and tobacco and salt and soap and a' the rest o' it. I estimate it'll cost nigh on two shillin's a day to keep a Kanaka frae now on, wi' his wages and a', if they pass it.'

'The Government wouldn't have been forced to bring in the

Bill if we'd given them decent rations to begin with,' said James, who had not spoken before.

'Aye, but these new propositions are reedeeculous. We canna afford it.' But he kept his head down, and did not meet his son's eye.

If world sugar prices were to drop, there would not be a hope of competing with Javan and Mauritian sugar, where the coolie got only sixpence or a shilling a day, without rations. And on top of it all, every pound of sugar that went south to the big Melbourne market had to pay duty at the border; and the Queensland Government charged a 30s import duty on every Islander. It almost seemed as if the Government was out to destroy the sugar industry, Angus grumbled to his fellow-planters.

Yet in the south there was a feeling that the growing of sugar-cane was a rather glamorous occupation; that the grower did nothing but sit on his spacious verandah in a planter's chair of woven cane, sipping whisky and soda and surveying his broad acres; and the poet George Essex Evans apostrophized Queensland in an ode beginning:

> Beneath thy coastline's rugged height,
> Wide canefields glisten in the light . . .

But in the year 1880, when the Pacific Island Labourers' Act became law, the sweets of large profits turned bitter in the mouth, like burnt sugar.

5 Marriage at Mackay

The massacre of the entire crew of the recruiting vessel *Esperanza* and of five men from the *Borealis*, had led to a new outcry against the Polynesian labour trade. The story of Captain Coath's grim end and the killing of his whole family had filtered back to Maryborough through new recruits who had heard the murderers boasting of it. Then the commander of a naval patrol vessel and three of his men were murdered while bathing on Mandoliana in the Floridas. There was an angry reaction in Australia.

'Do you think the Government will actually ban Kanakas from Queensland, Papa?' asked Helga, reading the gloomy prognostications of the *Chronicle*.

'Na, na. They will ban coolie labour from India, aye, and Chinese worrkmen who live on the smell o' an oily rag, and put honest Australians oot o' a job. But for why should they ban the Kanaka? He's a bonnie worrker, and who else would tak' on the "niggers' worrk" o' clearing and planting and trashing and cutting? Na, na, they winna do it.'

'I don't know so much about that,' said Dougal thoughtfully. 'In Mackay, they say, small farmers have taken up land and are working it themselves. And that's a lot nearer the Equator than we are.'

'Aye, and that's why it's imporrtant to get our new plantation established, to provide juice for our new mill there; for I dinna trust these sma' farmers not to gae bankrupt.'

He urged Graham Lindsay, therefore, to go north as soon as possible after the marriage, and take up his new position as manager. A honeymoon abroad could wait for a year or two, till the new plantation was running itself.

So Helga, much to her disgust and disappointment, found that instead of a glamorous trip to Europe, meeting Graham's titled relatives and visiting Covent Garden, she was to be banished to a small sugar town in the far northern tropics, to live in a wooden house set on stilts, like a stranded ship among seas of green cane which came in stifling waves right up to her door.

Her wedding was the event of the social season. Mrs Johnstone excelled in organizing functions, and Angus did not stint the money for sending off his only daughter in style. Marquees were arranged in the 'spacious gounds' of Chindera House, as the *Chronicle* inevitably described them. The wedding-breakfast was served there, but the reception was held in the house. Guests passed through the hall with its great, curving staircase and black-and-white marble floor, then through the drawing-room and out the open French windows to the terrace. The weather was perfect, warm with the first days of summer.

Julia Johnstone's one regret was that none of Graham's relatives could be present to see the stylishness of the arrangements. The native staff had worked overtime, with help from the caterers in town. Then in the middle of it all Estelle had fainted, and had to be taken off home by Tombua, who was doubling as butler for the day. It was most provoking; but it seemed that Estelle was 'expecting' again, and the event would be quite soon.

James had at first refused to be present, but agreed at last to come to the church, though not to the reception. Helga had chosen a heavy creamy satin, not to remind him of Rose's filmy, floating bridal gown, which had been buried with her poor remains in the family plot.

White and cream frangipani, heavy-scented, made up Helga's bouquet. They were like orange-blossom but large, more flamboyant and exotic. She threw the bouquet to the crowd from the top of the stair, and the happy couple left for a few days in Brisbane.

*

'What – in Heaven's name – is that!'

Helga sat upright in bed, her strong features expressing surprise, disgust and disbelief. She pulled at her nightdress, which Graham had been delightedly pushing up around her neck while he examined the prize which was his.

God! Those breasts! They were magnificent; they might belong to Erda the Earth-mother in some Nordic legend. She had been complaisant at first, lying sensuously relaxed and slightly smiling while he progressed in his slow worship from feet to chin.

For Helga's husband was a gentle *voyeur*. He had to see as well as feel; the sight of her breasts with their dark purplish rosettes, her creamy skin and the contrast of the demure dark curls that hid her sex, all had brought him to such a pitch of excitement that he could hardly wait. Yet he was determined he would wait till she was as ready as himself, and they came together as one flesh.

He would like mirrors all round and overhead so that he could see her from every angle. He had refused her timid request to have the light out. Then, after dwelling with his lips on the delectable mountains, he had thrown himself back, preparing to make the final assault on the gates of the city.

Alas! It was then that she caught sight of his weapon: engorged, erect, enormously ready and, as it seemed to her, about a foot long. At her exclamation he looked down at himself proudly.

'That—? Why, my darling, that is the equipment of a normal man. *That* is what fits there.' And he demonstrated with an exploring finger. Helga closed her eyes. Ah, yes, yes, yes, yes! She felt herself melting, yielding; she wanted him never to stop touching her.

But he drew back again. 'Look, dearest, it's not so terrible, is it? Open your eyes. Look at me, how you have excited me. See? Give me your hand.'

Strange, gristly object! Her eyes were unwillingly open. All the pictures she had seen in classical paintings had shown nothing like this. There was a delicate tassel of flesh, folded downward on a sort of cushion, and no more than an inch or two long.

Did every man carry about with him this great living monster, ready to start up in aggressive pose? She felt threatened, vulnerable.

'Oh, why are you like this? Why are you like this?' he murmured, as she lay cold and unresponsive.

'I'm afraid!' she protested. 'You will injure me, I know you will.'

'No, no, I assure you it is quite normal. Did your mother tell you nothing?'

'Nothing. Except that I must put up with whatever my husband demanded of me. I didn't think it would be like this.'

'It will be all right, I promise you.' He began to caress her again.

'Perhaps if you will put out the lamp.'

'Oh, very well.' He was beginning to get impatient. He fought his way through the mosquito net and turned out the gas-lamp. She felt the bed give under his weight as he climbed back.

'I'm cold!' she said fretfully.

'I'll soon make you warm.' He rolled all his weight upon her. There was no stopping him now. Helga bit her lip to keep back a cry. She was too proud to weep; but she lay silent and still afterwards with her face turned to the wall, while Graham, who had expected a night of endless bliss, stammered his regrets and begged her to forgive him.

Their wedding-night was a disaster. So was the rest of the honeymoon.

Helga had refused to let him touch her again, even the next morning. 'You see, you *have* injured me internally,' she said crossly. 'I am bleeding.'

'Of course, so you should be. Oh God, I do think your mother might have prepared you a little.'

'She was too shy, I expect. We have never discussed such things.'

'Well, don't girls talk among themselves? I mean, fellows tell each other things, and at least we know what's what.'

'I have never had a sister. And at home even the word "child-birth" was not mentioned.'

'Once we have a child you will feel different.'

'Giving birth could not be more painful, at any rate.'

'You are tired after the ceremony.' He made excuses for her. 'You will be all right when we get into our own home.'

But once again, on the first night in Mackay, he insisted on having the light, urging her to look, to accept him. She forced herself to do as he asked – hadn't her mother warned her that her duties would not all be pleasant? – but it made her head ache. He became angry with her 'foolishness', and longed for the response that never came. Yet somehow, after a few months, they managed to begin a baby.

Helga found that living in a small space did not make life easier or housework less. The amount of untidiness she could get away with at Chindera in her large, carpeted bedroom, simply looked squalid in Mackay.

And then she had always had someone to pick things up after her. Music-books scattered in her little living-room looked untidy, and the piano she had brought up by boat took up far too much space.

Still, it was rather pleasant sitting on the little glassed-in porch on the sunny days of winter, with a view across the tops of the waving cane. It was all right in the raised house, it was only at ground-level she felt shut in, overwhelmed, like a beetle lost in an enormous lawn.

Graham was busy, and away from dawn till dusk as the first harvest and the crushing-season began. Helga was content to experiment with cooking (though she burned her hand painfully on the wood stove more than once), and to play the piano and practise her scales.

Then it was time to begin sewing for the baby. She hated sewing, but felt she had to make some hand-sewn garments. Her only social contacts where there was music were the church and the choir. Word got about that Mrs Lindsay 'had a voice', but by the time she was receiving invitations to sing, she was becoming too large to be seen in public.

Then the wet season began. Life in Maryborough, though north of Brisbane, had not prepared her for a summer in the tropics. Toads, frogs and spiders invaded the house. Ticks embedded themselves in her flesh when she walked in the overgrown garden. Her piano grew mouldy, its tone slack.

'It's beyond *everything*!' she cried in despair, when one Sunday morning on getting out her best black leather shoes for church she found them covered with mould. Her whole wardrobe smelt musty. She longed for the gracious rooms of Chindera, for servants, for a carriage to take her out from this stifling house among the rows of twelve-foot-high grass. She felt that a desert, anything, would be preferable to this overabundance of moist green.

Her increasing bulk made her feel the heat more. And the humidity, she felt sure, was getting into her throat and making the vocal cords rusty.

She knew no woman well enough to talk to about her fears of childbirth. She dreaded to be hurt again by the baby forcing its way out, as he had forced his way in.

For week after week the rain fell without a pause. It drummed on the galvanized iron roof in an endless, deadening roar. Helga wrote to her mother:

I am very unhappy here, where there is no music, no nothing. My piano is mildewed, I am bothered by mosquitoes, bled by leeches and ticks; and in danger of being bitten by snakes. The air is so heavy with moisture that I can scarcely breathe, let alone sing.

How could I ever have come to this place? I long for Chindara ... Here the ceilings are too low even for us to install a ceiling fan, supposing we could afford it ...

Still the rain fell, straight down, enclosing her with its silver bars. She was beginning to loathe the prospect of endless green, stretching away in every direction. As she paced the house, staring out at the rain, she tried to compose a song with words and music to express her feeling of incarceration.

The final version came out like this:

Under a sky of Mediterranean blue,
In an Italian garden far away
I see among the flowers, the marble urns,
A crystal fountain play ...

Instead of that fountain climbing in the air,
Slow heavy rain that falls and falls
In silver bars; and I am kept close here
Within my prison walls.

When she had set it to music she felt rather proud of it, but she did not sing it to Graham. The prison bars were closing more tightly every day. Once the baby was born she would really be anchored here, in this provincial town of petty sugar-farmers and occasional 'Sacred Concerts' in the little wooden School of Arts with its dreadful acoustics.

She sat one morning on the end of the double bed, impatiently cobbling together a hole in the stocking she was about to put on – her last pair, and Graham said there was no money to buy more.

She thought of Italy, and London, where snow would be falling now in the streets, and hansom cabs moved quietly over the white and brown surface, and deposited a glittering crowd outside Covent Garden opera house. Yes, it would be night and winter over there now.

A crowd waited impatiently to see their favourite prima donna arrive ... In a diamond tiara and white furs, Dame Helga Lindsay descended from ... Damn! Oh damn! The needle had gone deeply into the ball of her thumb. She set her teeth, and drew it out. A bright drop of blood followed.

As if the blood had been a signal, she began to sob. She wanted to throw herself about in a paroxysm of grief, but her body was too cumbersome. Tears gushed from her eyes; her sobs grew louder.

Graham came in, his blue eyes looking troubled.

'My dear! What is it? Please calm yourself, you will do yourself an injury. Think of the child.'

'Oh, DAMN the child!'

'Helga! What happened? Now tell me calmly.'

'I ca-can't . . . I p-pricked my thumb.'

'You pricked your thumb!' He began to laugh. He lifted her hand and sucked some blood from the tiny wound. 'There, it will soon stop hurting. It's nothing to cry about, for God's sake.'

'I kn-know.' But she couldn't stop. Graham put it down to 'nerves', because of her condition.

6 Andrew Duguid

When Helga left the mansion of Chindera for a wood and iron box in Mackay ('a cardboard house', she called it), she was very conscious of the change. Emily Duguid was oppressed by no such feelings when she left her father's house for the verger's cottage attached to the Presbyterian Church, St Stephen's, in Maryborough.

It had grieved her to leave home without his blessing, for he was still deeply angry. The ceremony had been performed by Mr Stewart in his absence, and a friend of her mother's gave her away. Amelia Duguid was there. She had always liked Joseph, and she wanted grandchildren. She had quite come round to the idea.

Emily had led a fairly Spartan life in Bundaberg, after her unusual childhood in the Pacific. So she did not mind the tiny cottage and the small salary they had to exist on. Working as a missionary when he had first returned to Queensland, her father had often not known where the money for the next meal was to come from.

When any money came in, as when Amelia received a small legacy from her father's estate in Scotland, it was put into mission work: they held 'coffee suppers' and 'Sunday tea' for the Kanakas to counter-attract them from the hotels and the fan-tan games and opium dens of the Chinese quarter.

Emily, who as a child had been deeply hurt by her father's apparent coldness when she tried to show her affection, no longer cared very much about him nor even missed her mother. She was too unthinkingly happy with Joseph, happier than she had ever been in her life. He, who had his first initiation into the mysteries of sex by an older Island girl when he was only fourteen, and who'd had a few casual encounters since then, was skilled and gentle with her. She was utterly infatuated with him. She could not stop touching his crisp, curling black hair, his shining dark shoulders and arms with their rippling muscles under the satiny skin, his thin, fine-boned hands, and slender hips round which he would knot, carelessly, a length of cloth in a graceful sulu for wearing about the house.

Once she put a frangipani blossom in his hair, but he laughed sheepishly and removed it. He was an Australian now, married to a white girl; such playabout was strictly for Island-ers. He always wore a shirt when he went abroad, and a tie on Sundays. Graves were never dug on Sundays.

Andrew Duguid had found that the people in Bundaberg, though there was a Kanaka mission and the men were taught the Bible and to sing hymns, had not realized the Islanders' eagerness to learn. With Miss Young of Fairymead Plantation he helped to organize evening classes in the men's huts. The fame of the mission spread back to the Islands with returning labourers, who advised their friends to 'go 'longa Bun'aberg an' learn like I tell you.'

Emily too had helped for a while with this work, and he missed her. Apart from her help in the mission work, she was his only daughter and he loved her dearly in his austere, undemonstrative fashion. He could not forgive her 'desertion'. And though he had given his life to the Islanders, he could not reconcile himself to having one for a son-in-law. He felt like Desdemona's father.

Really, he preferred the Australian Aborigines, who were a milder and less proud and touchy people on the whole. Yet there were few of the original people left in Bundaberg, though it was said there were many still on Great Sandy Island, now called Fraser Island since the fatal wreck there.

On the mainland they had been systematically shot, poisoned, hunted down like vermin by the notorious Black Police. In the towns they more often died of disease, malnutrition and drink. Worst of all was the opium which the Chinese would give them, from the charcoal residue in the pipes used in their dens. It was a concentrated and debased form of the drug, which destroyed them mentally as the drink destroyed them physically.

Even the wild Kanakas, recent recruits from cannibal islands, despised them, and would sometimes organize Sunday afternoon hunts for the 'men belong bush', killing any luckless lone Aborigine they found with their cane-knives or tomahawks.

'Yet the Aborigines are not the low, sub-human creatures they have been painted,' Andrew wrote in one of his sermons. 'When I think what they were, and what they could have become, given a proper Christian education, I could weep. Man's inhumanity to man! There is no help now for the older ones; their habits are formed, bad habits which they have learned since the white man came here. They are sunk in drink and despair, their lands taken from them, very often their women stolen away or debauched by unscrupulous men. They gamble away their clothes and blankets. The only hope now is to get the young and educate *them*. The pity of it is that very few are being born. It seems the Queensland Aborigines are doomed to become extinct.'

Yet there were still plenty of half-castes being born, he admitted to himself, and some Islanders who elected to stay on in Australia married Aboriginal women because there were no others available to them.

It was a growing problem, and now here was his own daughter adding to it. Where would her children fit into this fragmented society, of white bosses and depressed black labour, of colour prejudice which if anything was even stronger against the part-coloured than the full native?

He suddenly felt tired as well as depressed. The summer heat had left him listless and feeling old, yet he was only just sixty. In a flash of insight he realized that he would not live to see his grandchildren. It was not his worry.

*

Amelia worried about her husband. They had reached a kind of pleasant neutrality, neither love nor hate, after the first bitterness he had shown over her decision to deny him her bed. At first they had quarrelled over all sorts of petty things, things like whether she had forgotten to put the cosy on the tea-pot, or her tidying away his papers before he had finished writing out a sermon. Behind the quarrels lay his hurt and frustration seeking an outlet.

Now, as she watched him growing thinner and more listless – he who had always been driven by a demon of energy, a fanatical wish to toil in the Lord's work for as many hours as possible out of the twenty-four – she realized how suddenly he had aged. Since Emily's marriage he had not been the same.

He even began lying in bed in the mornings, instead of getting up with the dawn; in the last years he had done with no more than five hours' sleep a night. He let her bring him a cup of tea in bed, though he would not eat breakfast there; to him this would have appeared self-indulgence amounting to a sin.

At last came the morning when he did not get up at all. He lay calmly with his large, curling beard – now quite grey, though his eyebrows were sandy-coloured still – spread on the coverlet. His eyes had greyed and faded: they had always been deep-set, with a fanatical gleam; now they were dulled, and sunken in his head.

Amelia sent for the doctor. He gave Andrew a thorough examination, looking carefully at the corners of his eyes and his finger-nails; then he took a small sample of blood from a finger and went away.

The diagnosis was anaemia. The doctor prescribed iron pills, raw minced steak and red wine.

'I'll not tak' it!' said Andrew with a flash of his old fire. 'The de'il's brew shall never pass my lips. And as for yon raw meat, let the doctorr eat it himsel'. 'Tis fit for none ither than wild beasts.'

He grew steadily weaker. The insides of his cheeks and his gums broke out in sores, began to shred away, so that it was painful for him to eat anything. He lived on a little milk and gruel. Amelia did not want to admit he was dying, but she felt she should send for Emily.

'I shall write for Emily tae come,' she said at last.

He had been half-dozing, lying inert with his hands outside the cover. They had always been sinewy, with large, prominent veins, but now they looked weak and pale as a woman's. His eyelids flew open at her words, revealing his sunken eyes.

'Na! I dinna wish tae see her.'

'But she will want to see you, Andrew.'

'Aye; I ken that I'm dying. The doctorr—'

'Has tellit me he cannot do mair, if ye will no' try the diet to make you well.' She began to weep.

'I'll not eat yon meat and wine, if that's what ye mean. Onyway, it's too late, I'm thinking. I'm not lang for this worrld, Amelia.'

She lifted his poor weak hand and held it to her cheek. Tears dropped over the hand.

'Dinna greet, lass. I'm gaein' Home.'

'Would ye like me tae read frae the Good Book?'

'Aye.'

Amelia kept a fire burning in his room all the time, for he complained of the cold though the weather was mild. One night a class of his 'boys' from a neighbouring plantation came and sang 'I will be safe on that beautiful shore' and 'Abide with Me'. A little colour came in his wasted cheeks as he tried to beat time.

The excitement exhausted him. The next day he was so low that Amelia wrote off to Emily at once. Going outside the next evening, after sitting by his bed most of the day, Amelia saw the Evening Star low in the west, above a band of clear orange light at the horizon. The sky above it was a pure blue-green, without any other star.

As she came in again, rested and refreshed, she heard a frail sound of singing from the bedroom. Andrew, re-installed in the comfortable double bed from which she had banished him, was sitting bolt upright, singing ... 'In pastures green He leadeth me, The quiet waters by ...'

It was his favourite, the 23rd Psalm. He fell back on the pillows, motionless, while the life and colour drained out of his face as it had from the sky outside.

*

Emily had arrived only in time for her father's funeral. She was filled with remorse that she had not been there sooner. She touched the clay-cold hands and dropped a kiss on the icy cheek. It was like kissing metal or stone. This thing on the bed had no relation to her father as she remembered him. It might have been a rather poor copy in yellowish wax, finished with a false beard.

After the funeral she stayed a few days, helping with the melancholy task of going through his papers and sorting his clothes for the poor-box.

Amelia was going to enter a home for clergymen's widows in Brisbane. Emily was relieved. Of course she would like her mother to come and stay, but the cottage was so small, their privacy would be gone. And soon there would be children to fill it; the first was on the way.

'He'll not see his grrandchildren; and forbye it's a blessing,' said Amelia heavily.

'Did he ask you to send for me, Mamma?'

Amelia Duguid hesitated. All her training was against the telling of a lie, even to avoid hurting someone. 'He'd ha' been gey pleased to see you, once ye'd arrived,' she said carefully.

'I feel guilty because I've been so happy. It wasn't a mistake, Mamma, truly it wasn't.'

'I pray you may be richt, child. But it worrit him.'

She wrapped Andrew's silver fob watch as a gift for her eldest grandson when he should be born.

7 Return to Chindera

A week before Helga's baby was born the cyclone struck Mackay. It came almost without warning, with a peak of a hundred-and-twenty-one-mile-an-hour wind about midnight. Afterwards, it was found that the lighthouse-keeper's log showed the needle of his barometer had dropped right to the rim, and could fall no lower.

The wind at first had been SSE at sixty-five miles an hour. Suddenly it reached eighty. His children, who were out walking, clung to the ladder over the rocks until he was able to rescue them one by one; but his youngest was nearly blown over the cliff when she let go for a moment.

Helga lay tense with fear, while Graham held her in his arms and told her there was no chance the house would blow away. But she felt it was no real protection, it was too flimsy to withstand the violence without. The whole place shook, as though plucked at by shrieking demons in the night.

It was fear for the life within her which made her so nervous. At another time she might have responded with exhilaration and excitement to the fury of the storm. Graham's only worry was that she might start the baby, and he would have to deliver it, for there was no chance of getting to a doctor in this weather.

A loose sheet of iron banged on the roof, and the wooden dunny out the back was carried away, unheard in the scream of the wind.

Helga fell into a fitful doze and woke to find the bed empty, and an uneasy lull in the air.

She got up and looked at the clock – 6 a.m. Dawn was coming, yet not a bird called through the uncanny stillness.

The air felt hot and somehow thin, as though it did not contain enough oxygen for normal breathing. She went on to the verandah and stared up at the sky. It was filled with swirling cloud, revolving round the horizon as though a giant stirred it with a stick.

Where was Graham? A sudden gust banged the verandah door back against the wall. With difficulty she dragged it shut. Then she heard someone hammering on the roof.

'For God's sake!' she cried, rushing down the stairs and outside. He was sitting astride the peak of the roof. 'Come inside, get under shelter, the wind is rising again.'

'I'm just fixing the loose iron,' he said calmly. 'We must be passing through the "eye" of the cyclone, the wind will come from the opposite direction.' His light hair was ruffled, he looked absurdly young and boyish. At length he climbed down and helped her into the house. 'I say, are you all right?' He looked at her anxiously.

'Yes, yes, but I hate the wind.'

The gale increased in severity until it came just as hard from the north-west; but it blew itself out by late afternoon, and they had suffered no more than a broken window from a flying bough. Next day, when the rain had stopped, they drove out to inspect the damage. The cane-fields were flattened. The flooded river had flowed right through the mill; 700 tons of raw sugar had dissolved and washed away out to sea.

'Your father will be furious,' said Graham glumly, 'even though it was an Act of God. He will blame me for the poor returns this year.'

With awe they looked at the ships which had been lifted bodily and flung high and dry on the river bank as if they were abandoned toys. They drove back into town over roads strewn with broken branches and one whole tree which had been sawn into sections and moved aside.

Outside the main hotel Graham put a nose-bag on the horse, braked the wheel and left Helga sitting in the sulky while he went into the bar to talk over the events of the night and day of damaging winds. The floods had subsided as rapidly as they rose.

Someone told him how 'Cranky Jenny', who lived on the river-bank with her fowls and goats, had refused to leave them. A rescue party in a dinghy found her sitting on the roof of her humpy, surrounded by livestock which shared the roof with her. 'Save me goats! Save me fowls!' she shrieked. They had taken her off forcibly just in time, before the tidal surge swept in at 6 a.m. with a twenty-five-foot wall of water.

The wave had swept up the river, knocking the middle spans out of the bridge. A moored steamer had sunk at the wharf, drowning her chief engineer.

Graham enjoyed the close, rowdy companionship of the bar. He downed two whiskies and forgot to watch the time. Helga, who could never bear to be kept waiting and was always on time for appointments, for whom inaction was a form of torture, sat for half an hour and began to grow restless. If only she had brought some sewing or a book! She gazed impatiently at the hotel, whence gregarious noises and laughter issued, from which she was shut out.

After nearly an hour she got down and paced up and down, but she was too heavy with child to enjoy walking. She began to wish her pains would begin, so that she would have some excuse for calling Graham from the bar.

Suddenly making up her mind, she unhitched the nosebag, took up the reins, and loosed the brake.

When Graham came out half an hour later, mellow with whisky and ready to tell her all the news, he found the sulky gone, and Helga with it. For a moment he panicked. Had the horse bolted, and thrown her out, in her condition? No, she must have released the brake herself and driven off.

He waited resignedly for her to come back for him. She did not come. In the end he was forced to go back to the bar and ask someone for a lift home, where he found the horse, still in its harness, grazing quietly on the small front 'lawn', which was merely a mowed space among the rich green growth on all sides of the house.

Graham was furious. He had been made to look a fool, left in the town without transport, and the horse might have damaged his newly painted sulky, left in the shafts like that.

(The sulky was a sore point, as he had had it done up with a smart coat of paint when Helga wanted the money for baby clothes.)

'He might have bolted with you, and thrown you out. I was worried stiff,' he said angrily.

'Ho, if you'd been so worried about your wife you wouldn't have left her sitting for hours outside a pub.'

'It wasn't hours, it was . . . well, an hour at the most.'

'And what was I supposed to do? While you're drinking and gossiping with your bloody friends, I sit and twiddle my thumbs—'

'You don't have to use barmaid language.'

'You would know what language barmaids use better than I.'

It ended in a blazing row. Helga picked up a pewter tankard from the shelf and threw it at his head, but she was too angry to aim accurately. Then she flung off to bed, refusing to get any dinner. She slept so far on her side of the mattress that she almost fell over the edge. The space between them was more than physical. It symbolized a gap which would never be bridged, even by the child who was born a week later, a black-haired mite.

Helga wanted to call her 'Brünhilde' but Graham was horrified at the idea. 'Fancy saddling a girl with a foreign moniker like that!' he cried. 'Helga is odd enough, but—'

'You used to say you liked my name.'

'I said it *suited* you, and it does. But I like a good old English name like Elizabeth, or Anne, or Sarah.'

'Or Mary, or Jane. They're so dull! What about Pamela?'

'Pamela? All right. She could be "Pam" for short.'

'Not if I can help it.' But at least they had agreed.

It was almost the last thing they ever agreed on. Two months later, with a protracted Wet still continuing, Helga's patience gave out. She could not get the baby's napkins and bedding dry; the child cried continually and came out in a rash from the sticky heat. Helga wrote to her father, from whom she expected more sympathy than from her mother:

'Papa, I must come home for a little and bring Baby with me. It is no use telling me to wait for the better weather of winter, for I truly believe that by then I shall be dead! Baby is not thriving and we get no sleep, consequently Graham and I get on each other's nerves. The break will be good for both of us — for of course he cannot leave the north at present, with all the work following the cyclone . . .'

She waited feverishly for an answer. Then her father wrote to say that she was welcome in her old home, but only if her husband approved: 'You made your bed, my girl, and now you must lie on it. A wife's place is by her husband's side. I realize that the cyclone, coming so close to the birth, may have upset your nerves, and Mamma thinks it may have affected the baby also, making her cry so much . . . If Graham agrees, take the first steamer south.'

Helga felt as if she had received a parole from prison. Graham agreed to let her go for the sake of the baby, which certainly seemed sickly, but he did not like it. He said he would come down and get them as soon as the weather improved.

But though Graham came to Maryborough, Helga was never to return to the far north.

Book Two

The Second White and the First Yellow

1 Aftermaths

1 At Chindera

Beneath James's window, the bower of pink and golden roses gave off a delicate scent. He had trained them up and over the top of a curved frame, beneath which he set a circular bench where he could sit among drifts of scent, the humming of bees, and the occasional soft caress of a falling petal. It was like a gentler version of Angus's stone eyrie on the highest point of his land. It had no view over a wide prospect. James sat there with his mind turned in upon itself, brooding over the past.

He felt at times that Rose was present, he even had the illusion of her fingers in his hair, though she did not speak. It was a peaceful, tranquil ghost that haunted the bower. Sometimes when he fell asleep there he dreamed of her, and woke with the vivid impression of a kiss still warm on his lips. It was hard to believe that it was only a dream.

Yet that other presence which wandered on nights of full moon – with ghostly hoofbeats crossing the fallow paddocks – could lift the hair on his neck. He had heard it more than once, though he had never seen the rider on the pale horse, in riding-habit and plume, that had so terrified Bella, the part-Aboriginal cook. He had even watched at midnight on the anniversary of Rose's death, but had seen nothing.

Then on the next night of full moon, while tossing sleepless on his bed, he had heard it: thud-thud-*thud*! thud-thud-*thud*!

It was the rhythm of a horse cantering, the hoofbeats muffled by dust. Some late traveller taking a short cut to the road? He rushed out on to the balcony and strained his eyes towards the sound.

Nothing! And the road lay white and empty under the cold, brilliant eye of the moon. There was no rider to be seen. The hoofbeats seemed to pass quite close, then gradually faded towards the Big Scrub.

James shivered, and went back to bed, but not to sleep. He lit the gas and read until morning.

*

Tombua had come to Mrs Johnstone and said he would like to resign. He had been coachman now for six years, and occasional butler: a big, handsome man, no longer very young, but trustworthy. She did not want to lose him.

'And Estelle?' she asked. 'Does this mean she will not be coming back?'

'Yes Ma'm. Estelle she have yeller-feller baby. We so 'shamed, we go somewhere else to live. Maybe Yeppoon. Estelle got people that place, Keppel Sand. We go.'

'Oh, Tombua! I'm so sorry ... I took some little garments down to your hut the other day, but Estelle said the baby was asleep and had not been well, so I couldn't see him.'

'Yes'm. She 'shamed. That why we go, some other place. Back to Islan's, maybe. But Estelle, she no want to leave Australia.'

'Of course she doesn't. Estelle is such a dainty, clever girl ... Oh dear, I shall miss her, and I don't know where we will get another coachman as good as you. I will give you both a good reference. Come back later, and Mr Johnstone will have something for you to help with your fares to the north.'

'We no want it Mrs Johnstone, Ma'm. We got enough.'

Julia Johnstone was amazed at his stiffness, almost resentment. They made excellent servants, these people, yet they had this queer pride.

'All right; please yourself, Tombua. But I will write you the references, nevertheless, and you can collect them with your wages at the end of the month.' She inclined her head regally, and dismissed him.

A thought niggled at the back of her mind. The father had been a white man – who could it be? The overseer? Or even possibly young Graham Lindsay? She determined to ask some leading questions of Helga, who had refused to talk of the reason she would not go back to her husband at Mackay.

'There must be *some* reason,' she had said to Helga more than once.

'Yes, of course there is a reason, Mamma. It is that we are

181

totally incompatible. And that I should go mad if I had to live through another wet season in Mackay. And then there is my music; Papa understands how I feel.'

'Papa agrees with me that your rightful place is by your husband's side—'

'If you say once more, "You have made your bed and now you must lie on it," I shall scream!'

'—And little Pamela, though she does not realize it yet, being so young, needs a father.'

'Then let him come down here and get a job in Brisbane or somewhere. For I am not going back there. I was a romantic fool. Love in a cottage among the sugar-cane! It sounded idyllic ... And besides he doesn't *need* me, Mamma. He has his men friends to go drinking and riding and shooting with, and he comes home only to sleep.'

'Nevertheless, since you have made your bed—'

Helga's chest swelled as she drew a deep breath. Her nostrils dilated. Her mouth opened, ready to produce an ear-piercing scream on the note of high C.

'All right! All right, I won't say it. But people will begin to talk if you stay here and don't go back. And – for men are all too human I'm afraid – you must face the possibility that he might console himself with someone else. Especially if there are any coloured girls about the place.' She gave Helga a sharp look.

'Never!' Helga was scornful. 'He may have sown some wild-oats in the Islands, or the outback when he was younger, but he would not deceive me. I almost wish he would, so that I'd have some excuse for leaving home which you could understand. As it is—'

'As it is, your behaviour is reprehensible. You know quite well that Graham cannot leave Mackay with all the losses from the cyclone, the replanting, the damage to the Mill. Your father needs him there more than ever. And another thing, Dougal is to be married soon, as you know, and they are going to live here at Chindera. I had thought to give them your old room which is bigger than his. It is only a matter of moving in a double bed and redecorating.'

'Oh, so that's it!' Helga burst out passionately. 'My room is preferred to my company! I thought Chindera was big enough for me and my child, but you want to turn us out!'

'Of course not, my dear. And I love to have Baby here; but it *would* be more convenient if you moved upstairs where her crying would not disturb your father. And then I can get your room ready for Dougal and Helen.'

'They're welcome to it!' Helga flung out of the room, smouldering with suppressed rage. She had never liked Dougal; she had always been jealous of her brothers, for Julia had made no secret of the fact that she preferred sons, and the house had revolved round the menfolk. Now, Helga raged, she was to be turned out of her room for Dougal and that horsy, buck-toothed Helen whose parents had made a terrible mistake in naming her after the classic beauty of Troy.

She had been enjoying life at Chindera, with servants to wait on her again and none of the dreadful chores of cooking and washing. And after life in the small settlement at Mackay, Maryborough was like a great city.

Gas lighting had been introduced recently, and Chindera was one of the first houses to be connected. The streets were brightly lit. A high, square white tower with a clock had been added to the Post Office building, a new brick church was being built by the Presbyterians, and a start had been made on the railway to Gympie.

The wharf on the Mary River and the basin beyond was full of activity, with a forest of masts – recruiters, traders, passenger vessels, timber freighters from Fraser Island.

Timber-mills on the river-bank, steam-driven saws, Walker's Foundry making heavy machinery and soon to start ship-building – the place was hissing and bubbling with activity like a great iron pot on the boil.

In all this ferment the original inhabitants took no part. Aloof and ignored, they wandered about the town, taking odd jobs for money which was soon spent on cheap wine; hanging about the Chinese opium dens for the dregs of the patrons' pipes, begging outside the hotels, huddling in winter under the warmth of Walker & Co's boilers; and every night at five in winter and six in summer, they were rounded up like so many stray sheep and shepherded over the river to their camp at Granville.

When the new Maryborough Gas & Coke Company Ltd was floated in 1878 with a capital of £10,000 in £10 shares, Angus Johnstone bought up as many as he could. He settled two hundred of these on Helga at the time of her marriage, adjuring her to keep the investment 'foreninst a rainy day'. The dividends meanwhile would bring her pin-money.

Helga decided to realize these assets. She would go to Sydney to stay with a married friend who now lived there and had asked her to come for a visit. There she would work hard at her singing and try to get some paid concert appearances, till she had enough to take her to Europe.

The shares were in her own name and had nothing to do with Graham, though if she had lived in England all her property would have belonged to her husband. She knew her father would be furious if she sold the shares; but she had to have money, and she would not ask him for it.

She picked up the scrip from the bank, though they seemed very reluctant to hand it over, and went to a young lawyer in town. She knew him fairly well from picnics and rowing-parties on the river in the old, carefree days.

'I want you to sell these Gas & Coke Company shares for me through a broker in Brisbane,' she told him.

'Does your father know about this?' he asked dubiously.

Helga's thick black brows almost met over her formidable nose. Her eyes flashed. 'George Wilson, do you want my business or not? My father settled those shares on me and they are mine to do as I like with.'

'Er, yes, well,' he blinked and coughed, shuffled some papers on his desk. 'It's just that I thought Mr Johnstone might like the option of buying them himself.'

'Yes,' said Helga shrewdly, 'but he would want to buy them back at the same price they were when he settled them on me.'

'Well, yes, perhaps—'

'And you know how the town has boomed since then. Find

out for me what they are on the stock-market today, and I will offer them to him at the current value.'

'Very well. I have a stockbroker friend, I'll tell him that they may be coming on the market but are not for sale as yet. You would certainly have no trouble in selling them.'

When Angus heard what she proposed, and the price she wanted from him, he sputtered with rage.

'How sharper than a serpent's tooth,' he cried, raising one finger to heaven, 'is the tongue of an ungrateful child!' Then, dropping his Shakespearean pose, he gazed at her with parental sternness from under his shaggy brows, still dark as her own although his hair was grey. 'Do ye realize whut ye are doing, wumman? Ye'll no' get anither penny oot o' me, and ye'll ha nae mair income frae the shares. It's a braw investment, ye ken, that ye're throwin' awa'.'

'I'm not *throwing* it away, Papa. I'm selling it, and at a good price. I'll not come back asking for help. I'm investing in my own future, and one day I'll be worth more than you. You'll see!'

He gazed at her with unwilling admiration, at the eyes so like his own, though they were dark and fiery where his were blue and fierce. Aye, she had her mother's nose and the same obstinate chin, and soon the deep-grooved lines, the Davenport lines, Julia called them, would appear each side of her mouth.

'Weel, lass, I hope ye may be richt. But I doot ye'll find the worrld a tougher nut to crrack than ye expectit.'

He took up a pen, dipped it in the inkwell set in a bronze eagle's head on his desk, and signed her a cheque for £3,000.

Triumphantly Helga put it in the pocket of her gown. 'And now,' she said, 'I am going to Sydney to begin my brilliant career.'

*

Dougal was relieved to hear that Tombua and Estelle were leaving. Not that the girl would ever say anything, of course, yet with the kid growing up on the property, Helen might somehow get wind of who the father was.

He met Estelle on the narrow back stairs one day, her brown arms full of clean sheets she was taking to the linen-cupboard on the landing.

'Estelle!' he said, barring her way. 'Look, I'm sorry about — you know. Tombua's mad at you, I suppose?'

She nodded, eyes down, without speaking.

'He beat you?'

Another nod.

'Did he guess who?'

'He know. That why we go, longa Yeppoon.'

My God, I better not use the carriage on my own, thought Dougal. He could carry a knife or a tomahawk under the seat, and you can't trust the black devils . . . 'Look, here's something for the baby.' He thrust a folded ten-pound note into the waist-band of her white apron.

'No-more, Mitter Dougal. He kill me, s'pose he find out I take money from you.'

'It's not for you, it's for the baby. He needn't know where you got it. Say Helga gave it to you.'

'Orright . . . He such a sweet baby,' she said, smiling for the first time and looking up. 'I callim George, proper whitefeller name.'

'I'm getting married, you know.'

'Yair. More better I go, h'm?'

'Yes, I must go too.' He took her to mean the immediate present, not wanting to admit that she still attracted him powerfully, now she was slender again. Black velvet! He had heard of fellows in the Islands, and on outback stations, who became so addicted to it that when they settled down to marry a white girl they had to use a burnt cork on their wedding night to make the bride seem desirable.

Yes, it was just as well she and her yellow baby were going. He hardened his thoughts against her; he had been feeling almost tender, for she was after all the mother of his first-born. He gave her a farewell pat on the bottom and pushed past her and her great pile of ironed sheets, and went down the stairs whistling.

Estelle dropped a big, salty tear on the pile of immaculate linen. She put it down on the stairs, and taking the note from her waistband, slipped it down the front of her dress.

2 White and brown

It was the end of winter and the height of the crushing season in Maryborough. Helga, though she had hated Mackay and the stifling fields of sugar-cane, was yet her father's daughter; and she felt a thrill of excitement and admiration as the tremendous operation got under way once more.

Angus Johnstone had trained as a ship's engineer and besides had a brilliant inventive mind when it came to things mechanical. At Chindera Mill the whole refining process was exact and efficient, streamlined and swift. Chindera had led the way with steam-jacketed copper pans for boiling the juice to the crystallization stage. These eliminated the chance of over-cooking as sometimes happened with the old iron pots over a fire, when the dreadful, bitter smell of burnt sugar signified another lost batch.

Instead of crude draining-boxes with holes in the bottom, Angus installed centrifugal machines which spun off the liquid molasses in hours instead of weeks. He was the first to realize that in the dried bagasse, the residue of crushed cane, he had good fuel for his steam-engines ready to hand. Sugar being so inflammable, the residue burned fiercely after being dried.

Watching from the balcony at Chindera while the baby Pamela slept in her crib, Helga saw how two gangs of Kanakas were working steadily from each end of the last patch of standing cane.

It had already been burned to remove the worst of the 'trash' of big dry leaves. The thick stalks towered above the men's heads. Their big cane-knives moved in a steady rhythm as each man attacked the next segment of cane. With a few well-directed blows near the base the whole sheaf was cut through, lowered in the crook of the left arm, the leafy or spearing top removed, and the bundle laid on the ground for loading on the tram. Slash, slash, cut, cut; an arm curved round the tall stalks, and with an easy graceful movement they were laid on the ground, lowered as gently as a woman. It was like a dance with fixed, endlessly repeated figures.

Occasionally a knife slipped and sliced deeply into a shin. With a tourniquet round his leg if the cut was deep, and a bandage of torn shirt, the Kanaka would be sent home to be off work for a week or two, but the wounds were usually clean and healed quickly, often without stitches.

Helga as a child used to watch the 'burning-off' which preceded the cutting, and which usually took place at dusk when a fall of dew would prevent the fire getting too fierce. Men with flaring torches would spread out along the edge of the canefield. Burning into the wind, the fire yet progressed with great rapidity, sending a red-and-gold, furnace-like flare into the darkening sky. It was topped by a dense cloud of smoke and black, spiralling cinders.

A loud, crackling, confused roar accompanied the fierce flames. Snakes, rats, field-mice and long-tailed pheasant-cuckoos fled before the conflagration. So swift was the fire that only the larger leaves and the tangled grasses between the rows were burned, leaving the main stalks, still green with juice, blackened but unharmed.

In 'the Season' the air was full of black smuts, whether from burning-off or from the mill chimney. The maids would close the upstairs window to stop the black snow falling on clean pillows and bedspreads, and smuts landed on the clean laundry on the line.

Today, while Helga watched, the last of the cane 'cut out'. The Kanakas vied with each other, racing towards the last clump left standing. It was quite dangerous the way they fell on it, knives flailing; then they fell back, laughing and panting, or flopped down on the ground where they were. As soon as they got their breath back they were chasing each other over the heaps of cut cane in a mock battle, brandishing knives or 'clubs' of bamboo, uttering wild cries. The hard work was over for another year. Now there would be weeding and planting, chipping and cultivating between the rows. The excitement of harvest was over.

But the mill-yard was full of activity. The little cane-trams with their jointed segments laden with long, untidy sticks of cane, jolted over the narrow rails to the unloading ramp.

Workers carried the bundles of cane to the moving belt which took them to the crushers.

Here the sticks were soaked in water, and chomped and crunched and squeezed of their sweet juice, which cascaded towards the first-stage reducing pots. The air was alive with the beat of steam engines and rollers; pumps pounded away, sending frothing rivers of juice through the various pipes.

Helga went over the mill with Dougal, fascinated as always by the sheer inhuman power of the grinding rollers, the stamp and thump of massive machinery, and the size of the great heaps of golden-yellow crystals, still warm, carried from the centrifuges and the drying-rooms to pour out into the waiting bags in the Sugar Room.

Here on her father's land was a great factory, symbol of the Industrial Revolution, yet out in the country among the green of growing things. Over all towered the mill chimney, belching out smoke, cinders and steam: symbol of power and masculine pride of achievement.

She shouted a question at Dougal over the noise; he nodded, and led the way up some steps to where, leaning on a safety balustrade, they could survey the whole operation. She sniffed at the sticky, syrupy scent of boiling sugar. It was sickly, but she was too used to it to mind. She would remember all this when she was away on the other side of the world.

There were fifteen other sugar-mills scattered around Maryborough, but they did not have their own refineries. Soon most of them were sending the juice from their cane to Chindera.

They pumped it through a series of fixed pipes to big storage-tanks at Chindera; or floated it down-river in 'sugar-tanker' barges. In the tanks a special lime solution was added to preserve it and prevent fermentation until it could be processed.

Dougal, who managed the mill, was in his element in the sugar season. He strode about importantly, giving orders, sorting out hold-ups and bottlenecks, exhorting the workers. When checking figures in the office with James, he noticed with surprise that one grower had an unusually high tally, for he was not noted for the quality of his cane.

Dougal had the curiosity to ride out one afternoon and take a look at this property. The standing cane that was left was poor and sickly; and the crusher was not working.

He rode back and checked the intake figures again. Yes, Petty's plantation had been credited with 500 gallons of raw juice for the day. Dougal was suspicious.

That night he waited till after the mill shut down, about 11 p.m. He traced the pipe from Petty's place and put his ear to it. There was a rushing sound and a rhythmical pulsing. Surely he was not pumping as late as this? Dougal went to the intake tank. Juice was not flowing *from* the pipe, but back into it. By reversing his pumps Petty was quietly filling his own small storage vats from Chindera's tank. In the morning no doubt the juice would be pumped back again, and added to the tally for which he would be paid at the end of the season.

Angus Johnstone was furious when he was told.

'The dom'd thief!' he cried.

Angus then proceeded to invent a one-way valve and fix it to the pipes, in case anyone else got the same clever idea. 'Aye, that'll fix 'em!' he said with satisfaction. 'The cheek o' him, selling us our ain syrup!'

But he had other worries besides recalcitrant daughters and swindling growers. It was getting harder and harder to obtain new recruits, for labour vessels were coming back empty from the Islands, or not coming back at all.

In 1882 a series of outrages culminated in the burning of Maryborough's own *Janet Stewart*, and the murder of half her crew. The Islands were becoming more, not less, dangerous, with armed disgruntled 'returns' leading the attacks. Even Royal Navy vessels were not exempt.

The Maryborough planters blamed Sydney shipowners and Fiji recruiters for the situation. More than 125,000 gallons of rum (a by-product of the sugar industry) had been exported to the Islands in the year 1880 alone; no wonder there was trouble.

Now there was talk of importing coolie labour from India as had been done in Fiji, though no-one was very keen on the idea. Mr Woodyatt of the *Maryborough Chronicle*, who had indignantly claimed that 'Queensland had done her best to guard the rights of the simple child of Nature who comes to her shores', now revealed his true attitude to these same simple children.

On the coolie question he opined that 'To most people in Queensland the Pacific Islander is less obnoxious than British-Indian coolies; but the sugar farmer will be *forced* to employ them unless the Kanaka trade improves.'

The blackbirders then turned their attention to New Guinea. They managed to 'recruit' hundreds of terrified Melanesians, who mostly decamped into the bush as soon as they were unloaded. Another scandal was brewing.

The newer plantations at Mackay were in greater need than those to the south. Graham Lindsay was one who received a batch of New Islanders, who had been battened down in the hold for the entire voyage. They were timid, sickly, small men, quaking with fear as they fully expected to be eaten. The first night they disappeared into the jungle, not so very different from their Island home.

Captain Williamson of the Pilot Station then found them hiding in the mangroves, evidently looking for a boat they could steal to take them home. Lindsay went with his overseer to bring them back, but the 'boys' dived into the harbour and swam off like fish. At last they were rounded up by a Government vessel and put on board another ship to be returned to their homes. Graham swore that New Guinea recruits were more trouble than they were worth.

The average price for each labourer delivered in Queensland was now £23 a head compared to £6–£9 a head in the early days, and 'the nigger business', as Mr Burns of Burns & Philp remarked, was a money-spinner. But he was a shrewd businessman, and he saw which way the wind was blowing. That hard-fisted Glasgow Scot, Thomas McIlwraith, with his sugar and shipping interests, had been replaced as Premier of Queensland by the lawyer Griffith, who had sworn to abolish the labour trade.

Then came the *Hopeful* scandal, and the trial at which the crew was found guilty of shooting natives swimming in the sea (in all, thirty-eight had been murdered in cold blood). The recruiter McNeil and his bo'sun Williams were sentenced to death.

Yet sympathies in the north of Queensland were all with the Europeans, and finally the sentences were commuted to imprisonment, though not for life. There were rumours that all Kanakas were to be sent home immediately. Mackay threatened to secede from the rest of the Colony, and Griffith's effigy was burned in the streets.

'This man Griffith!' said the chairman of the local Planters' Association to Graham at the hotel one night. 'He's trying to get the Kanakas out of the country, but we won't put up with it. It would mean disaster for us, man!'

'I don't know,' said Graham, who was shaken by his experience with those pathetic, terrified New Guineans. 'Some of the smaller farmers tell me they're managing with white labour.'

'Yes, for cutting; but what about when we want to bring new land, jungle, under cultivation? Can you imagine a white gang on clearing work in this heat? And then planting 20,000 cuttings by hand? No, that's nigger work. We'll just have to get Griffith out with his "White Australia" cant.'

Then the planters, by their own impatience, played into the new Government's hand.

Just after Christmas Day, 1883, when thirsts were long and tempers short in Mackay's steamy heat, there was a riot at the races. At the Boxing-Day meeting on Mackay Racecourse an old Tannaman, long assimilated and regarding himself as an Australian, went to buy a drink at one of the booths. He was not drunk, just thirsty.

'Bottle o' beer, t'anks,' he said, spinning down a coin.

The booth keeper, new to the north, tossed the coin back again. 'I doan serve drink to niggers,' he said. (Under the law, time-expired Kanakas could buy liquor anywhere, those still under contract had to go to sly-grog shops.)

Old Boslem was more than offended; he was furious.

'You stoopid Johnny-come-lately,' he shouted, swaggering away but turning to shout insults over his shoulder. 'What you t'ink, my money no good? What-for you no sell me beer? You jus' white rubbish, that all.'

He continued to rant until a crowd collected. A mob of forty or fifty Islanders, mostly from Lifu and Maré, some from

Tanna, gathered round him. Soon they started throwing empty bottles at the booth. 'Take your old bottles, we no want-em!' they cried.

Somebody called the police, but before they could arrive a white mob had driven the Kanakas out of the racing enclosure into the road. Then a group of mounted police and planters came riding down the road swinging stirrup-irons at the end of their leather straps – the weapons they used sometimes to brain a kangaroo or wallaby from the saddle.

Yells of rage and fear came from the Islanders. Soon they were lying in the muddy road, battered and bleeding. The horsemen rode on and over them, trampling the prostrate bodies.

Ambulances which had been ready for casualties on the race-track came and took the injured – all Islanders – to hospital. One of them died that night. The others, as soon as they were discharged, were brought into court on charges of being drunk and disorderly or 'creating a disturbance'. Fear had entered the minds of the white population. For a long time the streets of Mackay were deserted at night, and women did not walk alone by day.

Did they feel themselves threatened by the steamy heat, the languorous, tropical, frangipani-scented air, the velvety blackness of the night sky where the stars, when they showed, hung low and bright, yet yellowed, like yellow diamonds, not clear blue-white or sparkling with frost as in the colder latitudes to the south? This was the Deep North of Australia, violent and intolerant under the easy-going manners.

'Yeller-feller' was their derogatory term for a part-white, whether native Aboriginal or of Island blood.

There was no true place for such people in the northern towns, though many of the first generation were in fact highly intelligent and vigorous in mind and body. But unless they were very lucky or very determined – and George Tombua would be both – they sank into mere fringe-dwellers without status or prospects. Those who managed to acquire land of their own worked hard, made money, and so became respectable.

Of the others, like brown sugar they were not considered

good enough to grace the tables of the Europeans. These did not use the Second Yellow, or even the First Yellow, except for cooking; but imported fine white sugar from the refineries in the big capital cities to the south.

3 The Efate family

By 1883 Joseph's family numbered three already: one more each year since Tula, the first-born, arrived in 1880. He was very like his father. They all were, to the extent that they inherited his close-curling hair and dark eyes; but Tula was the darkest in complexion, and sturdily built like Joseph.

His younger brother, David, Emily thought, had something of her father in his long, Scottish head and thin frame. He was small for his age, just as Tula was a big boy for nearly four, but she had a feeling David would be tall when he grew up. But her greatest joy was her baby daughter, Fiona. She was such a beautiful child. Her complexion was a creamy olive, her brows were fine and feathery, her expressive, liquid-looking eyes, dark as peat-water, were shaded by enormously long lashes so that when she slept they made a great fan on her cheek.

Even Mrs Duguid when she came up to Maryborough for a holiday had to admit that Fiona was beautiful, though she still had reservations about the marriage. She believed that it had helped to kill Andrew.

Emily sat by the fire in the big kitchen, which was also their living-room, warming little David's feet in her hand after taking off his damp socks. He wriggled upon her knee; he was always a bundle of energy and hated to keep still. Emily was making sure her children learned to wear socks and shoes as a matter of course. Many white children went to school in the warm Queensland climate without shoes, but Emily wanted hers to be always 'properly dressed'.

Joseph, too, always wore boots to work.

'Is that you, Joseph?' she called as she heard his step at the back door. 'You're late – it's almost dark.'

'Yes, and you should lock the door when you're here by

yourself,' said Joseph, shedding his working clothes in the porch and coming inside in his white singlet and underpants. Against his dark limbs they looked dazzling. 'With all these wild black men about the place, you know—!'

They both laughed. Then Emily frowned suddenly. After all, it had been 'wild black men' who had killed poor Rose Lovelace. It was said that James Johnstone at Chindera had never got over it. She put David down and he ran to his father and hugged him round the knees, as high up as he could reach, tilting his head back to look at the big man. Joseph swung him on to his shoulder, and kissed Emily.

'Where's Tula?'

'I had to put him to bed early for being naughty.'

'Oh-oh! Chasing the fowls again?'

'Yes, he chased one until it fell down dead – of fright, I think. You'd better go and speak to him if he's not asleep.'

'I'll have a wash first.' He put David down and went into the little lean-to bathroom at the back, where there was an enamel basin on a wire stand and a bucket of water. Emily brought him some hot water from the stove.

'I have been digging a grave,' he said sombrely. 'Not a hard job – it was for a child of seven.'

'Oh!' Emily caught her breath. 'I wish you hadn't told me. I am so frightened sometimes for Tula – he is so venturesome; and you know I once dreamt he was drowned.'

'Dreams are strange, but not necessarily prophetic.'

But Emily, having lost her brother James when she was little, was always fearful.

After he had washed and put on a clean shirt and trousers, Joseph went to the small bedroom where the children slept. She heard him speak to Tula, and his tearful voice in reply. She had to discipline him though she hated to do it. Joseph absolutely refused to beat his sons, however naughty they had been.

Emily went on preparing the evening meal he liked: plenty of boiled root vegetables, and green spinach cooked in salted coconut milk with a little tinned fish to flavour it. Luckily they were both used to fairly frugal meals; Emily had been brought up on taro and sweet potato and fish.

Without much money, they were remarkably happy. Their family was a tight little unit, sufficient to itself. They were, of course, closely involved with the Presbyterian church, where Joseph still belonged to the Kanaka mission choir. But since he had left the plantation village he saw less and less of his men friends. The family went sometimes on a Sunday afternoon to visit at Chindera village and to gossip with Davita and Eliza, but though Emily felt at home with the people they were a little constrained with her. She was not one of them, and they made her feel conscious of it.

She preferred it when they took the children along the bank of the river for a picnic, or sat in the Queen Victoria Gardens and let them run up and down the grassy slopes among the park-like clumps of trees which had been planted so artistically by Mr Bidwill the botanist.

She always made the children keep away from the bunya pine with its huge nuts – though now she came to think of it, she had never heard of a child being injured by a falling coconut on Lifu. The bunya's botanical name was *Araucaria Bidwilli*, in honour of John Bidwill who had sent the first specimens of this strange 'pine' back to England. There was an Acclimatization Society in Maryborough which had helped to plant trees in Queen's Park since 1874. The banyan was growing and putting out a forest of aerial roots.

David and Tula rolled down the green slopes and chased each other round the flowering bushes while Fiona sat on a shawl in the sun, cooing at the sea of blue jacaranda flowers spread on the grass around her. The trees themselves were like rounded clouds of colour, looking more mauve than blue against the sky. Emily sat and dreamed that Fiona would go to the Maryborough Girls' Grammar School which had just been opened. She herself had had little formal teaching, just the lessons which her father had mapped out for her and corrected with teacherly sternness. She had never had the fun of playground friendships and girls' games.

Fiona would need a good education to counteract the fact of her colour. For there was no use pretending it was not a handicap. Emily had only to notice the glances, full of curiosity and a sort of censure, when she took the children into town shopping. They were attractive children, but they were all unmistakably a Kanaka's children, and therefore the other women looked at her oddly.

She did not care, she told herself fiercely. She preferred her beautiful dark-eyed, curly-haired brood to all their fat pink-and-white babies. The children were too young yet to feel their 'difference', yet she knew a difficult time awaited them. Especially Fiona. It was harder for girls. Every night she prayed that Fiona would one day find a good husband who would respect her. Brought up in faith in the efficacy of prayer, Emily thought it was never too early to begin reminding the Lord that Fiona needed special help from Heaven.

She leaned over and removed a blue flower from the child's mouth. Fiona screwed up her eyes and laughed. She grabbed a strand of her mother's long fair hair and pulled it loose from the tight bun in which Emily wore it now, drawn severely back from her face. Her expression was tranquil, serene, matronly; it was as if in marrying she had aged ten years.

Yet Joseph, looking at her proudly, thought her more beautiful than ever. He could hardly believe that he was the same person who had skylarked through these gardens with his friends when he was eighteen or twenty, half-intimidated by the white man's city.

Yet Maryborough was small then to what it had become. And further back, there was the little Island boy growing up on Lifu, hanging about the missionary's house, thirsty for knowledge and fascinated by the fair little girl-baby with her eyes as blue as the sea – who would ever have thought she would grow up to be his wife?

If it had not been for that thief-ship, that blackbirding vessel which had stolen them all away from their home Island, he would probably never have seen Australia and all the wonders of the white man's world; and when Emily left it would have been for ever.

Yes, he was glad to be here. He would never return. His sons and his sons's sons would make their home here for ever.

4 Graham

Graham Lindsay came down from Mackay as soon as he could get away, which was as soon as the crushing season was finished. He felt that his daughter was growing up and would not know him; and besides he missed Helga.

Of course the child must be with her mother while she was so young, even though Helga, he suspected, was not really a maternal type. But the wife's place was equally with her husband. He was determined to bring them back with him.

He had had the ceiling raised in the house and revolving fans installed, besides a new set of cane furniture. Helga had liked the north at first, before the wet season set in. She would settle down again.

He discussed his situation with a man friend one night at the Planters' Club, when he'd had enough whiskies to loosen his usual reticence on the subject of Helga's departure ('a trip to the south for the child's health'). He had been given some good advice for dealing with recalcitrant wives: 'Get 'em pregnant every year. Keeps them occupied, so that they haven't time for the megrims.'

But he had a feeling this would not work with Helga. One child was probably enough to satisfy her maternal instincts, though he hoped she would want a son later on. But to force her into unwilling childbearing would only increase her bitterness and hostility, her determination to get away.

And there was that old reprobate Angus Johnstone aiding and abetting her, allowing her to go on living in his house when he should have packed her off to Mackay months ago. It was well-known that she could twist him round her little finger.

Graham bought a new cutaway coat and a pair of smart checked tweed trousers in Maryborough before presenting himself at Chindera. He had purposely not let them know what train he would be arriving on. In his satin stock and with his fair whiskers curled and pomaded, he felt more like a young suitor than an established husband coming to get his wife.

In spite of herself Helga was moved when she saw him. He

came up the front steps to the terrace, hat in hand, with his clean light hair shining, his eyes piercingly blue in his brown face and his mouth straight and unsmiling. He had a well-formed mouth. Generations of breeding had gone into the fine cut of his lips.

The family ostentatiously kept out of the way while she led him inside, where he kissed her hungrily before they had passed through the hall. She felt the old weakness coming over her, as if her knees might give way.

'I have missed you terribly,' he said, a little breathless. 'How's Pamela – where is she? The photographs you sent were not very clear, but she seems to have grown.'

'Of course she's grown! Babies grow enormously in six months. She'll soon be standing by herself.'

'Well! Where is she?'

'Having her morning sleep. She will wake about noon. Meanwhile come into the morning-room and I'll ring for some tea.' She led the way.

'Tea! My God, do I have to drink tea? All I want is to have you to myself.'

Helga walked deliberately across to the bell-pull and rang. She had mastered herself now and when she turned to him her face was cold.

'Graham, I want you to understand one thing. I've told you in my letters, and I mean it. I am *not* coming back to Mackay.'

'But, God dammit, you're my wife! And my work happens to be in Mackay.'

'And mine is music. I need the resources of a big city and the services of a good teacher. I am going to Sydney, to begin my career, and then—'

'Your career! Just because you've sung in a few concerts in Maryborough! People praised your voice because you're the daughter of Angus Johnstone of Chindera, and you think the whole world is waiting to listen to you. Your proper career is in being a wife and mother first. Why did you get married if all you want to do is sing?'

Helga looked down, looked guilty for the first time. 'I made a mistake.'

'You made a mistake! And what about the child?'

'I'm not sorry about that. I think motherhood has added a certain depth to my voice, and I would not have missed the experience, terrible as it was. But understand me, I do not intend to have any more children.'

'Don't worry!' cried Graham, almost choking. 'You'll never be the mother of another child of mine!'

They glared at each other while Harriet came in answer to the bell.

'Tea please, Harriet,' said Helga absently. 'And would you tell Mrs Johnstone that Mr Lindsay is here? You remember Mr Lindsay?'

'Yes'm. Miss Helga — I mean Missus Lindsay.'

'Hello, Harriet,' said Graham. And to Helga when she had gone, 'Have you still got Estelle, and that Aboriginal cook, what was her name — Bella?'

'Estelle and Tombua left. She had a white man's baby.'

'Who was responsible, do you know?'

'I've often wondered. I wondered whether the baby might have red hair.'

He looked at her, startled, but before he could form a question Mrs Johnstone swept in, monumental in black taffeta and a jet-beaded cape. Her grey curls were topped by a small lace cap, like a dusting of snow on a mountain peak. She had put on weight but her face was still pink-and-white and almost as unlined as a girl's.

'My dear Graham! So lovely to see you. Helga has been here quite long enough without a husband' (she gave her daughter a grim look) 'and little Pamela has been missing her papa. You haven't seen her yet? Such a poppet! I am quite devoted to her, but she tires me rather, never still for an instant. Helga dear, are you pouring the tea, or shall I?'

'I'll do it, Mamma.'

'We've had such beautiful spring weather! Did you notice the wistaria on the balcony? It is quite divine, the best it has been for years. And of course poor James's bower is a mass of roses, with the most exquisite scent . . . You know he has never looked at another girl, he is still brooding over that terrible loss, I fear.'

'Your children seem to be unlucky when it comes to settling down, Mamma. Let us hope Dougal's match works out successfully.'

Julia Johnstone's eyebrows rose in their old intimidating fashion. 'I am sure I cannot think what you mean, Helga. Pass me the sugar-bowl, if you please.'

Graham sprang up to hand it to her, appraising the quality of the sparkling white grains, even-textured and perfect. She stirred her cup rather noisily, and dropped the teaspoon with a clatter, the only outward sign that she was very angry. 'And how is the weather in Mackay? This is a pleasant time of year in the north, I believe?'

'Yes, it is fresh and cool, with the south-easterlies blowing off the sea. But the political climate is a little stormy. They're burning Griffith's effigy in the streets and calling for secession.'

'That is ridiculous.'

'Of course; but feeling is very high. Some growers tried to bring in coolie labour from India, and there was almost a riot; the Indians had to be sent back again. Now with the fall in sugar prices and the shortage of labour, everyone is a bit edgy. If Griffith should ban all Kanaka labour in future, many of us would be bankrupted.'

Helga sat tapping her foot in the old impatient way he remembered, with that emanation of suppressed and smouldering energy which he had felt when he first met her. God! She was a magnificent woman, more mature and robust with childbirth, but still with a girlish expression about her large dark eyes.

'Sing to me, Helga,' he said suddenly.

She looked surprised and pleased. 'What shall I sing?'

'Why not "Home, Sweet Home", dear?' said her mother, not without malice.

'No!' Her mouth became sullen. She led the way to the drawing-room and turned over her music. 'I shall sing – I shall sing the Mad Song from *Lucia di Lammermoor*.'

They had read Scott's novel together, sitting up in bed – did she remember? Graham stood to turn the music for her. He marvelled at how her voice had deepened and become richer, yet still retained that pure, choir-boy quality. The notes floated, soared, flew out the window and away over the level fields like little jewelled birds. Ah-ah-AH-ah, her voice followed the climbing notes like an echoing flute to the pianoforte accompaniment.

Even Julia sat silent in the window-seat, intimidated by something that she did not understand. She had always said she had hatched a cuckoo in the nest with Helga. Now she suspected it might have been a nightingale.

When Angus Johnstone came down for a Scotch whisky before dinner, Graham was surprised to notice that he was showing his age. He had always been such a vigorous, lively speaker, all his movements decisive and brisk. Now he seemed to have slowed, though he had not mellowed.

His sharp blue eyes shot lightnings at Helga as he said, pointing the carving knife at her, 'Has she told ye what she has done wi' the investment I settled on her? Aye, two hundred shares in the Gas & Coke Company – she's sold them a'.'

'Is this true, Helga? You never consulted me. I thought your father meant you to keep them to provide an income, whatever might happen to me.'

'Aye, she didna consult her father, for that matter,' said Angus. 'Helga is pig-headed when she gets an idea, and naething will stop her. Like this mad idea of setting off for Europe, with a bairn and a', not to mention a husband.'

'Europe!' He stared at her, his face slowly turning crimson. 'Is this true? You've been planning to run even further away!'

'I started to tell you, Graham. In the drawing-room. But you interrupted.'

'Europe! You know I can't afford to come with you at present.'

'You can join us after a year. By then I shall know whether I am any good or not. And if I am as good as I think and hope I am, and as Signor Moi thinks, I shall have plenty of money for the two of us.'

'The gel is mad,' said Angus, nodding at his plate. 'She was always a bit "fey", was she not, Mither? But now her head is turrned completely.'

Julia's reply was to shake her head slightly, to his surprise;

but it was just to warn him that Harriet had come in with the tureen of vegetables. When she was gone Julia said grandly,

'Helga has no conception of the duties of a wife and mother. I am sure it is not my fault. I have tried to instil correct principles into her. I am sorry, my dear boy, that she has not been a better wife to you.'

Graham, looking at Helga's rebellious face, suddenly saw her as she must have been as a little girl: hating dolls and fancy-work, rebelling against the woman's role thrust upon her by mother and nursemaid; unwillingly learning to sew a French seam while the boys went riding and swimming.

He felt an irrational need to defend her against her parents' attack.

'Helga has a good head on her shoulders when it comes to money,' he said. 'And she *has* been a good wife, it's just that she didn't stick it long enough. The house at Mackay must have seemed unbearably small and hot after Chindera. Perhaps if she had another six months, taking singing lessons in Sydney, she would come back after the worst of the summer heat is over.'

Helga obstinately kept her eyes on her plate. He was being kind and conciliatory, which made it doubly hard. She could not lie about her ambitions, yet it would be churlish not to meet his overture. After all, anything could happen in six months.

'Come, Helga! Graham is being very understanding, I think.'

Helga looked up defiantly. 'Don't browbeat me, Mamma!' And then to Graham: 'All right . . . perhaps in the autumn . . .'

Graham had to be content. But six months, for God's sake! How was he to endure it? At least he would have his work, he would be busy. And he would see she never went away without him again.

*

Dougal and Helen Welltree had been married a few weeks earlier; they were still away on their honeymoon in the south. So Graham and Helga were given her old room, already fitted up for the newly-weds.

There was a certain poignancy for her in sleeping there in her new state. She put the baby to bed; and began thinking of the mystery of motherhood, the unbroken female line which stretched back to Eve, through her mother and her mother's mother and great-grandmothers all unknown. Their fragile link with the future was this scrap of humanity, flesh of her flesh, a bud on the everlasting tree of life.

She spent so long brooding over the baby's crib, lost in her dream, watching the dark fan of lashes sweeping one pale cheek, the thumb jammed between the soft lips, the little dimpled fist curled round it, that Graham became impatient.

'For God's sake put the mosquito net over her and come to bed!' he cried. 'I think she's absolutely beautiful, but I have duly admired her and now I wish you'd let her go to sleep. I suppose since you've made me wait six months, you think ten minutes more won't hurt me.'

Helga tucked the net round the crib and went to the dressing-table. She began brushing her long, dark curls, a ritual she always enjoyed. Suddenly her wrist was gripped in steel-hard fingers till the brush dropped from her hand. She was carried to the bed and dropped there unceremoniously.

'And that's where you belong!' said Graham with fierce satisfaction.

Without gentleness, he removed her dressing-gown and her long night-dress, and stared wordlessly at those breasts which never failed to take his breath away. With a swift movement Helga turned down the bedside gas-lamp until the mantle faded and there was only an eerie blue glow.

After the long drought he was carried away on a flood of rapture; but he did not carry her with him. Marriage, Helga was thinking, was invented for the man's pleasure, and she did not intend to let herself be a slave to Nature. But she put up with it good-humouredly enough for the present.

She said after a while: 'Graham—? You know I will never forgive you if I start another baby.'

Graham was chilled. 'Don't worry, I'm not a complete idiot. I have taken precautions against that.'

She sighed with relief and snuggled down against his muscular shoulder. Ah, life was so complicated! Ah if only she could be content with the simple joys of wifehood and motherhood, home-making and all the rest of it! But domesticity bored her, she shuddered as she thought of strings of wet napkins going mouldy in Mackay, the endless washing and preparing of meals, the sweeping and dusting. No! She was meant for something more than this. She felt her whole future, her singing career in Europe, was curled somewhere under her breastbone waiting to be brought forth to brilliant birth.

*

James, haunted for years by the memory of dead Rose, even physically haunted by her ghost as he believed, had squired several other girls at various times; but he was still not psychologically free to marry. It was as if all feeling and emotion had been atrophied by his experience, and any sensitive woman soon became aware of this, and resented it.

His greatest friends were the Grants, a couple with two schoolboy sons who lived in a long, low house set right on the river-bank in the heart of town. He spent many quiet hours on their shady verandah, watching the increasingly muddy flow of the tranquil Mary River. John Grant had come there as manager of a section of Walker's, the big metal foundry. The family had not known Rose, though they had heard the story of her tragic end. His wife Jean, prematurely grey but with a youthful, fresh complexion and the bluest eyes he had ever seen, was an amateur painter and sketcher of local wildflowers. She made him welcome with the utmost warmth and naturalness.

She made a sketch of his head in pencil, and gave it to him for Christmas. He took the boys over Chindera Mill in the sugar season. Sometimes he took his current girl to visit the Grants, waiting to see Jean's reaction, for he valued her judgement. And he suddenly realized, as he watched her calm, good-humoured face, that not one of them could compare with this grey-haired woman who must be at least forty. Bonnie Jean! If only she were free . . . But he kept his feelings to himself.

2 The second generation

1 David

School was a wonderful place to David. His elder brother, Tula, hated it so much that he used to catch bees among his mother's flowers, hold them cupped in his hands and shake them up until they were really angry. Then, with his fingers stung and swollen so that they could not hold a pen, he would be allowed to stay at home.

Once, when David had scarlatina, Tula was disgusted that he should be perfectly well and apparently unable to catch the infection, for David was strictly segregated from the other children. He slept in his parents' room, with a sheet soaked in disinfectant hanging over the door.

One day after school Tula crept round to the bedroom window, in behind the hibiscus bushes with their platter-like flowers of scarlet and gold.

'Hey, Davey!' he whispered.

'What?' David still had a temperature, and was drowsy.

'Hey, come over to the window. Don't make a noise.'

'Whaffor?'

'Never mind, you stupid David! Just do like I say.'

David came, clutching slipping pyjama pants around his skinny hips. 'I'm so hot. Is it hot outside, or is it just me?'

'Just you, I 'spect. Runnin' a temperature.' There was a fly-screen of fine wire mesh over the window. Tula put his face close against it. 'Now put out your tongue against the wire.'

'Why?'

'I'm gonna put my tongue against it too, and see if I can catch your germs.'

'You're mad!'

'All right, but I'd ruther have scarlatina than go to school. That old devil Johns belted me again today, just cos I got my stupid sums wrong.'

'What, *all* of them?'

'Yes. They was fractions. I hate 'rithmetic. Now, put your tongue out.'

The wire had a dusty, metallic taste. They held their tongues against it, one on each side, for perhaps half a minute. David tired first. 'I reckon the germs have had time to cross over,' he said. 'Erkh! Your tongue doesn't taste so good.'

'That was the wire. Gee, I hope I get it bad enough to stop home from school.'

'It makes you feel awful.'

'I don't care. Don't you tell Mum, young David!'

'Orright. I'm goin' back to bed.'

He staggered back to the temporary cot Emily had made for him on the box-couch. The top was padded, but it was too narrow and his bed kept coming to pieces. He wished he could get well and go back to his own bed, and to school. He was third in the class and top in mental arithmetic.

Mr Johns, the headmaster, did not like coloured boys to do well as it upset his theories of racial superiority, so he always made the tests harder for them. But David was so bright that he came near the top of the class all the same.

Emily was very proud of David and wrote glowing accounts home to her mother.

David, the one we gave the English name to, is the one who is most like Papa who was always so good at figures and loved writing his reports. Tula is more Islander in outlook, he is easy-going and good-tempered, and he takes after Joseph in looks more than either of the others. He finds school-work hard ...

Joseph continues to enjoy good health and likes his work. He has just been given a rise in salary because of the larger congregation with the new, bigger church. This is a help but it is still rather a struggle to get the children clothes and schoolbooks and especially shoes – I only buy essentials but the money goes so fast! And I will not have them running barefoot as so many do.

May is a darling, she scarcely cries at all, but keeps me busy as you can imagine ... Joseph never changes, he has not a fleck of grey in his hair. Indeed, I shall soon start to look older than he – as I keep very thin – instead of six years younger! He is the kindest, most indulgent of husbands. I wish Papa could have lived to see how well it has all turned out ...

That was the peak of her happiness, the year Fiona first went to school, the year after May was born, after so long an interval that they thought she was not going to have any more children.

That was before Fiona was old enough to get into trouble with men, before Tula set off for the Islands to find the place his father had come from, before David died. Every year on the anniversary of his death she used to shut herself in her darkened room, not eating nor speaking, going over in her mind what had happened, blaming herself.

It was while he was still home from school in quarantine, though he was up and about. Tula for all his efforts had not managed to catch the disease, which suggests that it was not as infectious as the doctor thought.

David had been cutting out pictures on the floor of the little parlour. He was always able to play happily by himself. Emily was busy tidying the house for a visit from the minister that afternoon.

'Oh run outside and play, do!' she had said impatiently, sweeping up the ragged bits of paper which stuck to the wooden floor. She wished they could afford linoleum, that new material which was so easy to keep clean. She was tired after the work of nursing him, and now she wished he could get back to school, away from under her feet. 'Go on, David, I say.' She wanted to finish the housework while the baby was still asleep.

'Oh-oh Mumma! I just want to finish—' he began in a whiny voice.

'Do as I say! This instant!'

Sulkily David gathered up his cuttings and scissors, his paste-pot and scrap-book. He put them on his bed and trailed outside, letting the door bang.

David wandered along the fence. There was a market-garden adjoining the verger's cottage, which the boys sometimes raided. Now he climbed through the place he knew, where the palings were loose, and searched for the feathery tops of carrots. He pulled a few baby rootlets to chew with a satisfying crunch.

Now he was thirsty; he wished he had thought of getting a drink at the house. Mumma would be crabby if he went back to the kitchen with muddy feet. Then he noticed a partly rusted tin standing in a furrow. It was half-full of rainwater which looked clean. His father had told him how, when working among the cane, they used to drink rainwater from the puddles between the rows when they were thirsty – no water-carts in those days, and no water laid on in the houses . . .

David picked up the tin and drank.

Ah! That was better . . . But the water had a bitter taste. He spat out the last mouthful, and wiped his lips with the back of his hand. After a while a violent cramp attacked his insides. Oh dear! He hadn't chewed those carrots properly, he thought. He walked on across the furrows until a new cramp squeezed his guts. It seemed to dart about inside him like a piece of forked lightning or a snake.

Suddenly he began to feel really ill. His palms sweated, his vision blurred, he could not walk straight. Another pain seized him, agonizingly. He ran, staggering, towards the fence.

'Mumma! Mumma!'

She heard the urgency in his voice and ran. By the back door was a slender, curly-haired little figure with eyes rolling wildly, showing their whites. He stumbled, and clutched her round the knees.

'Mumma! It hurts.'

'What hurts, darling, what is it? Tell Mumma where it hurts.'

'In my stomach.'

'What have you eaten? Quick, tell me!'

'N-nothing . . . I-I stole some carrots. Do you think God is punishing me? They were only tiny, little – Aieee!' He screamed and doubled up on the ground, clutching himself and groaning.

'God help me!' cried Emily.

She carried him inside and laid him on the kitchen couch. The baby woke and started crying, but she ignored her.

'I'm thirsty!' he whimpered.

She gave him a drink of water; he complained that it burnt him. The carrots, she was wondering, were they poisoned?

'I had a drink – a little while ago–'

'What did you drink – where?' He seemed to be getting drowsy. She shook him gently. 'What did you drink, Davey?'

'Some water – in an old tin. It was bitter.'

'Listen, Davey, I am going to give you something nasty to take to make you sick. It's better if you get sick, don't try to stop it.'

He bravely swallowed the mixture of warm water and salt; it immediately came up again. There was froth on his lips.

She sat down and with trembling hands wrote a note to the doctor who had attended him. She lifted the baby, patted David's cheek and told him to be brave. She would be back in a moment. At the corner of the street she stopped an errand boy on a bicycle, gave him the note and a shilling. 'Tell him it's urgent. I think my boy is poisoned.'

'Orright, Missus.' He pedalled off.

Coming back along the road bordering the market-garden, which here was fenced with barbed wire, she looked along the rows of carrots and saw a rusty tin lying on its side. Awkwardly, carrying the baby, she climbed through, catching her dress on the wire. With a violent tug she tore a piece right out, and went and picked up the tin. She sniffed, but could smell nothing but rust. Still, she took it home to show the doctor.

It seemed hours before Dr Burns arrived – a tall, thin Scotsman with a grave manner and grey sideburns. She rushed out to meet his gig. He strode rapidly up the path, talking to her over his shoulder. 'Ye say in the note ye think the lad's been poisoned. Ha'e ye given him an emetic?'

'Yes. Salt and water.'

'H'm. If it's caustic that's the worrst thing.' She silently handed him the old tin. He sniffed it. 'Frae where did he get this? It's contained arsenic!'

'He picked it up in the vegetable garden next door.'

'Weel, I'll try bluestone. It'll purge him, tak' the poison through quicker. It's too late for another emetic; but ye did right to gi'e him one.'

They forced the nauseous solution of copper sulphate through the child's lips, while he screamed and struggled.

Emily did not know how to bear it. She wished the poison was gnawing at her own vitals. God, my God, let this cross be taken from him, she prayed silently. Let me bear it instead. But it was David who was writhing and screaming there on the couch, his eyes staring, his lips drawn back in a dreadful grin, sweat beading his forehead.

'I'll gi'e him something for the pain, but we must get the wee lad to hospital.' Dr Burns took out a syringe.

'I must let my husband know!'

'Aye, it would be a good thing. I'll send the ambulance.'

He waited for a while till the child was quieter, lying still with his dark eyes staring dully from a face which had turned from a healthy light brown to a greyish putty colour.

Emily had forgotten about the minister's visit until she heard his step on the porch. She had held David while he had an enormous, painful evacuation, and now there was a strange chemical smell in the room, and on his breath.

'My dear! Am I too early?' Mr Stewart's hearty voice seemed to come to her through a cloud.

Too early, she thought. Does he mean too early for the funeral? 'Yes,' she said aloud. She rose, and led him through to the parlour.

'Mr Stewart, can you explain to me,' she said in a trembling voice, 'can you explain to me why a little, innocent boy should be made to suffer as that child in there has suffered? If you'd heard him! If you'd— But God is supposed to be merciful.'

'My dear Emily, your father and mother lost three little ones in tragic circumstances. We cannot know or understand the workings of Divine Providence. Perhaps this trial is sent to test you and Joseph.'

'But David! He is only eight. Eight years old! Why should he—? He picked up an old tin and drank some water. Now he is poisoned with arsenic, and may not recover. It is too cruel.'

'Would you like me to pray for him?'

'Yes! Let us pray that he will not suffer any more. I cannot bear to see him suffer.'

The minister began: 'O God, thou hast said, "My doctrine shall drop as the rain, my speech shall distil as the dew, as the small rain upon the tender herb, and as the showers upon the grass . . ." Lord God, have mercy on this young and tender plant, let thy mercy fall as the rain upon the parched earth . . .'

As they rose from their knees, Emily slightly comforted by the rhythm of the words, a little croaking voice came from the kitchen: 'Mumma?'

Emily ran to his side and knelt down. His eyes, heavy-lidded, half-closed, were fixed upon her face.

'Mumma, am I goin' to die? I don't want to die.'

'No, darling, Mumma won't let you die. You are going to the hospital where they will make you well.'

'I'm frighten'.'

'I promise you will get better.'

Mr Stewart tiptoed in. 'I will send Joseph home at once.'

'If you would. Just tell him – don't tell him . . .'

He pressed her hand, and left.

*

They sat in the hospital waiting-room until late that night. Emily was breast-feeding the baby still, so she brought her along. She had put Tula and Fiona to bed and asked a neighbour to sit with them till midnight, when Joseph would return. David was in a coma; they would be called if there was a change. She had noticed with half of her mind the surprise on the face of the pretty, pert little nurse when she told her her name. She had arrived before Joseph, and asked the way to the ward: 'I wish to see David Efate. How is he?'

'You mean the little Polynesian boy? I am sorry, he is still on the critical list. Only close relatives can be admitted.'

'But I am his mother. Mrs Efate.'

'Oh!'

Joseph when he arrived had been even more aware of an atmosphere of disapproval. One of these feckless Islanders, they seemed to be thinking, letting their kids wander the streets and pick up poison . . .

They would do everything to save the boy, of course, but really, how could a white woman – and nicely dressed and well-spoken at that – how could she bring herself to marry a black man?

In that shining, spick and span building, everything gleaming with paint and the nurses and sisters and doctors all in starched white among the white-sheeted beds, Joseph felt very conscious of his colour. And little David – how black his hair looked against the pillows, it reminded him of that 'funny' postcard, 'Far From the Madding Crowd', which showed a little Negro boy, just his head and his big eyes visible, in the midst of a huge, white double bed.

Sometime before midnight they were called. Emily, struck by a dreadful premonition, silently handed Joseph the sleeping baby. They followed the nurse along empty corridors, through swing doors. The ward was dimly lit, and round David's bed was a ring of white screens. The Sister in charge came out from her cubicle. She put a hand on Emily's arm. 'I am sorry, Mrs Efate. We did all we could . . .'

Emily walked stonily past. Behind the screens she flung herself on her knees and took David's fine-boned hand in hers, and felt it already growing chill. She stroked his forehead, his crisp, curling hair that seemed to spring with life under her fingers. How could he be dead? Joseph's hand rested silently on her shoulder. She buried her face, her dry, burning eyes, in the bedclothes.

Ages later someone, a nurse, brought her a cup of tea. She stared at it as if she did not know what it was for. Then Joseph put the baby into her arms, and feeling that living warmth she at last began to cry.

*

Joseph dug the small grave in the Presbyterian cemetery. On the day of the funeral it rained and rained. For a week afterwards the rain did not stop, the cemetery was running with water. Emily averted her eyes from Joseph's boots standing in the back porch. She knew where that clay came from.

She began to feel a kind of aversion to Joseph in his role of grave-digger. She could not bear the thought of little David lying in the wet clay, though she knew of course that his spirit was in Heaven with Jesus. It was a long time after David's death before she could bear Joseph to touch her. She felt oddly estranged from him, as if this child she had lost, flesh of her flesh, had nothing to do with him.

He had some of the Polynesian attitude towards death, over-laid by conventional Christianity. The dead were all about the living, though invisible; always present, not waiting in some vague Hereafter. The living could transport themselves at times – as they did in some of the Island dances – into communion with the long line of the immortal dead.

To Emily, daughter of missionaries, brought up to believe in Heaven, David's end was yet cruel and inexplicable. Nothing could console her for the cutting short of that young life.

David had been so bright, so clever, who knew what he might have become? Like the tall cane, that in one day was cut and crushed and dried and then utterly consumed in the mill furnace, he was gone, with all his green promise unfulfilled. 'For man is as the grass, which today is, and tomorrow is cast into the oven . . .'

2 Pamela

Pamela screamed: 'I won't! I won't! I won't!'

'Now then, Miss Pamela,' said the imperturbable English nanny, 'tantrums will get you nowhere. Your ma said you was to go to bed, and not wait up. She's bringing home a gentleman to supper, too late for little girls—'

'I'm NOT a little girl! I'm ten, nearly 'leven, and I will not be put to bed like a baby.'

'I'll tell you what, you can have the light on and read as long as you want. I'll just go and make some hot chocolate while you get undressed, and would you like a bit of shortbread with it?'

So with a mixture of diplomacy and bribery Nanny Turner

got her way. Reading in bed was a great treat which Pamela was not usually allowed, as Helga thought it might make her squint; she had read this theory somewhere. Pamela, full of hot, sweet milk and shortbread, both ruinous to her teeth, soon dozed off over the book as the nurse thought she would. She quietly removed it and turned out the bedside lamp.

In less than an hour Madame would be home from the theatre: radiant, talking nineteen to the dozen, ringing for ice and champagne and throwing off her white fox furs in that casual, impetuous fashion she had. Then she would dismiss the servants and settle down to a tête-à-tête supper with her latest admirer, who was no less than an English duke.

It was not for Nanny Turner to query the morals and behaviour of the rich, the famous and the titled; and Madame Helga was certainly rich and famous, even if she was only a Colonial.

She had taken Pamela along to the opening night to see her mother in *La Traviata* – not very suitable for a child, she thought, with all that living together without benefit of clergy; but the singing was really nice. Pamela had wept when Violetta-Helga lay dying, still singing away most beautifully as if her chest wasn't full of consumption.

Then the Covent Garden theatre went wild. From the front stalls to the slips away up near the roof there were stampings of feet and cries of 'Bravo!' The storm of clapping crashed in waves against the walls as the curtain rose again and again.

And there was Madame Helga bowing and smiling regally, stretching out her hands; then her arms were full of flowers, and more flowers were strewn at her feet. She kissed her hands to the audience and disappeared for the last time behind the curtain.

Pamela had sat with the tears still drying on her cheeks, looking ecstatic. 'Oh, wasn't she beautiful?' she gasped.

Tonight she had wanted to stay up to see the flowers, some of which Mother would bring home though she sent most of them to the hospitals. But Helga had made it clear to the nanny that Miss Pamela was to be in bed and out of the way by eleven.

Helga had got all and more than she had dreamed of in that

small, mouldy house among the sugar-cane. She had furs and diamond tiaras, beautiful beaded gowns and best of all the company of interesting people. She had met Gounod, with whom she conversed in French, and Puccini, who was delighted with the fluency of her Italian, which she had first learned as an 'operatic' language. She knew Paderewski and had sung with Jean de Reszke and Enrico Caruso.

The critics had praised her in extravagant terms: 'A voice of pure crystal ... Madame Helga not so much sang, as opened her lips and let the phrases fall, effortlessly, each one rounded and perfect as a pearl.'

(Madame Helga Davenport was the name she sang under; she was not going to be saddled with such a pedestrian name as 'Johnstone' or 'Lindsay'.)

A first night at Covent Garden Opera House was a social occasion in London, and the place was like a palace in which she was queen. When the lights came up in the first interval, and she looked at the glittering play of electric bulbs on crystal chandeliers and diamond tiaras, the tier on tier of beautifully gowned women and dress-suited men, the gilt and the red velvet and the great circular ceiling under which her voice had so recently soared, she seemed to float like a glass ball on a fountain, sparkling and sustained.

Sometimes as the applause crashed round her and she raised her arms to that vast house of discerning and wealthy people who had come to hear *her* – sometimes she felt quite giddy.

She had to pinch her arm severely to assure herself that this was real, that she, the Colonial daughter of a cane-grower in a small Queensland city, was the person standing here.

It would be no wonder if her head was a little turned; no wonder if she became rather arrogant and demanding, though her dresser adored her. No one else was allowed to use her dressing-room, even when she was away on an engagement in Europe or New York; it was kept for her alone.

Now she found it hard to remember her early struggles in a London which seemed indifferent to her voice at first. With the need to keep up a home for Pamela, and to pay a nursery-maid and a nanny to look after her, she had made heavy inroads on her capital before, after a resounding success as Marguerite in *Faust*, she had become the darling of the opera-loving public. She had been made to sing the Jewel Song three times over before they would let her go. But it was as Violetta and Mimi that she excelled.

She had never gone back to Mackay after getting her first engagement, singing excerpts from opera in Sydney and then Melbourne. Finally Graham had appeared at her flat overlooking the harbour in Sydney, and made a scene.

He had been drinking too much in Mackay. His aristocratic features had coarsened, his face had become red and bloated-looking, and he had developed a violent temper to go with his choleric complexion.

He had found Helga entertaining her accompanist, a lively, amusing man, in her room to afternoon tea. It was an innocent relationship as it happened, but Graham flew into a rage and rampaged through her bedroom, smashing the crystal clock which had been a twenty-first birthday present from her father and the hand-mirror which was among her wedding-presents.

She had told him contemptuously that there was no need to behave like 'a wild beast'. Pamela had cried when she saw him, which added to his fury. The child was growing up a stranger to her own father, he shouted, he would take her away by force if necessary...

'And I shall get a Court Order to restrain you,' said Helga. 'The Court would never agree to such a young child being taken away from her mother. You can come and see her whenever you want. I am not stopping you.'

'Bah!' And with that inarticulate cry Graham had flung out of the room and virtually out of her life. She received reproachful letters from her mother on the subject, and replied to them with what patience she could muster.

All that seemed far away now; she was enclosed in a glittering bubble which encapsulated her from the ordinary worries of life, and tonight she was soaring as well on the remembered fountain of applause.

Besides the praise of the critics and the plaudits of the crowd she had, as well, a real duke at her feet.

He was literally at her feet, for the dear idiot was at this moment kneeling to kiss the hem of her pearl-embroidered gown. Helga rested a hand lightly on his pale, fine, severely brushed hair, which would have curled if he had allowed it to. His yellow whiskers tickled her hand as he grasped and kissed it, still on his knees.

The poor man was besotted, he could not distinguish in his mind between the woman of flesh and the romantic, ideal creature who had sung from the stage – Violetta, the Lady of the Camellias. She was Violetta and Lakmé and Aïda and Marguerite, and the divine Mimi all rolled into one.

She felt for him a love that was part maternal, part gratitude; for with him she had for the first time reached that joyous climax she had never achieved with Graham. Now at last she understood why marriage was so popular, why women went on having babies year after year.

And it had affected her singing – how she had sung these past months! With a soaring richness, a depth of feeling that was quite new.

There had been no one else in all the nine years since she had last lived with Graham as man and wife: for one thing, she had been too busy working at her languages and her singing. She knew that many women envied her the glamorous role of prima donna, but they did not know the sacrifices it had meant. How many would have stood the long, long hours of practice, the denial of outings and pleasures, the lack of a true home and family life, the single-minded pursuit of perfection? All outings and pleasures that would interfere with her work had been excluded. Singing was her life; that and her daughter had filled it until now. She knew it was time Pamela went to boarding-school, but she had put off the day.

'Teddy, will you please get off your knees and pour me a glass of champagne?' she said. 'After all that singing I am parched, and you know I've sent the staff to bed so that we have to wait on ourselves.'

'Yes, I know,' he said tenderly. 'Heavens! How you held me off, all those months. I thought I should go mad, or just go "snap" like an overstretched bowstring' (the champagne cork popped on cue). 'Even now I can't believe that I have you all to myself, my beautiful Violetta.' He poured the champagne.

He circled her still-slender waist with one arm and led her to a sofa. He knew that tight-lacing contributed to it, but she was still a magnificent figure of a woman; and those great dark eyes, all fire and sensibility! They made you forget her formidable nose and chin. But she was a woman of character as well as talent and beauty. If only he wasn't married already!

*

Pamela woke with a start, to find the room in darkness. Nanny had cheated! She had meant to stay awake reading till her mother came home, and Nanny had let her doze off and then sneaked in and put the light out. She got out of bed and tip-toed to the door.

The door was ajar. Nanny was asleep in the next room, her door shut. Then came a sound she knew well – her mother's deep-throated contralto laugh. It was much lower than her singing voice, which was a soprano, clear and pure as a choir-boy's in Westminster Abbey.

Pamela crept past Nanny's door and down the stairs. She knew it was forbidden, she knew her mother was entertaining friends and did not want her. A light showed under her draw-ing-room door. She went down the stairs noiselessly on her bare feet in her little flannelette nightgown, without her robe or slippers, meaning only to look.

She opened the door a crack . . . and froze, while she felt the blood begin to pound in her ears. She pulled the door to and ran back up the stairs, back to her room, jumped into bed and pulled the bedclothes up over her scarlet face. Her eyes were tightly closed, but behind them was printed a picture she would never forget – of Helga half-reclining on the sofa, a glass of champagne tilting dangerously in one outflung hand, with her stiff brocade skirts bunched up around her waist. A man with thin hair and yellow side-whiskers tried to thrust them still higher, while he buried his face somewhere between her knees. And her mother did not object to this indignity but was laughing, more softly now, while her free hand played in his hair.

Pamela pulled the pillow over her head as well so as to shut out any further sounds from below.

*

It was after this episode, which she never mentioned to anyone, that Nanny Turner gave notice. Pamela became unmanageable and it was decided that she should go to boarding-school. She had travelled and lived in hotels a good deal in her young life, so she was not afraid to go. She was already enrolled at one of the best girls' schools in the country.

Then Graham arrived in London; his arrivals were always unexpected and unpleasant. He had heard the gossip about the duke, for Helga and her lover had been scarcely discreet, and he had instituted divorce proceedings. To avoid scandal, he had cited the grounds of desertion only. But he demanded custody of the child.

'If you don't give me Pamela I'll make him co-respondent and drag you both through the courts,' he threatened. 'You're not a fit mother as any court would decide. It's only a matter of time before she'll be legally mine.'

Helga wept and fumed, but he was immovable. He would, he said, take Pamela to Surrey to stay with his relatives, the Lindsays, and then back to Australia, where he had already put her name down at the Sydney Church of England Grammar School.

'She'll be able to spend her holidays with me; I'm in Bundaberg now, not so far north,' he said. 'Your mother and father would like to have her too. She is far too pale and thin, living in European hotels and in London with you—'

'I was about to send her to boarding-school—'

'In Australia she will have sunshine and swimming and riding. She will be much better with me.'

Helga had to give in. She put a brave face on it, but she suddenly felt acutely alone. She had never made women friends easily, and had no confidante of her own sex. She was aware of the gossip and disapproval over which she had shrugged in disdain in her triumphant love; but now the duke was frightened back to his wife, Pamela was gone, Graham estranged, and she had to fall back on her theatre friends for company.

There was no-one to share the luxurious, lonely existence of Madame Helga Davenport. For the first time since she had pricked her thumb in Mackay she broke down and wept with self-pity.

*

Pamela missed her mother at first, but not as much as she would have done five years earlier. She knew she was not the centre of Helga's life. Her father spoiled her, she was excited to be going to Australia, and she enjoyed the visit to the country.

Young Robert Lindsay, five years older than herself and the heir to the baronetcy, was home on holidays. He was just beginning to take a wary interest in girls. He showed her round the grounds and lent her his own pony to ride. When they were leaving he said, 'I say, I'd like to come to Australia when I leave school. Can I come and stay with you, Uncle? I suppose I'll have to come home when I inherit, but I could have a jolly good time in Australia first, hunting kangaroos and emus.'

'Wild pigs and foxes, more like it,' said Graham. 'Both introduced, both pests! Yes, we'd be delighted to have you, Robert.'

'By Jove! Wild pigs, eh? So don't forget, young Pamela. See you in Queensland.'

3 Tula

His brother's death made a great impression on Tula, who was not yet twelve years old. Of course he knew, as Mamma said, that Davey had gone to Heaven to be with Jesus. But it was very strange. One day he was there in the house, walking, talking, eating, laughing, quarrelling. The next he had utterly disappeared. (The minister and his wife had taken the two older children until the funeral was over; they had not seen David in his coffin.)

Tula wandered about the garden musingly, looking at the swing but not wanting to use it; at the tunnel which he and David had begun in a corner of the yard. He stroked the warm, vibrating, purring cat which was still so very much alive, while Davey was dead.

Not that he grieved exactly. They had been playmates yet not close, for they were in different classes at school and had their own friends, white children who had not yet absorbed the colour-consciousness of their parents. But he was more than puzzled and disturbed; he was appalled. It was as though the solid ground had opened before his feet, in a yawning black chasm.

It was there, waiting, and he himself could tumble into it at any moment, or little May; or – dreadful thought! – Mamma might die and leave them motherless, or Papa as well and leave them orphans. If anyone else had to die in the family, he thought it had better be May. He even put that request in his nightly prayers. Fiona was the family favourite, it was unthinkable that she should be taken, he told God.

A few weeks after the funeral the whole family went to visit David's grave, Emily bearing flowers, Joseph fetching water to fill the two glass jars that stood crookedly on the rough heap of clay which was still being allowed to settle before the grave would be made tidy. Emily wanted a simple wooden surround, like the bars of a cot, and a headstone shaped like a pillow – a sick fancy, Joseph thought.

While Emily wept silently, the baby May who was nearly eighteen months old but late in walking, sat tranquilly on her father's hip and smiled at the flowers.

Fiona ran among the graves, scarcely comprehending why they were visiting the cemetery. Joseph had sometimes minded her while he was at work, and she was used to playing among the marble scrolls and angels, the stone slabs and iron railings.

Tula stood silently by his brother's grave, staring at the raw clay and trying to squeeze out a few tears. What if he could not cry! What would they think of him? He felt anxious and self-conscious and somewhat sick. From somewhere a sweetish hateful smell was borne on the air, he had never smelt it before but he knew at once what it was. Suddenly he was crying, not with sorrow but with horror and revulsion. He hated that place! With its long, rank green grass, growing profusely after the rain; its rusty, fading chrysanthemums in empty jam-tins or smeared glass jars, its old graves in the far corner starting to subside beneath their blackened, tilting tombstones.

He never, never wanted to be buried in the earth. He would like to be a sailor and be buried in the clean blue sea.

Tula was infinitely relieved when Emily got up from her knees, took the baby back from Joseph and they made their way out along the overgrown pathways.

'I'll have to get the scythe out again,' said Joseph. 'The grass grows that quick, this time of the year. It's not long since I finished this section.'

'Yes . . .' said Emily vaguely. She was withdrawn, brooding, her face thin and hollow-cheeked under its smooth fair hair.

They came out on to the road and turned towards home. Tula took Fiona's hand as they crossed the street, though there was not much Sunday traffic, just one or two smart gigs out for an afternoon drive.

On the corner of the street they saw a half-grown pup chasing a cat. He was barking valiantly but not getting too close. Suddenly the cat stopped, turned, and crouched with ears back and tail fluffed out. The pup braked quickly, skidding to an abrupt stop, then made off in the opposite direction, barking vaguely.

Tula laughed aloud. Then he covered his mouth and stole a guilty look at his parents. Joseph was smiling at the pup's antics. Mumma's face was stony. Tula slipped a hand into hers contritely, and she gave it an absent-minded squeeze. I might as well not be here, he thought bitterly. I might as well be dead like Davey. Then at least she would cry for me.

*

On the first anniversary of David's death it was pouring with rain. When Tula said he would rather stop home, though Emily gave him a reproachful look she did not insist.

'Perhaps May had better not come either,' she said. 'She has a little bit of a cold. Will you mind her for me, Tula?'

Emily was terrified of the slightest symptoms of sickness in her other children. She understood at last her mother's feelings, having to leave those little graves behind in that heathen land.

'Do you know you have two uncles buried on Lifu, away out in the Pacific, where Papa came from?' she asked. 'That is one of the Loyalty Islands, you can look it up in the atlas.'

'How old were they?' asked Tula gloomily.

'Oh, just little tiny boys – one an infant, one about as big as May.'

Tula wondered how little infants who couldn't walk would get on in Heaven – would they be big enough to fly? He had seen pictures of cherubs, but they were fat, well-grown babies or small children, complete with wings. If God decided to take May she would become a cherub like the ones holding up the cloud below the Virgin Mary in Mumma's print of the Assumption.

Most cherubs (and this was puzzling) didn't seem to have any bottom ends, they were just wings and shoulders and heads. Tula, maturing early and with his curiosity stimulated by boys' talk at school, would have been interested to study the difference between boy cherubs and girl cherubs, had any been visible. He had watched while May's napkins were changed when she was little, and had been fascinated by that secret fold of flesh, so different from his own growing tassel.

When the others had gone out, Papa carrying Fiona on his shoulders, Mumma with her usual bunch of flowers from the garden, he and May lay on the floor looking at a map of the Pacific in the atlas that had belonged to the Reverend Andrew Duguid.

'Here you are – the Loyalty Islands,' said Tula importantly, shoving her curly head out of the way. 'That's where Papa came from when he was a boy. I'm going back there when I grow up,' he said, deciding at that moment. He stared at the little dots in the expanse of blue.

'Where Tula goin'?' asked May vaguely.

'I'm goin' in a ship, over the sea. I'll get a job as a sailor.' He measured with his fingers. 'I wonder how far it is?'

' 'Leven miles,' said May, who had just learned to count past ten.

He climbed on a chair and got down the two heavy volumes of the 1874 *Imperial Gazetteer of the World,* which also had belonged to Grandfather Duguid. He loved the smell of the thin paper, and the swirling coloured patterns inside the covers.

'L . . . Lima . . . Loyalties. Here it is: "Island of Lifu . . . The largest and most northern of the Loyalty Islands. S. Pacific, Lat. 20.27 s." (what does that mean?), "37 miles long, 10 to 20 miles broad. Of coral formation, and the highest point is 250 ft. Level on top and thickly wooded, including the breadfruit and the sandalwood tree . . . The only good ground is in low lands near the shore, where the villages are. The greater portion of the interior is destitute of soil." What's des-ti-toot mean, I wonder? – prob'ly "deep". "The natives are—" Oh!'

'Go on, Tula. Wead!'

᠎ "The – the natives are treacherous, cruel and cowardly, and have a history of eating human flesh. Pop. 3,000 to 5,000. Discovered by Captain Cook . . ." Well!'

He sat staring at the black print, aghast. How could they say such things about his father's people? He had always been taught to be proud of his Island blood. The Pacific Islanders were handsome, brave, musical, happy-natured. The word 'cannibal' had never been mentioned. And here it was printed in a book, that they were cruel, cowardly cannibals! His father's people!

Tula banged the big book together, catching May's dimpled hand and wrist as she was pointing to a wood-engraving of palms and beach. She cried, partly with anger.

'Never mind, kid . . . Pipe down, will you? Look, I'm goin' to get my boat and you can float it. Wait there while Tula gets it.'

He fetched the shallow enamel basin from the back porch, poured some water into it, and gave her the model boat with its sail made out of a scrap of straw matting. He had carved it with care from a piece of soft wood. But she wouldn't play sensibly; she splashed the water, tipped the boat over, and leant with both arms in the basin, getting her dress wet through.

'You silly idjit, May!' She smiled at him enchantingly. Tula took the basin away and mopped up the floor. Then he brought a clean dress, pulled the wet one over her head and put the clean one on her. Luckily she had not sat in the puddle. He felt her little drawers – they were dry.

225

It was then that temptation overcame him. He knew all about temptation from Sunday School. The Devil was just waiting for you, lining up mischief for idle hands.

He handed May the damp boat to play with, and said: 'Listen, I just want to put my hand inside your drawers a minute – just to feel if you're dry. I won't hurt you.' His voice was husky.

She made no objection, and continued to play with the sail while, with one hand, he explored that mysterious region hidden in the soft folds he had seen before. He was filled with a mixture of guilt and excitement. Occasionally she looked up inquiringly into his face, then went back to the boat. Suddenly she began to cry.

Guilt overcame excitement. He snatched his hand away.

'What's the matter? Shut up, can't you? I didn't hurt you, stupid. Shut UP!'

He began to panic. 'Listen, it's stopped raining, would you like a swing? It's dry under the carob-tree, anyway. Come on, I'll push you. Only stop crying! If you tell Mumma I'll – I'll beat you.'

Since Fiona and May were always asking for a swing, and since he could rarely be bothered pushing them, May soon stopped crying. He carried her out to the wooden seat slung from two ropes under the tree.

When the others came home soon afterwards he sweated with fear in case she said anything; and that night he prayed feverishly:

'Matthew, Mark, Luke and John,
Bless the bed that I lie on,
If I should die before I wake—'

Oh no, if he died tonight he would go straight to Hell, for sure! He substituted 'Forgive us our trespasses, as we forgive them that trespass against us.' He knew he had trespassed, and that he'd get into a terrible row if ever his parents found out. It was a long time before he felt safe, before he was sure that May had completely forgotten the incident.

4 Kanaka go home

In 1893 the Mary River came down in a great flood which swept away the bridge to Tinana. A lot of good cane-land flowed away out to sea as mud. Whole farmhouses came floating down the river, some with live hens on the roof; and dead cattle and drowned pigs drifted by with numerous wooden outhouses which had provided the local sanitation.

It was the worst flood in the town's history. It seemed to symbolize the flood of disasters which had begun with the run on the banks and restrictions of credit and the end of the land boom, and culminated in the shearers' strikes and general unrest of 1894. The cane-cutters, being mostly Kanakas, did not go on strike, and this made them even more unpopular with that mythical being, 'the Australian worker'.

'Chows, Kanakas and coolies' were lumped together as 'scabs' and bosses' men; it was not their colour, but their ability and willingness to live on a starvation wage without complaint, that riled the native-born Australians. To prove the point, they were equally hostile to the Italian indentured workers on the Burdekin, hounding them from the moment they arrived from northern Italy, late in 1891.

For after the *Hopeful* scandal, Premier Griffith had made it clear that it was only a matter of time before all Kanakas would be barred; and the riot at Mackay racecourse had clinched the matter. 1890 had been given as the death-knock, and recruiting actually ceased for a time in 1891–2; but after yet another Royal Commission a respite was given the growers.

The flood had been succeeded by a disastrous drought; it seemed that there was no moderation in Queensland, it was either drought or flood, bushfire or frost, and 'the poor bloody farmer always copped it', one way or the other. Sugar prices had fallen, production was down, and the shipping industry too was feeling the resultant depression.

So recruiting was resumed; the Extension Act was brought in, giving another reprieve. But with the new Commonwealth Government of 1901, one of the first Federal Acts passed was to the effect that 'No Pacific Islander shall enter Australia after March 31st, 1904'. No Queensland Government could have brought in such a law and survived.

The Minister for Labour was authorized to deport back to the Islands every Kanaka remaining in Queensland by the end of 1906. 'White Australia' had triumphed, and the Sydney *Bulletin* could stop raving about 'Chows, Japs, niggers, Kanakas, Ghans, coolies and Tommy Tannas' who took jobs away from Australian working men.

Everyone was happy except the shipowners (and the canny Burns & Philp soon put in for the contract for taking home again many of the Islanders their own captains had kidnapped in the past), the growers, and the Kanakas themselves.

Many of the less literate Islanders who had established themselves over the years in the coastal towns of Queensland and northern New South Wales, were frightened. Would they be turned out of their homes, made to go back to islands they had almost forgotten, where they were no longer remembered, and where they had no ties? They were used to European-style food by now, and the things that could be bought in shops: smart clothes, shoes, ice-cream, fizzy drinks, furniture; some of them even had pianos and phonographs.

But the new Federal Government, though resolved on 'Australia for the white man' (ignoring the unfortunate original inhabitants who happened to be dark), was not entirely heartless. Once more a Royal Commission was set up, to find out which Islanders should be exempt from deportation, and why. They interviewed Tombua's family at Yeppoon, now grown up, and the Efate family in Maryborough; spoke to hundreds of Islanders from Townsville to the border. Apart from the aged and infirm who should not be sent back, the Commissioners found that there were many individuals who had lived in Queensland for so long that they would find themselves complete strangers if they returned; and that 'others have fled from their Island homes to escape vendettas or punishments, and the deportation of such individuals to their own "passages" would be, in effect, their death warrant.'

So to the relief of many families who now regarded themselves as Australians, a man could claim exemption under the Act, under several conditions.

Under nearly all of these Joseph Efate was safe. He had been in Australia now for nearly thirty years. He had married a white Australian. He was also registered as the owner of a piece of freehold land, for he had bought a block at Piabla, on the coast opposite Fraser Island, with a sheltered beach and good fishing, where he hoped to retire on his church pension at sixty.

Apart from all this, he found that he and many of his friends were exempt because they came from the Loyalty Islands, so that they were technically French citizens and did not come under the definition of 'Pacific Islander' in the Act.

Sir Edmund Barton, Australia's first Federal prime minister, opined in Parliament that the new Act would be 'a handsome New Year's gift for a new nation'. But to the Islanders who were no longer wanted, it was a bitter pill indeed. They had helped to clear, to plant, to establish, to harvest; and now the annual crop of sugar-cane was worth more than a million pounds in export. They felt a strong sense of injustice.

'White men e say go along Queenslan',' they told each other in the pidgin English that was the lingua franca between one Island group and another. 'E say plenty good place, take Islander away from place belong 'im. Now bime-by e say "Orright, altogether coloured man, you clear out. This feller country im bilong white man." '

One of the more literate got on an empty soap-box in Bundaberg and began shouting, attracting a crowd.

'You-feller look all-about,' he cried. 'See plenty cane-field, plenty sugar-mill, big-feller planters making plenty money, and Island man do all t' work.' In his emotion he began to weep, as words and tears poured out in a torrent: 'White man no more want black man, use him up altogether, chase-im out, send-im back no money, go back poor to own Island where people belong-im all finish.' And in a final gesture of contempt he tossed away a handful of pennies, and pushed his way through the crowd.

'Him speak true,' they muttered among themselves. 'They no want us no-more. We just rubbish.'

5 Angus Johnstone

Helga came back in triumph to Australia, in the year when the Islanders who had made her father's wealth were being deported to their various Islands. She was the Queen of Song; thousands turned out in the streets of Sydney, Melbourne and Brisbane to welcome her as if she had been royalty. By then she was used to adulation and regarded it as her due. She waved regally from her open carriage ...

It was many years since she had been back, though she had made one trip to see her daughter. Then, as soon as she left school, Pamela had come to England to live with her mother. Graham did not survive long after; he died before his uncle, the baronet, killed instantly in a fall in an amateur steeplechase, dying with his boots on as Helga would have expected him to. Pamela was distressed at the news, but to Helga it was remote, as though this stranger who had died on the other side of the world had been her husband in another life. The girl who had married him had died long ago, she thought.

She had been disappointed to find that Pamela, who had a fair, English beauty derived from Graham's side of the family, did not have a note of music in her. Like her father before her, she preferred horses and the outdoors.

After coming to England to live she had spent several holidays with her Lindsay cousins, and her friendship with young Robert (who was also mad about horses) had grown with each visit. The future baronet had asked her to marry him, and one day she would be Lady Lindsay.

Angus Johnstone had been to Europe to see his famous daughter and hear her sing. Though he couldn't see why the critics made such a fuss about her wonderful voice, he was proud of her; and there was no doubt she had the hearts of the crowd. To Helga the applause, the living audience, was an essential stimulant, a drug she could not forgo. When she took her bow, and the thunderous applause rose to the arched roof of the great proscenium with its carved nymphs and gilded scrolls, she seemed to float somewhere above the stage, buoyed on those rolling waves of sound.

All the same, she valued praise from her dour Scots father, and tried to extract it from him; she should have known better. 'Did you like me as Gilda?' she asked him after a successful performance of *Rigoletto* at Covent Garden (when she had sung '*Caro Nome*' three times before they would let the opera go on).

'I didna like your dress,' he said. 'It was too low in frront.'

Angus was now nearly ninety, but still seeming as well and active as ever, though to her he looked terribly frail. She had become more solid and robust, and her face, as he had predicted, was deeply grooved by the two Davenport lines on either side of her mouth. Julia Johnstone was no more. That strong-minded, domineering woman had been conquered by illness and died last year at seventy-six. She had been nursed by young May Efate, just seventeen years old and beginning her training. (She had had to overcome the prejudices of the matron, who did not mind coloured girls as ward-maids but was convinced they would never make nurses.)

When Helga came home she stayed for two days at Chindera, in James's old room. A drift of rose-scent came in the window from the bower, now rather over-grown and ragged. James had recently married Jean Grant, who had been left a widow when her husband was drowned on a fishing expedition to Fraser Island. The boys were now grown up, so James had moved to her house in the town (which had officially become a city in 1905). Helga met Jean and liked her; she was glad poor old James had found happiness at last, though presumably it was too late for them to have any children.

Helga decided to look for a place overlooking Sydney Harbour, so that she would always have a home in Australia to come back to. She sensed that Chindera's days were numbered.

Angus continued to keep the financial affairs of the Chindera holdings in his own hands, much to Dougal's fury, and no changes could be made without his consent.

'Of course this place is an anachronism,' Dougal said to her as they walked on the terrace on her first morning at home. 'It's

231

ridiculous to have all this good cane-land tied up in drives and gardens and shrubberies, and this great house. The new planters grow cane right up to their doors. It's a wicked waste of land. I estimate that with the present price of sugar and an average of fifteen tons to the acre, the garden here costs us more than a thousand pounds a year, and the Old Man won't hear of cutting up even an acre.'

'H'm,' said Helga. She was always alive to the value of money, and yet ... Chindera was beautiful, an island of gracious calm in the midst of what was becoming a busy industrial city. She inhaled deeply the scent of the frangipani, dropping creamy blossoms on each side of the front steps, to lie like spiral stars on the grass. On each side of the steps was a carved stone lion. The lawns sloped down to the river, and up to the little Roman 'temple of meditation' where Angus still liked to sit and survey his domain.

'And it's getting harder and harder to keep a gardener,' grumbled Dougal. 'There are no Kanakas to be had, and wages are becoming scandalously high; while white servants demand ten shillings a week and their keep.'

She looked sideways at Dougal. He had changed too, grown rather fat and pompous, though there was not a thread of grey in the light gingery hair which went so oddly with his red complexion. His eyes were still that hard, bright blue. She wondered fleetingly if Graham had ever turned grey; she could not imagine it.

Pamela was in England, staying with the Lindsays in Surrey, and engaged to young Robert Lindsay her cousin. She would soon be Lady Lindsay, for the old baronet was gouty and apoplectic and not likely to last long. They were awaiting Helga's return for the wedding.

Angus had put up a memorial stained-glass window to his wife in the local Presbyterian church, where Joseph was still the verger. The old man missed Julia badly, even Helga with her shrewd searching glance at how he had aged did not guess how much.

'Sing tae us, lassie,' said Angus as they sat in the drawing-room after dinner on Helga's first night at home.

'What shall I sing?'

'Ma favourite, o' coorse – "Annie Laurie".'

So the voice which could command three thousand pounds for a single performance, which had charmed kings and commoners all over the world, soared out over the garden, the darkening rows of sugar-cane, as effortlessly and almost as purely as if Helga were not fifty-one years old:

> 'Maxwellton braes are bonny
> Where early fa's the dew,
> And t'was there that Annie Laurie
> Gi'ed me her promise true . . .
> And for bonnie Annie Laurie
> I'd lay me doon and dee . . .'

As the last notes died away, Helga looked round with her hands still on the piano keys, and surprised tears in her father's eyes.

'I sang that song to your mither when we were coortin',' he said. 'Aye, I hadna a bad voice in those days, my gel; it's whaur ye get it, nae doot.'

Helga doubted this; but she felt a pang, a shock of envy almost. She had scarcely thought of her parents as people who had once been young and in love. They had always seemed old to her. Yet they had been friends and lovers for nearly sixty years. How would it have been if she and Teddy had married? She'd had no ambition for the title, and soon had been created a Dame of the British Empire by King Edward, which was better than being a duchess by marriage; it was her own title.

But the basic loneliness of her self-sufficient existence struck her as never before.

'Oh, that was *beautiful*, Helga!' gushed Dougal's wife Helen, who was the daughter of a wealthy Maryborough storekeeper and to whom Helga had taken an unreasoning dislike ever since she had moved into Helga's old room. 'To think that you have sung in the great opera houses of the world! You have a *marvellous* voice still.'

Helga's black brows drew together, and the lines deepened

beside her mouth. She could have forgiven the fulsome praise, which was not necessary; she knew she had sung beautifully. She could have forgiven the intrustion of this stranger, as she thought of Helen, into a moment of family intimacy. But that 'still' implied she was getting old.

She crashed down the piano lid. 'That's enough from you, upstart,' she said coldly, and walked out of the room. Helen burst into tears, was comforted by Dougal. Helga went to her upstairs room, where she had a decanter of whisky, and drank moodily by herself.

Helga did not stay long, for she had commitments to sing in all the main capital cities; and now her mother was dead and another woman was running the Chindera house, she did not feel at home there. She enjoyed the company of her lively nieces, Julia and Elizabeth; but she felt tempted to tell their mother that Dougal had another child somewhere in Queensland, a part-Kanaka brat; for she felt he had fathered Estelle's baby. But she held her peace.

Her tour of Australia was both a personal and a financial success. Part of her feeling of triumph came from returning to Maryborough, to the place where her singing had been regarded only as a drawing-room accomplishment, like sketching in water-colours or tatting. 'That Miss Johnstone who sings rather well' had become world-famous as Dame Helga Davenport, the reigning queen of the Covent Garden Opera, and could command thousands of pounds for a single performance.

She returned for the English season, enjoying every moment of the sea-voyage, queening it in the dining saloon where special flowers stood on her table and the chief steward looked after her personally. But a letter was waiting on her return, black-bordered, written by her brother James: Angus Johnstone was dead. She wept when she read it. There was nothing at Chindera now to bring her back. That part of her life was closed.

Instead she looked to the future. She still had years of singing left, she hoped, and soon her first grandchild would be born. She hoped he might be musical, perhaps a singer like herself. She felt sure it would be a boy.

*

Angus had suddenly begun to feel his age after Helga left. He cut out his morning visit to the mill (much to the relief of James and Dougal) yet he still rose at seven o'clock every morning, resolutely refusing to stay in bed for breakfast.

One morning when the others had gone to the mill he decided to walk up to his eyrie and sit there for a while in the sun.

He took it slowly, leaning heavily on the stick he had used in the last few months. A pair of butcher-birds sang from the topmost twigs of the jacaranda, now covered in feathery leaves. Their clear notes, flute-like and pure, reminded him of Helga's singing.

He felt a bit short of breath and rather giddy when he reached the top of the path. He sat down abruptly on the sun-warm stone of the circular bench. There was an annoying ringing in his ears. Below, the lovely bend of the river reflected the morning sky in a purer, colder blue, dotted with puffs of white cloud. That meant a sou'easterly later, cool from the sea.

Beyond the confines of the park-like garden he saw the canefields stretching to the horizon, green and yellow and deep red-brown in the rattoon-crop paddocks, where the setts were just beginning to sprout with their new second growth.

The crushing season was underway. Smoke and steam from the mill chimney boiled up into the air and floated away, staining the watercolour blue of the sky, showering smuts and shreds of bagasse.

He was full of years, and content. His daughter, his favourite child, was now famous, and wealthy in her own right; and would come into more at his death. He had tied up his property as much as he could, for 'a life in being and twenty years after', so that the bulk of it remained in trust for his grandchildren.

The others could have the income from the estate while they lived, but they couldn't spend and disperse the capital, or sell the land.

'What I ha'e I hauld,' he muttered. His one regret was that as yet he had no grandson to carry on the family name. Pity Helga hadn't gone back to her maiden name ... James's wife, Mrs Jean Grant that was – a Scotswoman, so Angus approved – was too old by now to have any children; while Dougal's wife seemed to throw nothing but girls.

He looked back at the big white house with its green shutters and balconies and balustrades of Italian marble, its carved lions and massive front door of cedar. Dougal said that Chindera and its grounds were a waste of good caneland. It was all a matter of values. To him the house, the well-kept grounds, were the visible signs of success. What use was money if you had nothing to show for it?

The sun, in the clear air of winter, was too hot; he should have brought a hat. And there was that damned buzzing in his ears. Perhaps he had better go back to the house and lie down a wee while till he felt better.

He got laboriously up from the bench and took a few steps. Then the green mosaic of cane-fields and fallow seemed to tilt, to stand on end. He pitched forward on the path, insensible.

It was some time before he was missed; one of the maids looking for him with a tray of morning tea realized he was not in the house and went searching.

She found him lying on the path and called for help. He was carried inside and put to bed. He was still deeply unconscious when the doctor arrived, and James and Dougal were told that their father had had a massive cerebral haemorrhage. If he lived he would be paralysed and speechless.

Helen cried decorously into her handkerchief as she hovered in the bedroom. James could not help thinking that the old man, if he could hear her and speak, would have said 'Stop snivelling, gel, ha'e ye a cauld in your heid?'

He did not recover consciousness but died the following night, in the double bed where Julia had slept beside him. The last thing he had seen had been his broad property lying under the sun, while the butcher-birds sang their praises of the coming summer.

3 A tale that is told

1 May

Lady Lindsay, Pamela, as grand-daughter of a pioneer sugar planter and also a titled visitor from overseas, was being made much of in the city of Maryborough, after a tour of Childers and Bundaberg. She had been conducted over the Isis Mill and the great Millaquin Refinery, the largest in the southern hemisphere and the only factory making white sugar outside the capital cities. At Fairymead she had been asked to declare open a new section of the raw-sugar mill.

'. . . And I declare this great new complex open; may it function for many years to come!'

Lady Lindsay, holding her elegant white hat against the wind with a white-gloved hand, with the other cut the ribbon using the pair of gold scissors provided.

A group of cane-cutters gathered in the background cheered ironically. They didn't go much on titled visitors, even when they were Australian born and bred, and this one had a Pommy accent you could cut with a cane-knife: 'Ai declare . . .'

'They ought to give us a free beer, don't you reckon, George?' yelled one of them.

Pamela looked over at the group of brown-faced, tough-looking men. Most of them were Europeans, though about one in ten were Kanakas or part-Islander like George. He had the tight, short curls of the Islander but they were red, or auburn. He was a tall, striking-looking man, no darker than the sun-browned Australians beside him. 'Ar, they're too mean,' he called back.

Pamela glanced at him casually, then her eyes went back to the dignitaries on the raised platform with her.

The Mayor of Bundaberg was insisting that she should keep the scissors and a scrap of the ribbon as a memento of the occasion.

She, with her fine-spun golden hair, her delicate pink-and-white complexion, her grey eyes, might well have been English. She could be taken as an example of the First White, the fine-grained even-textured perfect white sugar which was the final product of the refining process.

A small girl, definitely Dark Brown, with shy, liquid dark eyes and a cap of tightly-curling black hair, was handing her a posy of carnations and roses. She bent to take it with a charming smile, but the little girl, too overcome to smile back, merely put one finger in her mouth and stared.

Pamela Lindsay was led away to a chicken-and-champagne luncheon, while the men went back to work. She was quite unconscious of the fact that the tall man with the reddish curls was her first cousin, son of Dougal Johnstone and the laundry-maid Estelle, and Angus Johnstone's only grandson.

*

George Tombua had met May Efate when he was cane-cutting in Maryborough. He had taken her to a local dance and a concert, and had sent her three post-cards since he came to Bundaberg. They were going to be married. It was on their second outing that he had 'put the hard word on her', and she had come across after a good deal of persuading. Afterwards, 'That was beaut,' he said simply but sincerely, kissing her gratefully. But May began to weep.

'Come now, it wasn't that bad,' said George.

She told him that she had been a virgin until tonight (he was aware of that already), and that she had always been frightened of men and terrified that she would have an illegitimate baby.

'Look what you've been missing,' said George, refusing to be serious. 'It doesn't matter, honey, I still love you. So stop crying, eh?'

She kissed the hard muscles of his arm. 'Dear George.'

'I suppose your old man'd half kill me if he found me here with you.'

'Yes, I expect he would. He's very strong for his age. But he never belted us as kids. Mumma was much more strict. She was very strict with Fiona and me over boys. You see her parents were Scottish, and they were missionaries on the island where my father was born; he met my mother there when she was a little girl. He was brought here by a blackbirder when he was only fifteen, and he's been here ever since. I remember my brother Tula showing me the Loyalty Islands on a map ... A big page of blue, and these three tiny dots ...'

Her voice trailed away. She had remembered something else. She became rigid with remembering. A dark brown hand beneath her little white knickers, fingering, exploring. She hadn't minded at first, and then it had hurt, and she had cried.

Was that perhaps why she kept knocking back coloured boys when they started to get fresh? Other girls didn't seem to mind. She liked George, she realized, because he was so light-coloured, so different from her father and brother, with his auburn curls and his pale, well-shaped hands, though the backs were scarred and sun-browned from working in the cane.

'Well, you're a half-and-half too,' he was saying. He lay on his back and looked up at the stars. 'But at least you know who your real father is, which puts you one up on me.'

'Yes. You know my father's verger at the Presbyterian church.'

'I'm not much of a church-goer, I'm afraid. I like to relax on Sunday with a few beers after a week's hard yakka in the cane.'

'I'm sick of church. We were taken every Sunday morning and evening, and Sunday School in between ... But George! What if I have a baby? I couldn't face Mumma. She worries about us so.'

He said lightly, 'P'raps we'd better get married and make it all legal. What do y'reckon?'

She sat up and stared at him in the starlight. 'Oh, George! George, dearest—'

'All right, don't smother me. You must have had lots of men after you, a good-looker like yourself. What about those young doctors at the hospital?'

'Yes, but – because I'm half-and-half they expect me to be easy, and when I'm not they get annoyed and don't ask me out again. I suppose you've had lots of girls.'

He laughed self-consciously. 'Aw, I dunno about lots. I've been around. But now I'd like to settle down a bit, have a family, p'raps get a small place of me own.'

He was saving steadily for his own farm, he told her. Now that white labour had taken over in the cane-fields, the old Kanaka rates of pay were no more. In spite of all the breast-beating by the big planters, the sugar industry had survived and was thriving; though some of the bigger plantations were being cut up into smaller holdings. They did not employ year-round labour as in the old days, but took on gangs of itinerant cutters who travelled up and down the coast, much as shearers followed the wool in the outback.

May was surprised at the amount George had saved when he told her. 'You don't spend much while the season's on,' he said. 'You're too tired at night to go on the binge, though some fellows blow the lot at the end of the season on a trip to Sydney, livin' it up with sheilas.'

He was sure he could get a cane-farm of his own; these days you didn't need a big acreage, you didn't need a crusher; you just took the load of cut cane to the nearest mill and they paid you on the c.c.s.

'What's the c.c.s.?'

'The recoverable sugar content. It's highest in a dry winter and spring, before the summer rains, because there's less water in the sap. I've read it all up in a book I borrowed from the Mechanics' Institute. Fascinating stuff, sugar. Though I've cursed it often enough in me time, all covered in sweat and black from the burnt cane, and sweltering between the rows.'

'It must be worse up north, around Tully and Mossman.'

'Yair; terrible. My people are at Keppel Bay, near Yeppoon, out from Rocky. There's a bit of sugar grown there, but you have to worry about dry years. It's not nearly as steamy and wet as further north, but warmer than Maryborough in winter. Anyways, one day I suppose they'll have machines to do all the cane-cutting, like they have harvesters for wheat.'

'I don't see how a machine—'

'It'll come, don't you worry. Then the poor bloody cane-cutters will be out of a job. That's why I want to get on the production end. You can't go wrong; the stuff grows itself.'

2 Fiona

George took his friend Chukka Brown along for moral support when he went to meet May's parents. He was a bit scared of her mother, a missionary's daughter and strict, according to May; though she must have been an unusual type of girl to marry a full-blood Pacific Islander, an indented labourer.

Not 'Kanaka'; that was a term of white-man contempt. It meant literally 'man' just as in Africa all natives were called 'boy'. In the old days it had meant less than that. Kanakas then were a commodity to be bought and sold, shipped here and there like copra or sandalwood. And not just 'Islander' because there were plenty of Australian Aborigines who were from one of the islands on the Queensland coast, like Fraser or Palm or Thursday.

No, May's and Fiona's father was a Pacific Islander, like George's mother and the man he called father until he grew up and realized that he was different. Tombua, to his credit, had never shown any difference in his treatment of George and the other boys in the family.

It was funny about Chukka Brown's name, George thought, because while Islanders were naturally brown, Chukka was in fact 'white', though his face and torso were brown from working in the Queensland sun. He liked to work in nothing but a pair of trousers and boots, and his chest, back and arms were in fact darker than George's. George, with his red hair, was inclined to sunburn and always kept his shirt on when working.

Emily gave them tea in fine china cups that had belonged to her mother. They sat on the edges of their chairs, drinking it awkwardly; they were more used to an enamel mug and a billy of tea in the open. The old clock that Andrew Duguid had brought from Scotland in 1853 ticked away quietly on the mantelpiece. Beside it, behind a magnifying glass and frame, was a picture of David Efate taken not long before he died. On the other side was a large, pink-lined shell, and beyond it a paper nautilus.

'That was our youngest son,' said Emily, noticing George

looking at the picture. 'He died when he was only eight, did May tell you? Our other son, Tula, decided to go back to the Islands. He writes that things are very disturbed on some of the smaller islands. There are too many firearms and not enough jobs. Some of the returns are recruiting straight away for Fiji.'

'I reckon it's pretty crook, just packing them off to their home islands like that,' said Chukka warmly. 'Chucked out like a worn-out tool. As long as they were useful, clearing new land, establishing the cane-growing industry, that was fine. Now it's "Out! We don't need you any more." '

(He had got his nick-name from his fondness for the word 'chuck', which he used in any context: to chuck out, to chuck up (get sick), to chuck it (i.e. give the game away, give up), to chuck a sixer (throw a fit), to chuck in when a round of drinks was being bought, and to chuck a rock at someone.)

Fiona, silently passing her mother's home-baked shortbread, looked at him with interest. She liked his rugged, bony, weather-beaten face, his sun-bleached hair as straight and light as straw. It was so different from her own, which she tried in vain to smooth down with oil and water.

'It was a rotten thing to do,' she agreed. 'An insult to my people.'

He looked a little amused at that. 'Your people? But the people responsible for the White Australia policy are your people too.' Was she trying to deny that side of her being, he wondered? Yet she was very fair, lighter than her sister, with a smooth magnolia complexion and large dark eyes 'like pools in a paperbark swamp', thought Chukka, who wasn't given to poetic comparisons as a rule.

'I know. But the others need me. I've joined the Aborigines' and Islanders' Advancement Association. My sister-in-law is Aboriginal you know,' she added defiantly. She felt him appraising her, and looked back warily. She had learned to distrust white men, especially cane-cutters. They were here today, gone tomorrow, and always out for a good time. She thought that one of them who had come back regularly for two years was going to marry her; but he shot through. In an emotional over-reaction she had taken up the coloured side of her inheritance. She was working at the Church mission (still called Mission to the Kanakas) and visiting poor families in their homes. When they had to leave under the Deportation Act she helped them pack up their belongings in their pathetic boxes and imitation cedar-wood trunks.

Some had tried to avoid being deported, when the police would come and take them in chains to the ship. Others dressed as for a long-awaited cruise, their children beautifully turned out: little girls in frilled muslin and flower-trimmed straw hats, little boys in sailor suits and white socks.

All these children had been born in Queensland, had gone to school there and yet they were not allowed to claim Australia as their home. For they were not white, or even yellow, but dark brown and therefore unacceptable: 'a black spot, a contamination of our race', as one speaker had thundered in the Commonwealth Parliament debates on 'the Kanaka Question'.

And among those to go on board one of the returning vessels had been her brother Tula: armed with exercise books, writing materials, hymn books and Bibles, he was going back to his father's island to become a missionary and teacher of Sunday School.

He did not need to go, for his parents both were technically Australians and he was married to an Australian Aborigine; but Tula, who did not appear to take after Emily's side of the family in appearance, had inherited some of the missionary fervour of his grandfather.

His wife Maud had cried openly, her big bosom heaving, as she saw him standing on the deck of the *Sydney Belle* dressed in a white drill suit, a sun helmet and canvas lace-up boots. But Tula's face was shining with purpose, for he regarded himself as divinely called to this work. Fiona thought he was crazy, but she felt proud of him all the same: a fine-looking Island man, big and dark and solid.

Fiona had comforted Maud as best she could – a big woman in every way, generous, outsized and energetic, left with her two sturdy, dark brown, curly-haired boys, Billy and David. She had become interested in trying to bestir the local Aborigines, long sunk in apathy, to stand up for their rights, and had enlisted Fiona in the Aborigines' and Islanders' Association of Queensland.

She was known to everyone as 'Aunty Maud', and she had relatives everywhere; she had been born on Fraser Island just off the coast. She had refused to go to Lifu with Tula. 'That not my-country,' she insisted. From Hervey Bay near Maryborough she could look across the sheltered waters to 'her' island, and sometimes went fishing over there with her two boys for tailor and flathead. She must go and see Maud next weekend, Fiona was thinking . . .

*

'—I can't see no sense in slavin' your eyeballs out for a boss,' George was saying to her father. 'Better to get your own place and work for yourself.'

'Yair, I'm goin' to chuck it in, cane-cutting's a mug's game,' Chukka chimed in. 'You can save money in a year, but then most blokes go and blow the lot down in Brissie or Sydney, in one big bender . . . Eh, chuck us the sugar will you, George? Use the local product, it supports you.'

(The sugar was pale brown, which Emily preferred, having been brought up on it because it was cheaper.)

Joseph in his quiet way was studying the two men. He smiled – his big, strong teeth as white as ever in his brown face – and said, 'You don't know how lucky you young fellers are. D'you know what we worked for in the old days? Six quid a year and our keep.'

'Yair, Kanaka rates,' said Chukka, and then looked uncomfortable. 'Oh, the pay's good today if you can stick to the work.'

George said, 'A gang today can average four to four-and-a-half tons per man of cut cane – that's for an eight-hour day. They used not to equal half that.'

Joseph looked down at his big brown caloused hands, which had known the cane-knife and the chipping-hoe, and now were accustomed to the poor crooked scythe and spade. 'Yes, but it was hard at first, living on strange tucker and working twelve hours a day without a proper meal at the end of it. Some of the younger blokes out from the Islands – just keeled over and died in their first year. A lot did.'

'Shit, eh!' Chukka clicked his tongue in consternation. 'Makes you want to chuck up, doesn't it, George? To think the poor bloody – sorry, Mrs Efate – the poor blokes had no unions to stick up for them, so they were just got at, right and left.' He seemed unaware that the first word he had used was more reprehensible in his hostess's eyes than 'bloody'. George looked mortified, but Fiona laughed.

Chukka turned to her with relief. 'So you're working with the Aborigines; I hear they're trying to get some land set aside for them on Fraser Island? But they're not "your people".'

He was teasing her, she realized, looking into his kindly, pale-blue eyes with their fan of lighter-coloured crinkles in his tanned face.

She smiled. 'No, but we have the same problems. We are all dispossessed.' She added angrily, 'Do you know the Queensland Government wants to round them all up, wherever they come from, and banish them to Palm Island away up north? Out of sight, out of mind! It's a thousand miles from Brisbane and thirty from the mainland. They treat them just like lepers.'

A faint pink tinge showed in her pale cheeks and her face became animated as she talked. Chukka thought she was 'rather beaut', as he told his friend afterwards. He was what is known as 'a quick worker', and before they left he had managed to get Fiona aside and arrange to take her to the pictures the next Saturday night.

'All right,' she said, 'but I'm coming straight home afterwards.'

'Yair, right-oh, why not?' said Chukka disingenuously.

He walked her home from the pictures, taking a short cut through a vacant block shaded by palms from the street-lights and soft with mown grass. Their progress was punctuated by a series of fierce struggles, and when he delivered her to her father's door he complained: 'Gosh, you're hard-hearted, Fiona.'

'I'm not hard-hearted, just experienced. And I'm not falling for any bloody cane-cutter with a good line, again.'

'Just because some bloke chucked you up—'

'He left me cold.'

'More fool he.' He grabbed her again and kissed her long and insistently. She suddenly went limp; then she pushed him away, and sighed.

'I do like you Chukka. But you know how it is – once bitten, twice shy.'

'Hell! It's cruel, what you're doing to me. I never felt like this about a sheila before.' (This was not strictly true.) 'When can you come out again?'

'I don't know – next week, perhaps. You can come to the meeting of the Council of the Aborigines' and Islanders' Advancement Association, if you like. At the School of Arts on Wednesday.'

'All right. As long as you'll be there.'

'I'll be there. I'm making a speech.'

She did not really expect him to turn up, but she saw him on Wednesday sitting near the front, looking quite well-dressed in long drill trousers and a blue shirt with a tie. He applauded her speech loudly, looking round and daring the rest of the audience to disagree.

On the way home, in 'a moment of madness' as he told George afterwards, he asked her to marry him. She still didn't give in, however, but promised to think about it.

He left for Bundaberg in the train, still chafing with unappeased desire, and something else besides – a feeling of loss, of tenderness, an inability to think of any other subject than Fiona.

Good heavens, could this be love? He had actually bought a tie and worn it to impress her. He was amazed at himself. It had never happened before.

3 Joseph

The next cutting season he came to Maryborough, Chukka went straight to the Efate home and asked for Fiona. Emily told him her daughter now had a job at the local library.

'Thanks,' said Chukka, preparing to go.

'Oh, but won't you stay and have a cup of tea or something?'

'No thanks, Mrs Efate.' He turned at the gate, lifting his battered, broad-brimmed felt hat for a moment in salute. 'I've got something to say to her, and it won't keep.'

He started to stride away while Emily stood holding the fly-screen door and staring after him. He stopped in mid-stride, turned and came back.

'Eh, I suppose – she isn't, er, married by any chance?'

'No, she's not married.'

'Whacko!' And Chukka set off for the library at full speed.

The librarian, a grey-haired lady with a large bun of hair on top of her head and a large bosom below, looked rather disapproving as he strode into the building without tip-toeing. He walked straight up to Fiona who was sorting cards at a filing-cabinet and said, 'When can you get out of this place?'

'Oh, Chukka! You're back.' She smiled radiantly. 'About five I knock off.'

'I haven't written because I wanted to tell you to your face. We're going to get married, you know.'

'*Are* we?' She smiled again, her head tilted to one side. 'And when was this decided?'

'While I was comin' down on the train. I couldn't think of anything but you. Crikey, Fiona! Chuck us a kiss.'

'Shh! Not here. Miss Pemberthy is glaring at the back of your head as it is. You're supposed to speak in whispers.'

'Why? There's practically nobody in here,' he said loudly, looking round the empty tables. 'You'll have to chuck this job and travel round with me. I don't trust these wanderin' cane-cutters round this town.'

'Meet me outside just after five. I can't talk any more now.' She could see Miss Pemberthy squaring her shoulders preparatory to battle.

That night after dinner in town, Fiona and Chukka went home and told her parents. Fiona said she had always made her own decisions and it wasn't necessary for him to ask permission, because her mind was made up. 'Me marrying a bloody cane-cutter!' she marvelled. 'I can't believe it.'

'Don't worry, I'll be a cane-grower before long.'

Chukka, like George, was a hard worker and was saving to

buy some freehold land. George already had a leasehold of seventy-five acres of good land at Childers. He and May had a high-set home built at the side of the road, with sugar-cane growing almost up to the walls.

Emily, whose golden hair had turned grey long before her husband's, wept a little with happiness. Fiona was so attractive, and so vulnerable; she had feared the worst for her always, that some white man would seduce her and leave her with his baby.

And Chukka Brown was such a nice fellow, a bit of a rough diamond perhaps, but genuine. She felt sure he would treat Fiona well. She couldn't help liking him for wanting to marry her daughter. It was ridiculous to be so pleased about this, Emily told herself. She had been perfectly happy with Joseph yet she was glad that one of her girls was 'marrying white'. Fiona's children, unless they inherited the stubbornly curling frizzy hair, would not be noticeably different from their playmates.

Joseph, sitting quietly smoking with his toes curled round the rungs of his chair (for though Emily had always insisted on the children wearing shoes, Joseph had gone back to bare feet in the house), mused on the strange pattern of his life.

If that blackbirding vessel, the *Jason*, had not come to his village on Lifu, if Providence had not decreed that he should be captured on that sunny day in 1871, he would not have married Emily, he would never have come to Australia. His grandsons now would inherit some of his adopted country, to which he, Joseph, had been brought against his will, as a virtual slave.

Old Angus Johnstone, his first employer, was dead now. His son Dougal and his wife no longer kept up the old place, he supposed it was too big for them. Joseph had gone past there recently and had seen the garden neglected, the shutters loose and in need of painting, the balcony sagging from the top floor.

It had pained him, almost as if Chindera House had been his home. The old days were passing away, and the old life of the plantations with their native villages, their feasts and singing and dancing; and their cruelties as well. Samuel McGriggen, the former overseer, was dead; some said he had fallen, drunk, into the river, others that a gang of his own men had thrown him in.

Soon the gardens at Chindera were to be ploughed up for a crop of cane, and the house would gradually fall down. Joseph thought of the 103rd Psalm which Mrs Duguid had made him learn by heart, all those years ago in Lifu: 'For the wind passeth over it, and it is gone; and the place thereof shall know it no more . . .' He watched the smoke wreathe upward from his pipe towards the dark ceiling.

'What was that, dear?' asked Emily. She stretched out her hand and rested it on his.

'Nothing. I was just thinking aloud.'

In a few years he would be sixty, and he and Emily were going to retire to his place at Piabla, not far from Maud's. There he could have a little boat, and row on the quiet waters of the bay, and take his grandsons fishing; or just sit and look at the sea across which he had sailed so many years ago, and which he would never cross again.

He knew that Emily didn't quite approve of Tula's family. They lived in a rather ramshackle wooden house on low stumps, set back from the beach among a grove of casuarina trees which sang in the salt winds through their long, drooping leaves.

Tula had kept bees, and there were still rows of white hives set among the paperbark trees. There was no garden, just a sweep of uncut grass with a path trodden through it, the grass growing over a collection of old junk brought home at various times: a wheel off a cart, a rusting square water tank, an old scythe, a broken harness and some lengths of chain.

Maud was easy-going and never made the boys mow the grass, though she would grouse at them if they forgot to cut wood for the stove. She hid her grief at Tula's desertion, but still hoped he might be disappointed in the Islands and return to his family.

4 Helga

She was walking up the drive at Chindera, between the dark green shady mango trees burdened with summer fruit. The yellow globes, some half bitten-through by flying foxes, fell with a soft 'plop' in the grass.

Beyond the shadow-banded drive, painted in yellow sunlight and framed by green leaves, she saw the flowering garden: the brilliant clashing colours of magenta bougainvillaea, red poinciana trees, and the purple-blue of jacaranda. Each tree stood in a ring of fallen blossom.

From the cane-fields beyond came a smell of crushed grass, of burnt cane, smoky and sharp, and under all the heavy syrupy scent of boiling sugar. The air was warm, languorous, soft and moist. As she emerged from the drive into full light, the sun felt pleasantly warm but did not burn.

The gravel crunched beneath her shoes. The two stone lions lay guarding the mildewed steps, their sightless eyes gazing down the drive. Beside them was a hitching-rail for horses. There Rose Lovelace used to tie up her part-Arab mare, Graham Lindsay his big grey.

She heard a beat of hoofs ... and woke to hear a knocking on her door. 'Go away!' she growled. '*Avanti! Lasciami dormire!*'

Helga flung over on her other side and tried to get back into her dream of Chindera. It had been so vivid, so full of colour. How could people say that you dreamed in black and white?

The shutters were closed, but a bright Mediterranean sun shone through the chinks. She was resting in a *pensione* at Lerici, on the Ligurian coast, a quiet place recommended by her throat specialist. Queensland and Chindera were far away – the garden did not even exist any more, James had told her in a letter – yet she was homesick, heartsick for all that warmth and colour ... It was early spring in Italy, with snow still on the peaks of the Apennines and the days bright but cold.

She lay and thought about Chindera and her first pony, the little Shetland she had found tied to the bedpost on that Christmas morning long ago. She could recall the faint grey light of a clear summer dawn outside her window – how long since she had celebrated Christmas in mid-summer? – and the exciting rustle of paper parcels on her bed, overflows from the stocking that hung bulging there.

Oh, was there ever such pure happiness to be found again in

life? If it were only possible to go back to that bright uncomplicated world of youth! She remembered how in summer the flying foxes used to squabble all night in the mango trees. They came at dusk, flying on translucent membranous wings against the fading brilliance of the western sky. On her last visit she had seen them, now that electricity had come to Maryborough, tangled in the wires, the victims of progress: their bodies charred, their brown wings spread helplessly like dead veined leaves.

Impatiently she flung on her other side and tried to get back into the waking dream of Chindera homestead.

So she sentimentalized, forgetting the tears, the days of cold and rain, the disappointments. It was only since her present life had become less exciting that she had started brooding over the past.

She had unwisely attempted to sing *Tosca* at La Scala, and it had been one of the few failures of her career. The Italian audience, she sensed, was not *simpatico*; she was past sixty, and Tosca demanded a strong voice and dramatic acting. Her light coloratura was not suited to the part.

Now the specialist said she had overstrained it. A dreaded 'node' had appeared on her vocal cords; only a complete rest could cure it.

'You are tired; you have overtaxed your vitality,' he said. 'Stop singing entirely for three months, and you will find your voice again.'

If only she could be sure! She felt as if a tame bird which had been hers as long as she could remember, a beautiful blue bird she thought of it as, had flown away and left her desolate. She must lie here in silence, hoping it would come back. It was death not to be able to sing.

The Italian *padrona* had gone away, but now she sent one of the girls upstairs to demand if la signora would like a *citrone con ghiaccio, un po' di caffelatte* . . . ?

'*Niente.*' She turned her face towards the wall. '*Grazie,*' she added grudgingly. Her secretary-companion had gone back to London to make arrangements for postponing her third 'farewell' performance at Covent Garden, since now she could not sing at all. Yet she was the same. Nothing but a tiny swelling on her vocal cords stood in the way.

Her figure had thickened, yet she had sung Mimi last year in *La Bohème*, for her voice was a girl's still, or had been. She rolled over and pulled a hand-mirror towards her from the dressing-table. She threw back the shutters. Her large, dark, melancholy eyes gazed back at her – ringed with heavy pouches, the iris surrounded by a grey ring of age.

Her cheeks had sagged, forming a jowl, and on either side of her mouth ran the deep-grooved 'Davenport lines' she remembered on her mother's face.

She threw the mirror across the room.

Of course, she could go back to England and stay in the country at the beautiful Lindsay home while she recuperated. But her instinct was to hide like a sick animal. She did not want pity, nor fussing over. Besides, Pamela's twins were rather exhausting; it would be impossible for her not to talk and use her throat there.

Pamela had as yet not managed to produce a son and heir to the baronetcy. Strange, how the female principle seemed to prevail in the family! There was Dougal with two girls, and herself with one daughter, and James with no offspring at all. Chindera Estate would be carried on by Dougal's sons-in-law, she supposed, though the big places were all being cut up now.

She did not want to see Chindera House again, broken down and shorn of its gracious garden. She might, though, rescue the stone lions for her place in Sydney. As soon as she had given her last farewell concert she would return to Australia to live.

There she could sit on her own patio, lean on the marble balustrade twined with wistaria like the one at Chindera, and watch ships from all over the world gliding past. She had plenty of friends there in the musical world, and besides she would be a big frog in a rather smaller pond, Dame Helga the great prima donna.

She buried her face in her pillow and wept.

5 Tula again

Tula leant on the rail of the *Sydney Belle,* watching in a dream the side of the ship slipping, hissing, through a sea like dark blue glass. Occasionally a shoal of flying-fish would break the surface, to go flitting away from the ship on stretched membranous wings of silvery blue.

He could not have seen all this before: the deep, rich purple-blue of ocean far from land, the flying-fish in silver shoals, yet it was as if he were remembering it from some former life.

'The memory must be in my blood, in the cells of my body,' he thought. His ancestors had sailed these waters in wooden dug-out canoes, long before the white man came. They had sailed often far out of sight of land, travelling from island to island, with fresh coconuts for drink and dried fish for food.

The gentle dipping motion of the schooner, like that of a gull riding the waves, soothed him like the rocking of a cradle.

He was reversing the process begun thirty-five years earlier when his father was taken to Queensland, never to return. What emotions filled his breast as the ship turned north by east and, sailing into the sunrise, left behind the country where he had been born but where he felt he did not belong!

Then came his first islands, low coral atolls that looked at first like dark lines on the water against the glitter of the morning sun. As they came closer, they resembled gigantic green wreaths flung floating upon the sea.

At last they reached the island of his ancestors, not just a ring of coral but with some high land and rock: green palms waving a welcome, the white breaking waters of the reef, the emerald lagoon enclosed by dark blue sea, and the curve of glittering beach. How yellowish and dirty had been the sand at Piabla and Hervey Bay, compared to this! How murky those sheltered waters beside these crystalline depths!

As they stepped ashore the green jungle towered over them, full of flowering trees and bright-plumaged birds, humming with life and heat. At once he felt at home. Was it possible that this beautiful place was the 'land of heathen darkness' the missionaries talked about, a place of cruelty, head-hunting and cannibalism only a generation or so back? He remembered the *Gazetteer*'s remarks on the Lifuans, and that blue expanse in the atlas with its little dots of black; his resolve to go there.

He had heard Roman Catholicism was getting strong in the Islands, and he would be fighting Popery, as a good Presbyterian, as much as heathenism.

Some shocks awaited him when he had unpacked his Bible, his portable lectern, his hymn-books and bundle of tracts. The local chief was still powerful, and he wanted a white missionary to give him status.

Tula wrote to his parents:

I enjoyed the voyage very much, and was not seasick once. I think the weather was good. But the chief here seems very hostile to me, though he has now allowed me to set up my mission in the village. I heard him say to one of his henchmen, 'I don't want these bloody black missionaries here'! And this is the attitude of our own people! He thinks a white missionary would give him more prestige.

However I have managed to gather in the children. Some of the returned ones are running wild and getting into all sorts of bad habits. I have started a Sunday School, but many are sick and cannot come. Their shoes soon wear out and their feet are badly cut by the coral. Then the wounds turn septic.

It is not very easy to be a Christian here, but I feel called to the work. Perhaps if you could send some ointments and bandages, and medicines for fever, I could start by looking after their bodily health and perhaps spiritual grace will follow.

Tula started a garden to help feed the children, but tribesmen from the hills came down and raided it just as his taro was ripe. He set up a coloured tract Emily had given him, with a picture of the crucified Christ, like a scarecrow in the garden, and it worked. The men from the hills were terrified.

'Eh, man belong God here, plenty strong magic,' they told

each other, though they could not read the English words, '*He suffered for us*'. They scratched their heads, and decided, 'More better we clear out.'

Gradually Tula collected more of the local children, and then their parents came along to get them from Sunday School and stopped to pray. They were having a hard time. Many of their children fell sick with fever and died because there was no doctor or hospital. Blood poisoning, dysentery, yellow fever saw to it that only about one in ten survived.

In Queensland meanwhile Tula's part-Aboriginal, part-Scottish, part-Islander, wholly Australian sons carved themselves a place in the white man's world.

Maud, who'd had a letter from Tula saying that he had found contentment in his work and would not be coming back, came to see Fiona. She seemed resigned.

'Oh well, I have me sons,' she said. 'And Tula was never that good as a husban' – you know what I mean? He not much interested in, you know, lovin' me. These last years I'd bin sleeping by me own self most nights. He always prayin', and callin' out to Jesus.'

'Poor Maud,' said Fiona. She had no complaints on that score, her happiness showed in her smooth, fulfilled features, her satiny skin. 'I suppose there was some conflict there, between the Scottish missionary and the pagan Islander, pulling him apart. It's funny, but I never felt it.'

She liked Maud, and wondered how she could be so fat and jolly-looking after such a disappointing life. Perhaps she ate a lot to make up for it; and she had her boys.

Dave, named after the uncle who had died, was only thirteen, but everyone said he had the makings of a champion boxer. He was a dark, solid, nuggety boy, light on his feet as a dancer. He already trained every Saturday morning.

Billy, the elder, was more like Maud, less Islander in appearance. He was always winning races at the school sports, and would have been top of his class if he could have brought himself to do his homework.

He liked best to be out of doors, and spent his whole weekends fishing and prawning in the boat he had built himself. He wanted to leave school and give all his time to fishing.

Fiona's daughter, Anna Brown, wanted to be a ballet dancer; so far there were no sons. Her cousin John was Emily's favourite. He was a sensitive, dark-eyed boy who collected classical records, and preferred music to either fishing or fighting. Emily had given him her mother's piano; Maud's elder boy had the silver fob watch.

After saving his pocket money for a month, John came home with his latest acquisition. He wound up the turntable and set the shining metal needle on the revolving disc.

He listened entranced. 'Hey, Mum!' he called. 'Listen, isn't she a beaut singer? Just like a bird!'

Pure and true, the notes of Lucia's aria followed the flute, climbed, floated out through the open windows and over the wide green fields of cane: Helga's voice, timeless and changeless, though she herself was dust.

*

At Childers, Bundaberg, Maryborough, Mackay, Rockhampton, Townsville and along the Tweed River south of the border in New South Wales, the descendants of the Islanders who remained in Australia can still be seen. The cane still springs from the red soil, turns to a green wall topped by lilac spears, is burned in crimson flame and slashed by the cane-cutters in their slow, rhythmic dance along the rows; or more often, these days, by a mechanical monster which chops and spews out sticks in an endless stream. Shaped like a giant pre-historic bird with long neck and chomping jaws, and driven by one man, it can cut forty tons of cane in a day.

The little cane-trams still run along their narrow tracks, though driven by diesel instead of steam. The cane is carted to the mills and washed and crushed into juice and spat out in shreds, and the juice boiled and spun and separated into molasses and golden syrup and brown crystals and yellow crystals and, finally, at Millaquin, into white. The dry bagasse is flung into the furnace and consumed in the fierce heat; but some obstinate black smuts remain, which are carried high into the air and descend to smudge the clean white sheets of housewives washing their linen in the sugar towns.